Sivad & Chorn

The Adventures Begin

Steven J. Davis

Order this book online at www.trafford.com
or email orders@trafford.com

Most Trafford titles are also available at major online book retailers.

Printed in Victoria, BC, Canada.

ISBN: 978-1-4269-2005-9 (sc)
ISBN: 978-1-4269-2006-6 (dj)

Library of Congress Control Number: 2009941116

Trafford rev. 2/4/2010

www.trafford.com

North America & international
toll-free: 1 888 232 4444 (USA & Canada)
phone: 250 383 6864 • fax: 812 355 4082

For Cassandra

Endeavour always to expand the imagination.

Contents

The Adventures Begin

Sivad, a twelve-year-old Akanian boy, lying on his back in his well-organized room, bounces an oblong ball off the wall, with a ruler stretched out next to him. He looks up at the star systems he has drawn out on his ceiling and mumbles to himself,

"There are constants in our universe—planets are round, elements that make up life are identical, all species breathe some variety of oxygen, and evolution requires chaos."

He swiftly tosses the ball into the air, catches it, and then bounces it off the wall again. As the ball lands, he excitedly rolls over to measure the distance then springs up to jump on the bed. While continuing to jump, he writes a mathematical equation on the wall for the velocity, force, and energy projected from the ball and impact. He lies down on the bed again and starts the sequence over.

Suddenly, a voice yells from outside the bedroom door and down the hall,

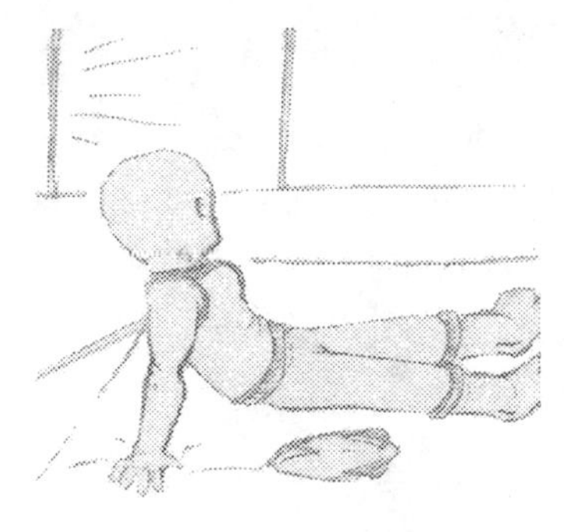

"**Sivad!** If you could only stay out of trouble for two minutes, you could be something someday. I have no idea what, but you could be something! Now get your Akanian butt down here, RIGHT NOW!"

Sivad turns and looks at the door with wide-open eyes, saying,

"**OOPS!** The Ferbos!, mom found the Ferbos."

Sivad runs out the door and down the stairs to the food preparation area, or FPA, where his mother is looking up at the ceiling, with a broom in her hand, trying to knock fifteen small, furry creatures off the ceiling.

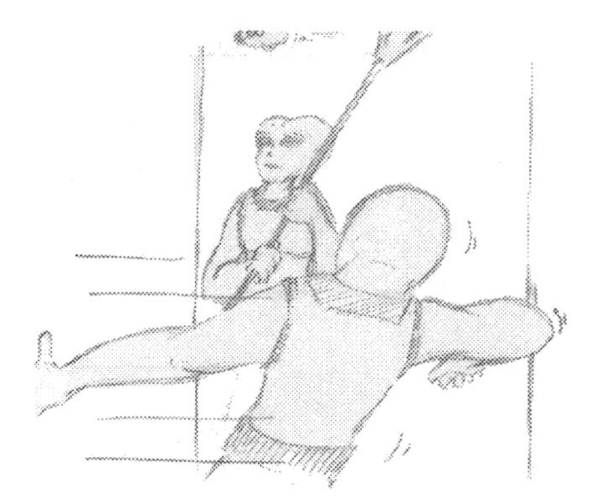

"**Mom, stop!** You don't want to hurt them."

"Sivad, what are you trying to accomplish here? You and your experiments! What kind of experiment is this one? To see how high I jump in fear when I see these horrible creatures on my ceiling?"

In a relaxed voice, Sivad replies, "No, Mom, I was just seeing how long they would stick and slide around with the Teflon glue. Besides, they're cute," he says as they watched the Ferbos glide around across the ceiling.

"Well, get them down and get ready for school. You're already running late."

"The compound will wear off in approximately thirty minutes or so, and they'll just fall down, unless they figure out how to pick up both their feet at the same time. And I still have two minutes before I need to go to the school transport," Sivad says to his mother with a mischievous smile.

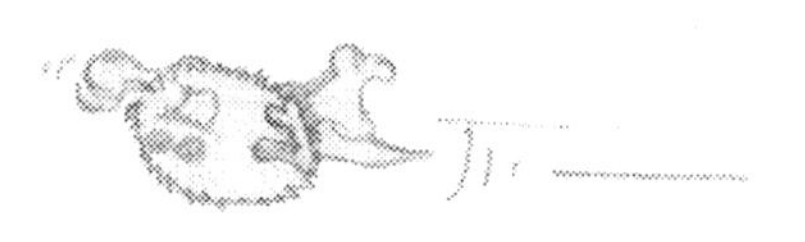

"They'll just fall down when they're ready? Then what? I'll have these ratty things sliding across the floor? The sticking compound may wear off shortly, but the Teflon does not. What am I supposed to do with them then?" she asks with a smile, almost proud that Sivad had the ingenuity to conduct the experiment.

Sivad shrugs his shoulders as his mom says, "Now go get ready for school."

Sivad tears off, running up the stairs to get out of the situation and stay on time.

"*That boy*. I don't know where he gets all that energy. If we could only habituate him to think farther ahead, then he would only get into *HALF* the trouble he gets into now," Sivad's mom says to herself as she watches the boy run out of the FPA. She could hear him thumping above her as he changed and prepared for school.

She turns and grabs Sivad's lunch in anticipation of him stampeding through the door and off to school. As expected, the FPA door opens, and Sivad runs through no more than thirty seconds after the scolding. He casually catches one of the dropping Ferbos behind his back as his mom turns to hand off his lunch bag.

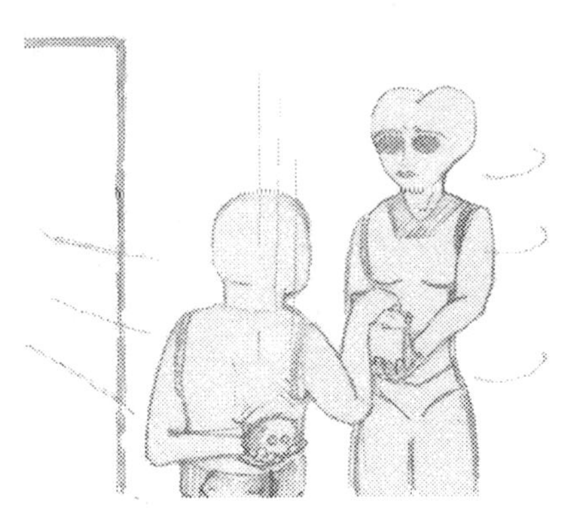

"Got to go! Uh, here you are." Sivad gives the Ferbo to his mother as he grabs his lunch bag from her other hand.

"Yuck! What if it excretes? You're cleaning it up after athletics tonight," his mother says as he runs out the door and down the street.

"Okay, see you!" Sivad's voice fades away.

His mother is left standing in the doorway, smiling, then she looks down at the Ferbo in her hand.

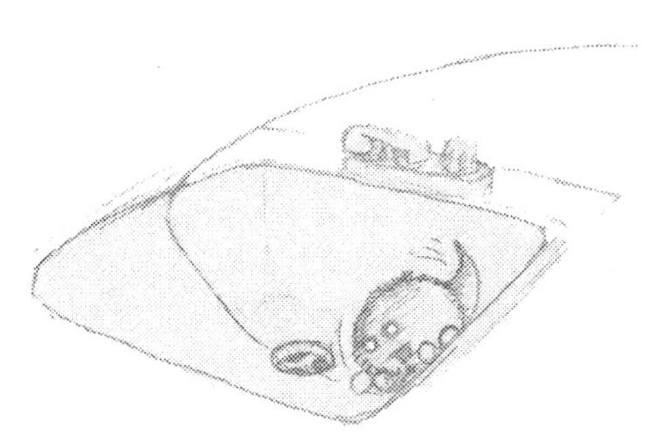

"Aaaeeeah!" she says as she quickly tosses it into the FPA sink, where it continued to slide around.

*****

A few blocks away, an alarm clock sounds. A tired, lazy arm reaches up from under the covers to grab the clock and, with one brisk movement, throws it across the messy room against the wall. It lands next to a pile of mechanical parts spread out across the floor. Also on the floor, small rustic robots are moving and hopping about, serving no apparent purpose other than to move.

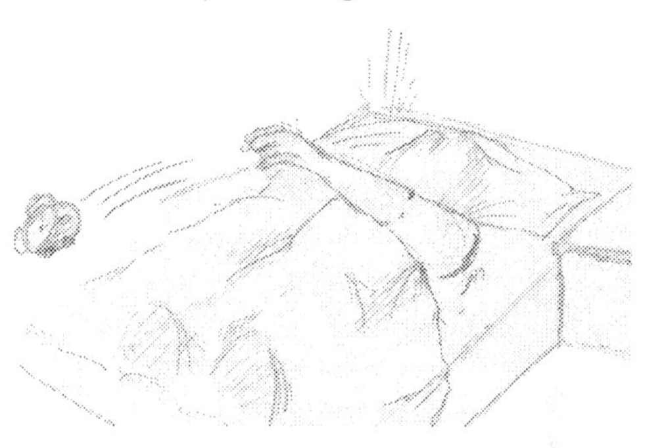

Two eyes pop out from under the covers to see the door crack open and a little Akanian girl, about three years old, enter. She picks up a small hammer-shaped robot as the covers are tightly pulled back over the peeping eyes with a groaning sound.

"5 MORE MINUTES, COME-ON"

The young girl walks over to the bed and proceeds to beat the covered Akanian boy with the toy hammer-shaped robot as it moves in her hands.

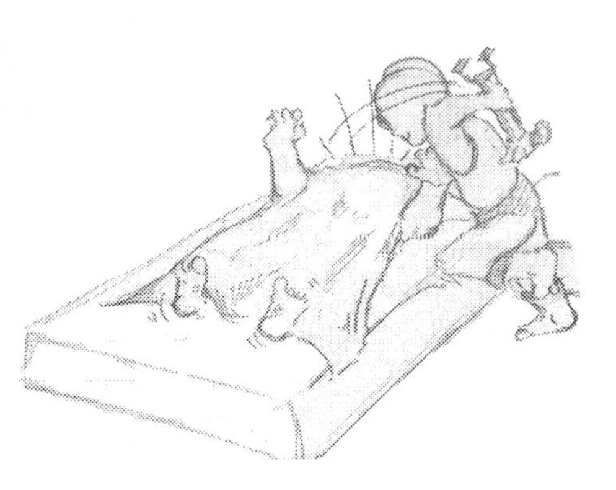

"Hey, stop it!" a voice says as a figure pops up from under the covers.

"**Chorn**, stop picking on your sister!" a voice cries out from the hallway.

Chorn looks at the built-in clock on the hammer robot and jumps up. "Shoot! I'm late!" he cries as he trips over some robots on his floor and hops over to the hanger, throws on his pants, and runs out the door within a few seconds of waking.

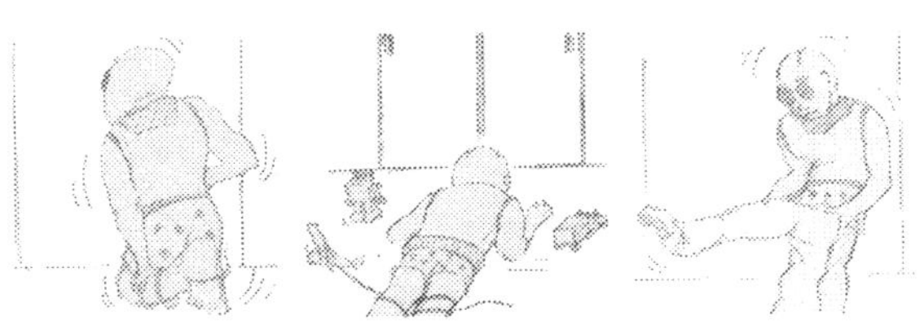

Chorn runs through the FPA, past his mother, stops, runs back, and grabs his lunch bag and heads for the door. **"Bye! I'm late! I'm late!"** Chorn yells as he spins quickly and bounces off the screen door, which needed to be pulled instead of pushed. As he springs back, still holding the door handle, he gracefully pulls the door on his recoil and charismatically spins, heading out.

"Look out for—" his mom begins to yell when she hears a clattering sound outside.

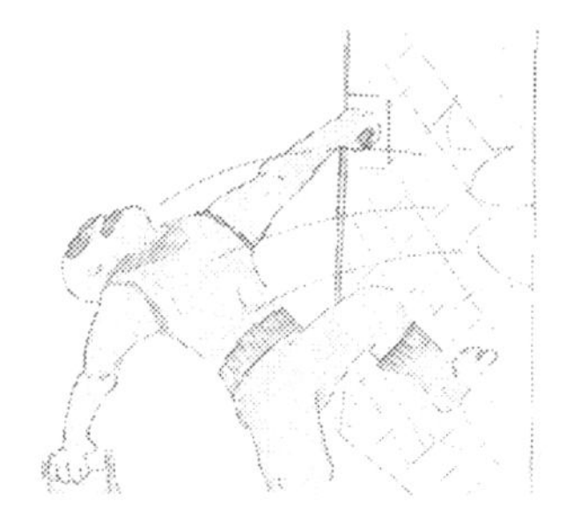

"CRASH@%$!"

Chorn lies on the ground, a tipped-over can next to him and garbage all around. He gets up in a bit of a tiff, looking back at his smiling mother and little sister as they hold back their laughter. He looks down, quickly grabs a bag, and takes off with a grunt heading down the road.

Chorn's mother walks out and picks up the lunch bag she made for him. "He'll be surprised to see that his lunch isn't what he expects it to be. That's what he deserves for not getting up earlier and not taking out the garbage, among his other chores." She sighs and smiles.

"I guess we're going to the school AGAIN just before lunch to deliver this. Do you want to go for a ride?" Chorn's mother says to the little girl, and the girl jumps in excitement.

*****

That morning in the classroom, Sivad and Chorn sit a few seats apart, looking bored as the instructor speaks about twenty million years of Akanian physiology:

"The planet, Akan, is large and dense, and its five moons cause heavy gravitational forces. Our relatively close proximity to the sun, mixed with the dense gravitational fields of our five moons, causes high humidity and many shaded times. The high humidity, mixed with the temperature, causes moisture to rise up from the surface and condense in the atmosphere. The shaded times keep the moisture low to the ground. This has caused our bodies to adapt to the environment with our strength, larger eyes, hairless skin ..." Blah, blah, blah.

As the instructor speaks, Sivad takes his magnetic pencil cover and flicks it off the corner of his computerized, interactive writing board, bouncing it off Chorn's head. Chorn, who is diligently looking forward and trying to listen, growls and waves his hand for Sivad to stop messing around.

Sivad, seeing that Chorn is annoyed, smiles and finds a small clip, flicks it at Chorn, and bounces it off his head once more. The other students turn to look at Sivad being mischievous and are also annoyed, as conformity and discipline are societal practices of Akanian culture.

Chorn looks over at Sivad and says in a harsh whisper, clenching his teeth, "**Stop it!** You're going to get us in trouble!"

The professor turns and declares, "**Chorn!** Disruption is unacceptable. Discipline and conformity are not only rules, but also practices for optimal educational performance. Please write on your interactive board how and why Akanians became the first species to travel the galaxy."

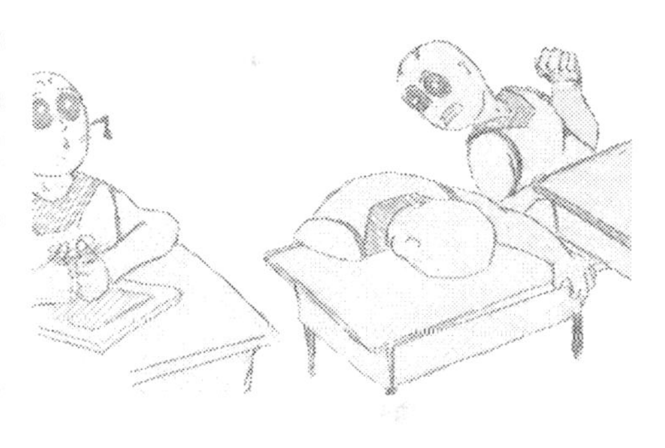

"Yes, sir," Chorn says while smiling at the professor and giving Sivad an evil eye.

The disrupted class looks back at Sivad, whose head is hung low, as he just got his friend in trouble.

The professor, seeing this, looks at Sivad with a glare. "Sivad, you are always getting yourself and Chorn into some kind of trouble. The two of you having perfect grades does not excuse disruption. I want you to write, one, what you expect you will be able to do in the future if you do not maintain the conformist values; two, what will happen to our society if we do not have discipline and harmony; and three, what will be the impact to our efficiency levels? You two will never reach a level of intellectual insight unless you have discipline and focus."

"Yes, sir," Sivad says as he begins to write on his interactive board.

First Mission

After ten years of study and training Sivad and Chorn prepare their shuttle to take off from their home planet of Akan. They have been chosen to embark on a special mission to the other side of the galaxy. This mission is usually known to be given to more experienced travelers with a strong sense of process and intercultural relations. Why they were chosen over the more senior travelers never entered their minds. Their confidence and the excitement for their first adventure overshadowed the uniqueness of the voyage.

Akan is known for its dense jungle forests and high humidity. It is a tropical planet where the standard temperatures run between 90 to 120 degrees, with humidity levels at 80 to 90 percent during non shadow times. Blocked by five large moons, much of Akan is under shadow and is often dark. During Shadow times the temperatures can drop down to as low as 30 degrees; In turn, they have extreme high and low temperatures throughout the day. When the sun does shine on the planet, it charges ionic partials in the mist, helping the Akanians absorb electrolytes that augment their neuron dendrite development, allowing them to learn faster than most species.

Because the planet has five moons, there exists an uncommon dense gravitational force, making the Akanians 1.5 meters tall on average and very strong. The Akanians have developed high durability to external environmental changes.

The Akanians are a peaceful race, relying on logic, objectivity, and efficiency more than emotion. They very rarely act out of anger or spite and are generally happy and supportive of each other. Akanians reached their technological peek along with the rest of the galaxy over three thousand years ago. Operations are as efficient as ever, but due to the lack of technical growth, there exists the constant question of "what is next. Is the best we can be? What about all the questions we couldn't answer?" Spiritual cognition and exploration of the inner mind is one of the main areas of study. It is believed that the Akanians were the first species to evolve in the galaxy and the first to travel through space with their first rocket launch over five thousand years ago.

Because Akan is located in a remote solar system on the outer belt of the galaxy, the planet is far away from neighboring systems; thus Akanians are more isolated and self-sufficient than most other species. They tend to have their own technologies and are known as the most evolved and advanced species in the galaxy. Most systems do not have many interactions with Akan because of its remote location and solitary society. Akanians are not seen traveling very often, unlike other species that have roamed, colonized, and settled across the galaxy. When Akanians are seen roaming the galaxy, they usually have a specific goal in mind and ostracize everything around them, making others curious about their mission's purpose.

As Sivad and Chorn ascend from their planet on what appears to be a simple mission dedicated to information collection, their destination, the *Miniloc Moon Exchange Port* (or *Miniloc MEP City),* located on a remote desert moon across the galaxy.

On the surface, their mission is to explore the progress of the old moon space station used as a trading post for the more nefarious of species to conduct their gray market trade. The gray market trade is known for its questionable morality and product- and service-exchange protocols. Most often, the traders and buyers don't want to be known for selling or buying certain questionable items.

From the beginning, their mission was basic in design and, for Akanians, oddly ambiguous. Akanians are usually very detail oriented. This mission's structure, goals, and design have been brief, as if the original writer wrote it to be vague on purpose. And with Sivad and Chorn as the data-collection designates, mean anything could happen.

The Akanian senior chancellor and one of his executives watch from a high terrace just above the forest's tree-covered hood as Sivad and Chorn's shuttle prepares for departure.

Because of the spiritual cognition beliefs and inner-mind exploration of his people, the senior chancellor suspects that there is a higher reason for the selection of these two specific Akanians. He also knows that the mission could very well be of no great importance and that there are a million variables that could go wrong because of an ambiguous mission scope.

The senior chancellor's executive advisor, however, does not share the same optimism and does not believe Sivad and Chorn are the right Akanians to go on this journey. He speaks up, saying, "Sir, do you believe that Sivad and Chorn are the right Akanians to send on this mission? They have not ventured out before and still have minimal experience. And, their behavior is, well... peculiar. Sending them to Miniloc Exchange Port is irregular, even for a simple mission as this, and could be dangerous. We Akanians do not travel that far very often. It has been over fifty years since our last visit."

In a slow, calm-toned voice, the senior chancellor replies with dignity and confidence in his decision to send the two. "The choices we make not only determine the outcome but also how events may begin, and the chain of events that follow. Because of their 'peculiar' attitudes, they may have the best chance of succeeding." The Chancellor continues, "I have been watching them and believe that Sivad and Chorn will soon realize that the current mission and objectives, for a simple task of information gathering, are not congruent with the requirements of what must be done."

The senior chancellor looks out toward the jungle interior and takes a deep breath, feeling the air around him, and continues, "I understand your concern. Sivad and Chorn are a bit odd for our species. Compared to other Akanians, they possess a slightly higher IQ, which is strange since they were both raised in the same controlled Akanian educational environment. It is this slightly abnormal IQ that is believed to be the explanation for their odd inventions and operational tactics.

"Some believe that they do not take anything seriously and are daydreaming goofballs; I have seen this at times as well. Others have told me that they believe their mischievousness is due to our over-controlled environment; thus nature is taking back a piece of what is *hers*; I do not believe that this is the case. The elite, however, are the majority, and they think that they have developed the personalities through their strong friendship, making their creativity more clever. In turn, they have the potential to somehow change the constants," he pauses, "out there." He turns to walk back indoors, stops, and looks at his executive advisor, saying,

"*They seek adventure* whereas *we seek conformity*."

The executive looks at the rising shuttle launching to the sky and says under his breath, "This will be interesting," gives a small laugh, and follows the senior chancellor.

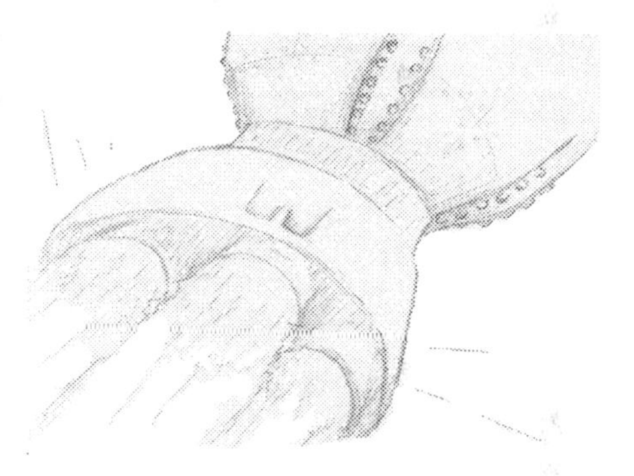

Just Trying to Get There

Upon clearing the atmosphere, Sivad and Chorn settle into their vessel and, with a process-oriented aura, immediately begin rustling around, checking monitors, setting navigation sequences, igniting the engine thrusters, seeming professional and serious about their mission. Chorn disappears for a moment then brings out a pot of tea, sits down, and casually pours himself a cup. He begins to work using small watchmaker's tools on a little device that looks like a short headset.

Once finished with his duties, Sivad joins him and pours himself a cup as he looks out into space. Sivad turns toward Chorn with a half-mischievous grin and says with some excitement,

"Let's fly by the Blue Planet?"

They look at each other with excitement and then hastily get up and proceed to change navigation systems to their new course.

The *Blue Planet* is known throughout the galaxy, and all worlds are excited because the *Blue Planet* species are in their final stage of evolution before they begin space travel and join the

federation of species in the galaxy. The *Blue Planet* is expected to join the federation within the next one hundred years. All federation species are interested in the *Blue Planet* since there have been no new planets joining the federation over fifteen hundred years. The federation has been consistent and somewhat stagnant; it needs new species to join its mostly peaceful alliance.

The Blue Planet has been a site of observation for a few millennia and, because of its uniqueness, has not been disrupted. The evolution is late for the galaxy, and the planet is much smaller than the average, which is thought to explain why they are evolving differently from the rest of the federation. The galaxy is excited to see what the *Blue Planet* species are capable of.

As Sivad and Chorn begin flying through the *Blue Planet's* solar system, they drop out of light speed and hurry over to a small side window to see the planet with their own eyes rather than through the sensors. Because their heads are so large and the porthole was constructed low and small, it is difficult for the two excited Akanians to see through the same porthole.

Sivad and Chorn begin to slap fight over the window, playfully pushing each other so each can see.

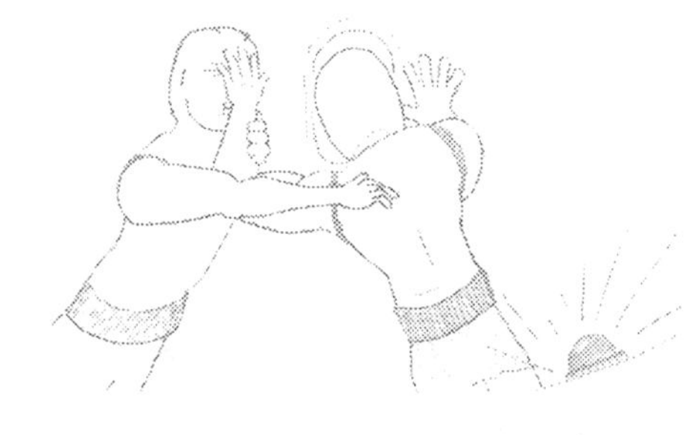

As they are fighting for window space, a sensor begins to glow, and a faint alarm sounds. However, Sivad and Chorn are too involved in seeing the *Blue Planet* to notice it. After a few seconds of battle over the porthole, there is a sudden crashing sound and a jolt.

Sivad and Chorn rush back to their command stations and continue to monitor the sensors and identify the root-cause analysis. After quick research, they identify it as an isolated incident, a minor encounter with unexpected space debris, and continue on their way.

As Sivad and Chorn return to light speed and get back on their mission course, they decide it would not be entirely necessary to further identify what they hit and report the incident into the logs with any more detail than required.

What Sivad and Chorn did not know was that the impact was with an object from the *Blue Planet*, damaging it and sending it spiraling off course. They had no foresight that they had just inadvertently changed the trajectory and future of this device.

The Improbable—Out of Control

The satellite originating from the *Blue Planet* spirals out of control, off course and excreting radiation from its power source as it approaches an oncoming vessel. However, this vessel is no ordinary ship. The commander is Caption Galleon, a loyal and trusted executive in the Shobo order, and his ship, called the Gigil Pain, is a science slave vessel used for unorthodox research and experiments. Their primary goal is the search for profit and power through technology. Galleon will leverage his abilities, slaves, and drones to gain scientific advantages for the Shobo order, the most powerful and controversial society in the galaxy. Shobo, the master of the order, is a powerful and feared individual. No one knows where he came from, and he is seldom seen. According to legend, he is half Akanian, created from an Akanian experiment gone astray.

Galleon, the most powerful captain of Shobo's reign, controls an army of drones that he created. The drones are half living tissue and half machine, an army highly trained in quickness, strength, and blitzkrieg battle tactics. These small, mirrored-faced creatures are abominations to other species in the galaxy, and when traveling in numbers, they are feared by all. Having all emotions repressed, algorithmic thinking, and bodily implants and enhancements, they have absolute obedience and calculate every move.

Traveling at minimal light speeds, Galleon sits on his sky bridge, overseeing his drone operations crew below. His security drones are strategically placed around him. Galleon, with his resolute mind, looks out through the deep abyss of space on the large screen monitor.

Suddenly, the Gigil Pain loses all navigational control. The vessel drops out of light speed and comes to a dead float in space. The operations crews are flung to the front from the immediate slowdown.

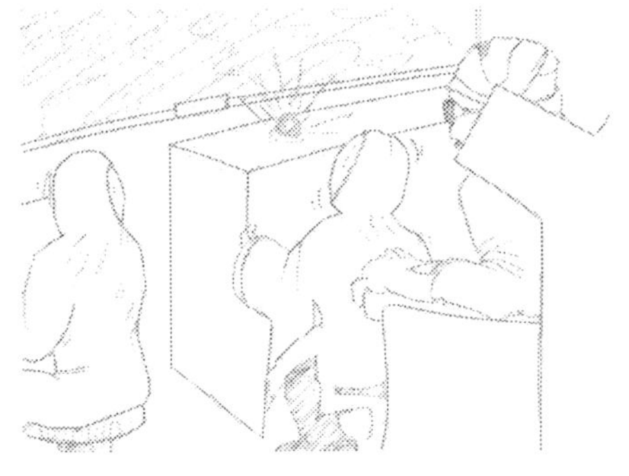

Captain Galleon yells out his commands,

"**ALERT, READY STATIONS-** Get to battle stations **NOW!**"

The crew gets up off the deck, shakes off any bruises, and returns to their stations as fast as they can, Galleon himself was thrown from his chair, but his drive picked him up quicker than the rest.

Oddly enough, the Gigil Pain's power is still intact and online. The event appears to have had no impact on anything else.

"**STATUS REPORT!**" Galleon orders, thinking to himself, What kind of malfunction or rip in space could this be since our sensors could not pre-identify any known anomaly or ship in the area?

His crew, at attention and conducting their analysis accord to procedure, were quick to report any abnormality to their captain.

The computer sounds a report,

"Incident appears to be an isolated navigational problem. Cause unknown"

Just seconds later, dead ahead, Galleon and his operations crew see on the monitor an object coming out of a shroud of smoke. It is a small device with a long stem and a large disk array coming straight at them. The object, covered by the thin gas cloud, could not be identified by the computer and was not on any of the known ship registries.

Galleon, not knowing if this object is aggressive or not, proceeds with caution, as the object has had such an adverse impact on his ship, dropping it from light speeds and forcing the engines to shut down.

With the Gigil Pain still at a dead float, Galleon orders "**SHIELDS**".

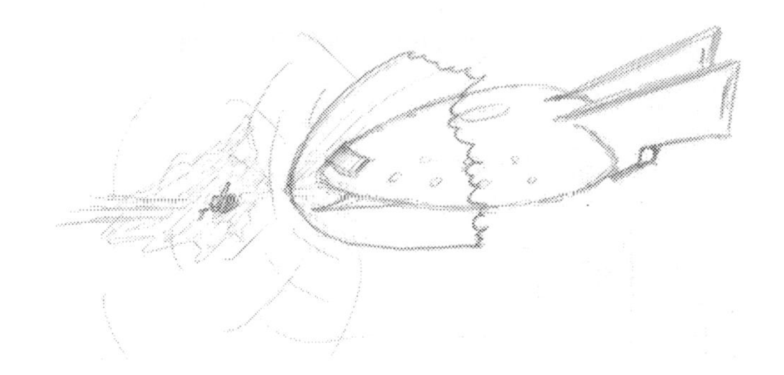

As the magnetic wave of shields cover the Gigil Pain, the monitors light up to indicate that the engines have resumed normal functions.

The computer sounds,

"Navigational control back online."

Everyone is confused by the event, stops, and waits for their didactic captain to give them directives.

Galleon stares at the monitor, analyzing this foreign image, waiting to see if there will be another aggressive move, watching the object tumble and float in space as it heads directly for the Gigil Pain. Galleon debates the options in his mind: destroy the device, disregard and continue on, or explore more. The crew, silent, hands on the controls ready for his decision, stand at alert.

As the object nears, Galleon commands in a calm, curious voice, "Move out of the way of the object."

As the Gigil Pain moves to one side, the object flies by, tumbling out of control on its same course.

One of the science officers informs Galleon that the smoke trail and gas cover is radiated and appears to be emanating from one of the cylindrical stems sticking out of the device.

The monitors zoom in on the origin of the gas cloud, which appears to be a leak, as the Gigil Pain continues to slowly follow the object.

The communication officer informs Galleon of a strange frequency-modulated radio wave being sent by the device with plasma-charged radiated particles. Another science officer reports that the structure of the device is very basic, with technology that has not been used in a millennium

Galleon thinks, curious and unsure, What kind of device is this?

The answer occurs to him when one of his officers informs him that something looking like solar panels for energy collection is connected to the chassis of the object.

Galleon orders, "Calculate the place of origin based on its flight path."

"Flight path unknown, sir," answers one of the crew members

"This object is damaged?" Galleon replies with one eyebrow raised above his old gasmask glasses. "Could it have been hit and redirected by an asteroid?"

"We are within the solar system of the *Blue Planet,* sir."

Galleon perks up and replies, "Is this object from the Blue Planet?"

The entire crew looks up at Galleon in shock and intrigue. The crew quickly traces back and locates a possible point of impact where it would have changed course from an origin from the *Blue Planet*.

Galleon commands over the intercom to his science slave team, "Let's take a closer look at it. Isolate it and bring it in. Let me know once you have an idea of what disrupted our navigation systems."

Galleon stares, still fearing that it could be a new weapon.

The science slave crew gains control of the object, and in a controlled environment, they quickly seal the radiation leak.

After reengineering the object, they contend it is an exploration satellite. It has very basic monitoring devices for ultraviolet, infrared, radio, charged particles, plasma, and cosmic ray spectrometers. The downlink is a simple two-frequency channel radio. The power source is a technology understood but not used, which is defined as a high-risk volatile power supply (plutonium-based radioisotope thermoelectric generator).

The science team, working as fast as they can for fear of Galleon's wrath, finds that, because the object was damaged, it was sending and receiving data in a firm single-layer phase. With the charged particles from the radiation leak on the radioisotope thermoelectric generator, it charged the wavelength, which matched the Gigil Pain's navigation command modulations.

In turn, the root-cause analysis of why the satellite disrupted the navigation systems of the Gigil Pain is defined as a complete coincidence. The species from the *Blue Planet* are on to something, but they take high risks in doing so with their power source. The science officers joke at the primitive technology and are amazed that the *Blue Planet* species still use radiated particles for energy. This information was reported to Galleon over the intercom.

"Radio-iso-what?" Galleon asks to the science team

"Radioisotope thermoelectric generator. It is the plutonium extraction device that emits energy."

"Radio-iso-you're-an-idiot generator?" replies Galleon.

"It's the battery, sir," says the slave over the intercom.

"Don't get feisty with me, or you'll find yourself playing with that thing without protection," Galleon replies

After further review, the elite slave team finds something critical as they mumble to each other in a circle around the alien device. They talk over one another finishing each other sentences and moving to the next revelation theorizing that the navigation disruption may not have been a coincidental disruption:

"However, an external re-modulation command, from an external source, *was able to enter into the system due to the radiated particles* mixed with the low modulated frequencies. *It is then theorized that* this might have some benefit, whereas, *in a radiated environment*, we can readapt and protect navigation modulations *and stabilize control under severe radiated conditions*. The satellite was able to send and penetrate the Gigil Pain's navigation systems *through its radiated cloud. When the Gigil Pain raised shields,* the magnetic field from the shield protected the ship's navigation system, then, it is theorized that, *a smaller isolated magnetic field centered in the navigation core* may also protect the navigation systems in a more severe environment *such as that which is similar to a wormhole.* If the frequency modulation was not an isolated disruption, *but a stable connection*, then we could possibly use this technology *with our own systems*, protected by the core magnetic field."

"To enable consistent navigation through a wormhole".

The entire science team pauses at this extrapolation and looks at each other in surprise. Then, continue with their group discussion even more excited:

"In a wormhole, *time and space fluctuate*, changing at an extraordinary rate, *and this technology might be able to* stabilize the navigation systems, *protecting us and enabling* wormhole travel between galaxies, *and possibly universes.* Currently, if a ship entered into a wormhole, *they would be lost forever.* The highly radiated tunnels send ships *from galaxy to galaxy*, all the way to different universes *at random.* No one has the technology to stabilize the navigation systems to enable consistent wormhole travel *and get back again.* This could be it?"

The Science team discussing the discovery together transfers over to Galleon's computer board as he finishes reading the report, he then visualizes the high potential of this discovery and the glory for him to be the first to attempt stable wormhole travel. Galleon orders his science slave team to carry this research farther and build and test simulations until they have a stable system, one that is not vulnerable to high radiation and tackyon fields.

The elite science slave teams begin working, and Galleon knows that, if they succeed, he will have the most valuable technology in the galaxy.

Galleon thinks with a half-cocked grin, *The* ability to navigate through wormholes ..."COOL!"

Miniloc MEP City Adventure

Sivad and Chorn arrive at their destination, the Miniloc Moon, with one large City called Miniloc **MEP City**. MEP is a galactic trading post where the scourge of the universe goes to trade their questionable services and products. As in any boarder town or trading post, there is a variety of species and cultures working to coexist, which means they do not always get along; in turn, it is often a precarious location where delicacy and diplomacy should be followed. In any intercultural dealings, one could inadvertently cause an unstable incident that could lead to physical violence, especially when dealing with the more nefarious of each species.

Miniloc is a yellow desert moon, with a low mega-sphere overlooking a large gaseous planet called Elnido. On Miniloc, there are several large craters where asteroids had impacted the moon long before it was inhabited. Miniloc is one of several moons of the Elnido planet. It is also the only inhabitable moon.

Outside MEP City, Miniloc has somewhat primitive but peaceful outlanders residing in villages. These residents often come into the city to try and get rich by scamming newcomers, begging or selling worthless trinkets.

MEP City for the most part adhere to interstellar laws, or their interpretation of those laws, which are respected and seldom broken; however, there is a gray zone where new and ambiguous issues have not been decided by the law council and are not yet defined under the interstellar law. These new negotiations and transactions usually take place on this remote spaceport. If the interstellar monitoring agencies do not know about it or cannot track it, then it is fair game.

Sivad and Chorn sit on top of a large sand dune overlooking Miniloc MEP City. They decided to land their shuttle outside the city so as to draw attention to themselves. Akan is located on the opposite side of the galaxy from this space station, so there are not too many Akanians who frequent this area of space.

Sitting on the sand dune, Sivad and Chorn plan their visit. Sivad, however, is quiet for a while. Chorn turns to him.

"Sivad, you have a dark cloud over you today. What's up? Are you bummed about something?"

"Yes," Sivad responds as he looks away at the spaceport.

Chorn tries to cheer him up and changes the subject. "Sivad, have you been working out? You look bigger."

"Yes, I've been doing space calisthenics once a month. I am getting HUGE." Sivad states as he flexes his arm jokingly.

After sitting silently for a time, Chorn says, "Are you thinking about that female at the academy in the Quadra system again?"

"No, why?" Sivad replies.

"You do seem rather bummed, and on a day like today? This is our first mission since we graduated from the Celestial Aerospace Academy, and this is our first adventure outside our solar system. This

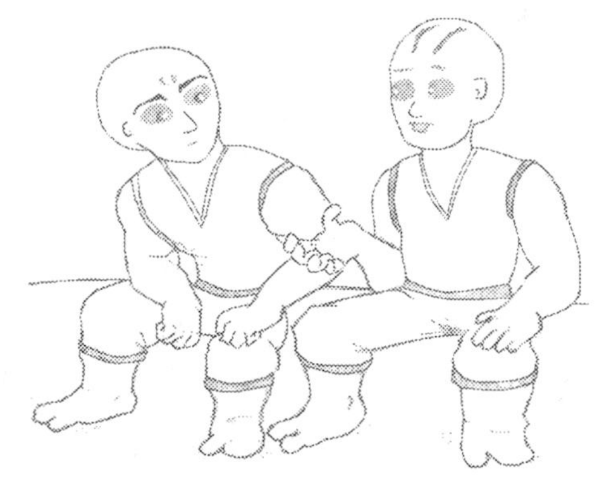

is a great day! So what is up with the dark cloud and gloom? It's not like you."

Sivad decides to open up a bit. "Yes, you know, I have been doing some soul searching lately, and since we passed the *Blue Planet*. I was thinking about the *Blue Planet* and how fast it is developing and how slow we are. Do you realize that our society has not changed in over three thousand years? That's pretty ... pathetic. Look at this colony. It's a decaying society. Most of the solar systems don't even intercommunicate, let alone interact. Because everything seems stagnant, there is little need to integrate with other cultures. There needs to be more interaction, more joint projects to reunite the galaxy. This colony, for example, probably hasn't seen an Akanian in over one hundred years, not the fifty stated in the report. Their leaders only see our species at the federation council meetings. They are all like those small creatures on, you know, that planet only twenty light years away from here, with all the colonies. You know, the species that refuses to evolve."

"The Gen Planet," Chorn jumps in.

"Yeah, that one," Sivad says.

Chorn gave Sivad a scolding look. "I told you not to sleep in astro-anthropology class. Besides, what do you mean? We have had lots of developments."

Sivad jumps back in. "Development, yes, but what significant changes? Societies are on a decline as far as evolution. Our society has even stopped evolving it seems. We are now looking at the inner ability to feel time and space. That is not evolution! That is going back to spiritual beliefs. We must go forward, not backward."

Chorn intervenes, "Hey, our spiritual insight that you think so little of is evolution. Our species is on the verge of not only telepathy but also telekinesis and clairvoyance as well. That is evolution, my little, bald friend. And there have been a lot of change like, you know, and, um—"

"Yeah? SEE!

"Well, what about our new steagora device?" Chorn challenges, a bit frustrated, for he cannot think of any significant event that has changed anything.

Sivad is curious about what Chorn just said regarding the new gadget he has been working on, as Chorn is always coming up with some strange inventions. "What? The stegra device? What is that?"

"The steagora device. You know, the headset to tap into the thought wavelength of another?" Chorn reminds Sivad of the device.

"Oh, that one.

You're still working on that? It's been a while. I thought we were going to call it thought tapper or thorapper?" Sivad says.

"Na, I thought it would be more appropriate and funky to mix a couple other words for it. You know, the stegarwana root and aura. I would expect some strange results from this thing. And the programming is very complex for this to get the right results, so far forty-nine million lines of code," Chorn replies

Sivad, with a diligent and cynical face, says, "Our science board has not even condoned it. Besides, that's nothing compared to the development of the *Blue Planet*. Plus, the steagora device is just a toy. We developed it only for our own amusement."

Chorn reasons, "Sivad, think about it this way, we haven't had that many significant changes because we are already advanced. We have accomplished everything we have imagined and more." Chorn looks out the corner of his eye with a satisfied grin. "I don't know why you're bummed. We're doing alright."

Sivad replies, with a bit of frustration, "That just isn't good enough. Mediocrity is not greatness. What do we have to show for the advancements from the past three thousand years? I mean, you and I are unappreciated geniuses, like most *conditioned* Akanians in our society. But what have we done? What have we accomplished?

"Look at this port. These species are all barbarians, but they're happy and content. Life is exciting for them. This place looks like a boring desert, but I'm sure it's still a new world for them. We, on the other hand, never do anything. Everything is so controlled, conformed, and over-evaluated. It takes the fun and excitement out of everything. Our species are just too conservative."

Chorn says in surprise, "Wow! *You* are really boring today. You must really be going through a psychological phase now, huh? Hitting puberty or something? Have you ever asked yourself if maybe YOU ARE abnormal? You've always been that way, always getting *me* in trouble. Let's face it, you're strange for an Akanian."

Sivad responds with a half grin and in a more cheery mood, pleased at what Chorn just said, "If I'm abnormal, what does that make YOU?"

Chorn, a bit impatient and pointing at Sivad, replies, "Smarter than you- Eh? Uh oh-, you know what, you always get this way before something terrible happens. And besides, you're wrong about us not developing anything new; we have been working on the steagora device."

Sivad, a little more excited and cheery, says with a mischievous grin, "We haven't even tested it yet. How do we even know it works?"

Chorn shrugs down. "Boy, aren't you Mr. Exciting today?" He pauses then looks back at Sivad, having a very good idea what he is thinking. "Uh-oh. Here we go again!"

Sivad says with a playful grin, "Do you want to try it?"

Chorn, a bit nervous, sits back and says, "I thought you wanted to try it."

Sivad, with a convincing voice, says, "You said you wanted to do it."

"You said that you wanted to do it," Chorn replies right back at Sivad.

Sivad leans forward, **"Okay I'll do it!"**

"Are you sure?" Chorn asks with a quizzical tone.

"Yes, we have to test it sometime, so let's do some information gathering with the steagora," Sivad says, determined.

"But we don't know how it will affect you here on this moon."

"The lack of electrolytes in the atmosphere should augment the initial effects we saw in our experiment on the Ferbos."

"The Ferbos? But we haven't tested it on our chemistry. Do you think it will work? There are a lot of unknown variables," Chorn says with concern. He continues, trying to make Sivad more nervous, "I never told you that the Ferbos blew up after you left!"

Sivad shows his selective listening and ignores what Chorn said for a moment. "Our planet is moist and full of electrolytes—**BLEW UP?** What do you mean, blew up?" Sivad's apprehension shows.

Chorn smiles and looks with a glare out the corner of his eye. "We should have doubled the effect due to this dry atmosphere."

"According to my test results, we could have some unpredictable and exhilarating effects." Chorn, staying calm, is happy he got Sivad to be nervous about something for a change.

Sivad starts getting restless in the sand where they are sitting. He has a renewed excitement but also shows his uneasiness. "Exhilarating? But no bad side effects, right? *RIGHT?*"

Chorn, in an agreeable tone, replies, "Uh, yeah, sure, right. No worries ... I think."

Sivad figures out that Chorn is pulling his leg and leans forward to get up. "Okay then, there's nothing to worry about. Plus, it will create some excitement in our lives. Let's go have some fun!"

"Sivad, sometimes I worry about you. I think you ate too many paint chips when you were young," Chorn says as he leans over to stand.

As they get up and brush the sand off their paints, they start walking down the dune, leaving their prints in the sand.

As they continue to walk, Sivad turns and asks Chorn, "So, did you lock it?"

"Lock what?"

"The ship."

"No, I thought you did."

"So it's not locked?"

Sivad and Chorn say together with a staggered tone, **"Oops, back to the ship**."

Ask the Clark

It is late afternoon. A bit dusty from walking through the hot sand, Sivad and Chorn enter into the more civilized MEP from the desert. The MEP roads turn from pure sand to dirty pavement, becoming more soiled from usage rather than sand-covered erosion. Sivad and Chorn walk past MEP City outlanders, who usually stay on the edge of the city. The outlanders, dirty, homeless-looking creatures, watch as Sivad and Chorn pass.

A bit unnerved by the outlanders' appearance, Chorn walks close to and behind Sivad. As they travel deeper into the city, they begin to wonder where they should go, looking around all directions, nervous and curious. At a crossroad, where the buildings grow higher, shading the streets from any sunlight, and where a mass transit system overpasses, Chorn asks, "Okay, now which way?"

"This way; it smells better," Sivad says as they both crinkle their noses from the bad smell emanating from the other direction and turn at the same time to walk away from the repulsive smell of rotting garbage and vermin.

Walking on, they pass by a few street vendors, some selling miscellaneous items, others selling food. Chorn, looking at one of the food vendors, makes a distasteful face when, all the sudden, Sivad stops with his nose in the air, taking a big whiff. "That smells GOOOOOOD-."

"You cannot be hungry for *that*, Chorn replies.

"Why not? Food is food," Sivad says. "We should try new stuff while we're here. That's all part of information gathering, right?"

The chef of this particular street-vending stand, called the **Clark**, is a scary-looking humanoid with solid, dark eyes and an emotionless face.

Sivad, leading with his nose, leaves Chorn and walks over to ask the chef of the Clark kiosk, "What are you cooking? It smells delicious."

"MEAT," the chef replies with a large blunt of tobacco hanging from his mouth.

"Obviously a species with few words and an attitude," Chorn mumbles while he drops back a step, nervous about Sivad starting a conversation.

Sivad said confidently, "I'll try one."

The Clark vendor flips a piece of meat onto some bread and tosses it onto the counter. Sivad takes the burger and starts to eat it. After the first bite, Sivad has a satisfied look on his face.

"Hey, ask him where we should go and where there is a lot of action around here," Chorn says to Sivad as he began to stuff the burger into his mouth.

"You ask him," Sivad says in the middle of a bite.

Chorn shakes his head no when Sivad pushes him forward with his elbow as he eats the burger. Chorn, falling forward while looking back at Sivad, hesitantly sputters out, "Excuse me, sir?"

"Yes? What, you want one too?" answers the bold voice from the Clark chef.

"Uh, no, sir, uh, can you suggest where we should go for information gathering in this area?"

Sivad jumps in, popping his head in front of Chorn as he chews the burger. "What my old boy is trying to say is where can we get some good action around here?"

"**Ganda**," replies the Clark chef, still short on words.

Sivad and Chorn look at each other curiously when, all the sudden, the intimidating Clark chef becomes a chatterbox of information,

"Ganda, I once went to Ganda. Talked to a girl there. Almost had a date as well. What a cutie pie she was. I called her my hamster girl—bark like a hamster for me! Ha-he-he. She didn't know what she was missing. How could she have known that I would become a fancy restaurant owner." The Clark chef lets out a jolly laugh, and his belly shakes.

"What do ya wanna go there for anyhow? All the action is out here." The Clark chef leans forward with a grin on his face, tobacco hanging out one side of his mouth, and stares at Sivad and Chorn. "Heck, one time, I saw a man get killed over a rock there. Heck, what I like is when people fight over my meat; that's a good time. Little do they know, it does not cost me a cent. I just pick it up off the street from desert animals that wander through and get themselves killed. He-he."

Sivad, with a grossed-out expression, interrupts, a bit upset knowing he is going to get roasted by Chorn later, and says in a curt voice, **"Ganda. Which Way?"**

The Clark chef rattles on about his adventures at Ganda and points down the road to his right. Sivad and Chorn quickly turn and run, hearing the Clark chef's voice fade away behind them yelling,

"**HEY!** What about my payment? That was high quality meat strangers." Then he continues with his story reminiscing to himself about the Ganda experience.

Chorn, with a nonchalant smile, bites his tongue as Sivad gives him a dirty look to warn him not to say anything yet.

Finding Ganda just down the road, Chorn could not hold back any longer. Sivad had eaten some street food that turned out to be road kill, because he wanted to try something new.

"Did you bring your intestinal medicine?" Chorn sparks. "I wonder how long that MEAT is going to last before it liquefies and **blows up** in your stomach," Chorn says with the low voice of the Clark chef.

Sivad repeats, "Shut up. Shut up. It's not funny. Quiet," as they walk to the door of Ganda.

Chorn, continuing on, says, "MEAT, meat, MEAT, meat. BOOM!" in a low, loud voice, still imitating the Clark chef, with his hands in the air.

Ganda Exploits

Ganda is a medium-sized, dim-lighted bar known for engineering and communication elites who fritter time away and conduct underground business. It is one of Miniloc's most influential and nefarious establishments, and can be ruthless. Although Ganda is located in what is known to be a nighttime party area of MEP City, it is not a place to party or get wild. For those outsiders on leave in MEP City, out to have a good time, soon realize that, once they pop into Ganda, they have stepped into the wrong pub. They realize that Ganda is not a place for them and their merrymaking and usually leave calmly within a short period, ensuring that they cause no disturbance.

It is a dodgy bar where all new business negotiations for technology and data are transferred from one to another, at a price. It is a bar where, to be accepted into the local crowd, the attendee must have the tenacity of a guerilla fighter and a brainpan that is usually a higher IQ than others of their species. At Ganda, there is the usual crowd of technology dwellers and drivers who form an alliance within their groups, but they watch each other closely, with distrust and opportunistic patience.

Under a fog of tobacco, a beautiful and mysterious singer named Cas stands on the slightly raised stage, singing with a voice that sooths the soul. She has a voice that even the great singers of history could not contend with, the sound that truly tamed the savage beasts in Ganda, the voice that maintained harmony surrounded by chaos. Cas, caped in a seductive hooded gown, draws attention

from all in Ganda and calms possible violent outbreaks by the sound of her voice. Her singing is not only for entertainment, but also to ensure that all species are relaxed enough to stay objective about their business dealings. Cas's planet of origin is not known, as she does not talk to many strangers outside the usual crowd and, much like the others who frequent the bar, never talks about her past.

Sivad and Chorn walk in with smiles on their faces as they noisily joke about the Clark chef. All the patrons in the bar stop what they were doing, turn toward the new entrants, and gaze emotionlessly at them. Akanians do not frequent this area much, let alone enter into a barbaric bar such as Ganda. Sivad and Chorn stop as they enter the bar and take a look around. Chorn turns to Sivad, yells, "MEAT!" and starts laughing loudly.

The rogues, seeing this strange behavior and no apprehension from the two Akanians, accept them as no threat and return back to their own dealings, and the bar regains its usual character.

Sivad and Chorn walk through, too absorbed in their own conversation to notice anyone staring at them as they look for somewhere to start their steagora experiment.

Some in the bar recognize their species as Akanian, causing a slight disruption and feelings of uneasiness in Ganda. Many hear that Akanians are smaller but smarter and stronger due to the high gravitational forces and high electrolyte content on their planet. The stories of the Akanian arrogance make a few in the bar insecure. Since Akan is located on the other side of the galaxy, there is not a lot of space commerce.

So what brings these two Akanians to Miniloc? There must be something big going down! Such thoughts cause some patrons to quietly leave the bar in fear, as they do not want to become involved in whatever is about to happen. Sivad and Chorn, not recognizing the tension, continue with their mission goals and jokes. They do not have an understanding of what others feel about their species.

Nonchalantly, Sivad and Chorn go about their lighthearted business, sitting down at a small, centralized, round table flanked by plants, large columns surrounding them. The young Akanians look at the variety of species in the bar, many looking away when Sivad and Chorn's eyes fall upon them as they search for good targets to try out their new entertaining invention.

They mumble back and forth about each species. "What about that one, with the long pipe and small red hat?" Chorn asks as the character looks away.

"No. He doesn't have anything interesting to show, and he probably hasn't left his barstool in weeks," Sivad responds, snickering back at Chorn and wrinkling his nose as if he smelt bad.

"What about that fat one there? He looks like he might have had some action lately," Sivad suggests.

"Not unless you want to find out where he has eaten. That doesn't sound like fun, knowing this place," Chorn replies with a big smile. "Want some *MEAT*?"

Sivad smirks sarcastically back at Chorn. "**There!** That one, with the space suit," he says excitedly, moving to grab the steagora device from Chorn's hands.

"Are you sure? He doesn't look very friendly," Chorn says while looking at the armored man. "We don't want to get shot and vaporized by choosing the wrong karma victim here. We're just trying to have some fun. He looks like he might shoot us."

"Karma victim, I like that ... he-he," Sivad says as he starts to place the steagora device on his head.

"It's backward, knucklehead," Chorn informs him. He knows he cannot stop Sivad, so he puts his chin on his hand and waits.

The steagora device developed by Chorn is a basic mechanical device that taps into the brain receptors through thought wavelengths. Once a connection between the steagora device and the user is made, the device taps into the karma wavelength that follows us all and remains cached in the buffer memory. In this case, it can measure the stress levels, IQ, species, age, and images of the past twenty-four hours remaining in buffer memory or the latest, most stressful experiences of the target specimen.

It is a creative device Chorn intends to use as entertainment, but like most geniuses, he did not know how to apply it to better use, especially when it comes to making a profit. Every invention or technological gain has a process and is presented to the intergalactic science council for approval. Since Sivad and Chorn are just playing around, they do not realize that this device could be of importance to the rest of the galaxy. Thus they do not consider bringing it before the intergalactic council yet.

As Sivad prepares the steagora device, in the background, the door of Ganda swings open. A breeze blows through, and a morbid silence captures the room as the patrons watch a lone security drone enter into the room and turn to stand in a dark corner at attention near the entrance, with the simple intention of minding his own business but monitoring all.

The bartender leans over to a nervous patron who was about to leave because of the security drone's arrival and says in a low, gravelly voice, "At Miniloc, the feared and powerful security drones are ignored when out in singles. Everyone knows that, as long as they're not provoked and as long as no one has anything to hide from the Shobo Order, they don't bother anyone and leave as quietly as they entered."

The barman leans forward and grabs the patron's forearm to say, "Sit! Stay! Don't worry yourself. When the security drones are out in singles, such as this one, it means they're probing the area for something or someone. As long as nothing sudden happens, there will be no complications with more of Galleon's drones. Just hope they're not after YOU?"

"What? What did I do?" asks the patron with a guilty tone.

"Did you do something? No one here cares, but better not call attention to yourself especially - NOW," the barmen replies.

Sivad looks up at the ceiling as he turns on the short headphone-looking steagora device on his head. He looks up and sees the ceiling fans spinning around, four of them becoming one, spinning in sequence, and becoming a single fan. Sivad begins to feel a bit dizzy from the stimulation of the receptors on his head. "I feel a tingling sensation. Ooooooooh," he says with a strange stretched face.

Chorn replies with curiosity, "What is it? What do you see?"

Sivad says nothing and looks down toward the forbidding-looking creature dressed in an armored space suit, wearing a helmet and an oxygen pack on his back, feeding him air. Sivad begins to feel a montage of information start to stream in.

"It's ... kind of like a data dump. I can't make sense of all this," he says as he stares at the spaceman, his eyes moving back and forth so as to catch the data entering his head.

After a few seconds, Sivad says again, "Oooooooooh."

"What? What is it? What do you see?" Chorn asks with a very curious tone, looking from Sivad back toward the spaceman, trying to see what Sivad is encountering.

Sivad takes a step forward, still staring at the man, as a montage of information begins to appear.

Through the montage, Sivad sees shapes and images coming into view: sparkling palace walls, jewels, knights lined up in black armor, servants, and a beautiful waterfall streaming through the inside of the palace.

The image becomes more clear, and Sivad feels as if he is there himself.

An older, distinguished-looking man with a beard begins to scold a young, big-eared man: "You are a spoiled brat with no experiences outside these palace walls. How can you ever think of taking over as ruler of our people with the minimal accomplishments you have shown. Everything you have, I have given you. You do not command respect. Everything you have done has been an embarrassment to our family. You cannot even command the respect of a ferbo, let alone your servants. The maidens joke about you, as you being their boy-toy. Are they your servants, or are you theirs?"

The young, cracking voice of the prince replies with a whine, "I have experiences. I read all the time and know the history of our world and solar system."

The king picks up some animation books and tosses them at the prince.

"These are dirty comics! What experiences can you get from these fantasies?"

The king turns and walks a few steps away, one hand on his shaking forehead.

"I want you to take a leave." The king pauses before continuing,

"I want you to leave this place and go out and EARN some respect. Hopefully, you will learn something along the way.

"Do not divulge who you are to anyone. If you are old enough to get into trouble, then you are also old enough to take responsibility for your actions. I want you to go outside our solar system, where you do not have the luxury of my leadership or confidence to hide behind."

The king leans over and looks the big-eared prince dead in the eyes and says, "Regrettably, do not come back until you have something to show me and can prove that you are worthy of my crown and the respect of your peers."

Sivad is unable to see why the big-eared young man was in trouble, as it was not important enough for the man to have in his cached memory. Sivad says out loud, "Harsh!"

Chorn, curious as ever, hovers around Sivad, waiting for an answer. "What? What is harsh? What do you SEE?" He leans over Sivad's shoulder as if trying to see the karma spin.

Sivad's face becomes more determined to pull more information out. He clenches his fists, eyebrows down in absolute effort to dig deeper into this situation of the spoiled kid. As the karma spin continues, Sivad sees a large knight dressed in black armor, speaking with a low, powerful tone,

"Hey, kid, Pops isn't too happy with you, huh? You *know* he's right thourgh. You have to earn leadership.

On this sabbatical, let me give you some advice: be strong and look for adventure, then, when you return, you can claim your true birth right as *Prince Grant*. That's what the king wants. So good luck. He-he"

The knight gives a low-tone laugh, keeping the situation lighthearted.

Prince Grant sits and sulks on his bed, shrugs his shoulders, "Thanks, Phelan."

Sivad, staring at the armored man with all his focus, says out loud, "Prince Grant."

"WHO? Who is Prince Grant?" Chorn immediately asks, wanting to know what is happening.

Sivad takes off the steagora device and places it on the table, taking a deep breath as Chorn sits and leans over the table, anxiously waiting to hear the report.

"Well?" Chorn says.

Sivad pauses then begins with his extrapolation of the steagora device and how it functioned, "Well, it worked. I felt some tingling on my head as steagora made contact with me, then what seemed like a data dump of information was received. It was quite exhilarating. It felt like I was actually there."

"So, what did you SEE?" Chorn is not curious about the impact on Sivad or how his device worked, but he wants to know more of the actual events Sivad saw of the creature.

"It was difficult to process the information at first," Sivad says as Chorn grabs his shoulders.

"Stop toying with me. What did you see?" Chorn impatiently interrupts him.

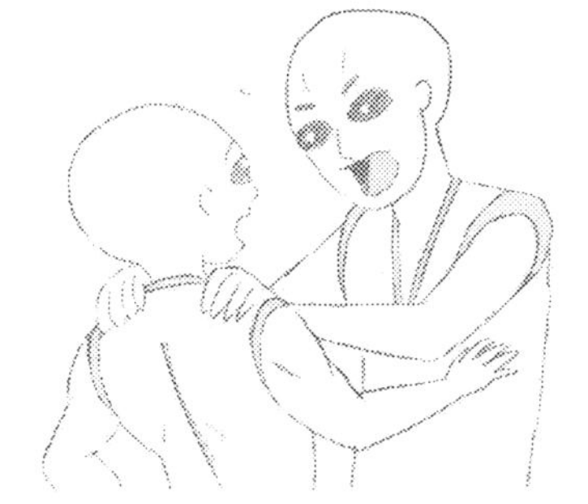

Sivad casually slaps Chorn's hands off his shoulder and brushes away the wrinkles. "I'm getting there.

Be patient!" Sivad says, knowing Chorn is waiting for the actual information. He starts speaking about the philosophy of the karma spin, "Exhilarating as this is, it is interesting to find what and where people have been; it defines the motivation of our actions."

Chorn falls back, putting his elbow on the table and one hand on his chin with a bored look, and his other hand taps on the table top. "Yeah, yeah, yeah." He knows Sivad is purposely delaying now. He accepts a drink from the waitress as he listens to Sivad ramble on.

Sivad stops, leans forward, looks at Chorn, and says in an eager tone, "He is the spoiled prince of Farthe, *not* scary at all! I would call it dressed in drag right now. I really don't know how he got that helmet on with those big ears." Sivad put his hands by his head, drawing out the prince's big ears, then emulated a struggle of putting a helmet on with no success.

"But he's not who he is pretending to be. His name is Prince Grant and ..." Sivad begins to tell Chorn the story about what he saw.

Giggling to each other, they look around to find their next karma victim.

"If Prince Grant looks dangerous and he's not, then take peek at that fat-bellied big guy over there."

"Where?" Sivad asks.

"THERE." Chorn points with his finger, drawing attention to the fact that the two Akanians are talking about the big outlander.

The creature they refer to is a barbaric outlander named Ragun, whose appearance is much like a traditional augur. Wearing a vest with no shirt underneath, large boots, and an old, beat-up pair of pants, with a large weapon strapped to his waist, the outlander sits and looks at Chorn pointing at him with a perturbed expression.

"That guy there with the fat belly," Chorn points and says a bit too loud. The big outlander, hearing Chorn, stands up and walks over to Sivad, who was looking away, putting the steagora device back on his head. Sivad turns to the large outlander directly in front of him. He sees nothing but belly as he looks up. "Wow!"

The karma spin begins to flow to him from the outlander; he is in the desert, eating a small, live creature as it screams. Sivad sees that this outlander, is a local denizen of Miniloc Moon.

The large-bellied outlander stands in front of Sivad and speaks in a foreign tongue, very upset. Sivad, too busy in the karma spin to pay any attention to the outlander in front of him, continues with his experiment. Chorn, in a panic, draws attention and moves his pointing hand to another direction while looking up at the large creature. He whistles nervously to get Sivad's attention.

Akanians, though strong, are pacifists and do not believe in confrontation unless absolutely necessary. It is fortunate that they have strength and wisdom, but when they have to defend themselves, they do so very well.

This particular outlander at Ganda is a representative of a more evolved local village. Still, barbaric in nature, he is ready to squash Sivad for what is perceived as an aggressive action.

Sivad takes off the steagora device, begins to turn to Chorn, and says, "This guy is boring. He has done nothing but—" Seeing Chorn's whistling face and hand waving while he is looking at the outlander, who is directly in front of Sivad, he takes a big look up, stops for a moment, and says fearlessly, "Damn, you're big up close."

The outlander again speaks in a non-comprehensible language. Chorn sits petrified and glued to his chair, when suddenly; Sivad reaches up and firmly grabs the outlander's nipples, twists, and nods his head in the direction of the outlander's seat, saying in a stern voice, "GO SIT DOWN!"

The shocked outlander turns with a very disappointed look on his face, his head slung down, as he submissively complies and returns to his seat.

Chorn, in shock of what just happened, looks at Sivad, who was just about to get pulverized, twisted the outlander's nipples, and LIVED? Chorn is speechless.

"This thing is *really* handy!" Sivad says to Chorn, whose mouth is still wide open. He holds up the steagora device and continues to talk more about the device than the event that just took place.

At this time, Chorn is not the only one with his mouth wide open. The music had stopped, and everyone in the bar was staring in amazement. The Ragun was known to be dangerous, and Sivad got away unscathed.

Seeing the shock, Sivad began to explain to Chorn with a confident, calm attitude that, by using the steagora device, he had discovered that it was this outlander's custom to show dominance by twisting nipples. Thus Sivad abided by customary traditions.

Ganda does not take long to regain its usual composure of business after any event, no matter how strange it may be. The music began to play again, and Cas's voice surrounded the hazy room.

Sivad and Chorn talk more about the device they have created.

The small, lone security drone still in the corner took notice of Sivad and Chorn and these events. While watching them with his mirrored face, he transmits the interesting information to Galleon. The transmission appears as blue text on the inside of the drone's mirrored face. Part of the transmission reads, "**Why are there two**

Akanians in this part of the galaxy, and what is this device they're using?"

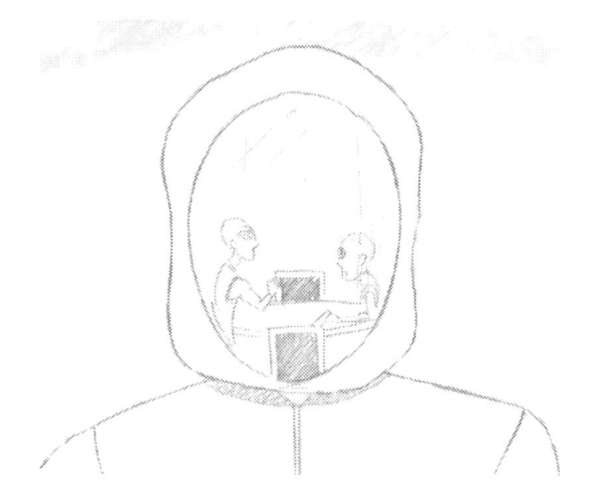

The fierce drone's algorithmic thinking knew that this information would be valuable and could trigger more curiosity and research among the order. He continues to monitor these two Akanians. The last part of the transmission states, "**Possible candidates for science slaves**."

Sivad and Chorn go on quietly speaking to each other about the steagora device and begin looking for another karma victim so Chorn can try the unit. "So, do you feel any adverse side effects?" Chorn jumps in to say.

"Nope, all worked well," Sivad replies, busy adjusting the device.

"Who should I try it on this time?" Chorn asks, with the question about the device's effects still in his mind.

"Well, let me try it one more time with the latest adjustments I've made. We might be able to get a longer buffer recollection and clearer imaging with the receptor valves open wider," Sivad says, working on the device.

Chorn agrees as he stands up and walks around Sivad, watching where he places the steagora device on his head.

Suddenly, in through the door enters an older humanoid with long gray hair and a beard, wearing beat-up, dirty clothing, one shoe, and a shackle around his ankle. He is immediately perceived as a homeless man.

The old man stumbles across the entrance and leans on the wall to catch his breath. He bends and falls forward just as Chorn turns to look at the commotion. The dirty creature falls over, grabbing Chorn, knocking him to the ground, and pinning him down underneath his foul-smelling clothes.

Sivad crouches down to the old man with the steagora device on his head just as the karma spin begins to take effect. The intention was to help Chorn get out from under this reeking creature, but the adjustments Sivad made were stronger than expected, and the karma spin took hold of Sivad with a series of intense images.

Stunned, he stops and focuses in on the man, preoccupied by the images. The images appear as a series of data dumps of a space vessel from the Shobo Order, a foreign object, a major discovery, and images from the *Blue Planet*.

From the corner where the security drone lifelessly observes, a dart springs from a small weapon and strikes the old man in the butt. The dart is not seen by anyone else in the bar, as all were focused in on the commotion with, again, the Akanians. The security drone quietly disappears into the chaos.

Chorn, upset at this stinking, dirty creature falling on top of him, tries to get up but falls again from the old man's struggling weight. Having been struck by the dart, the man falls forward once again, this time arching his back from the dart's impact.

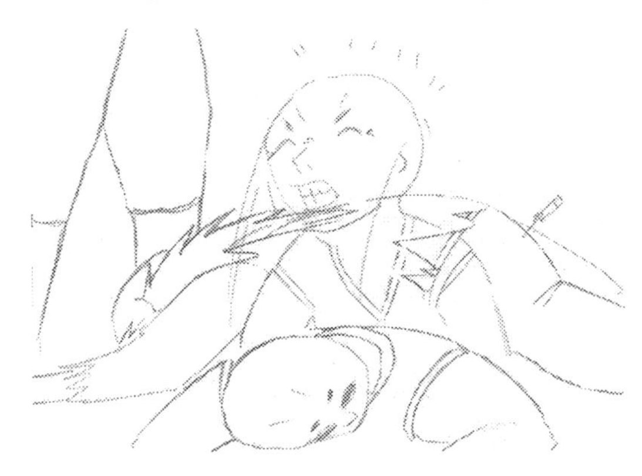

Chorn, almost sickened by the smell and germs from this transient creature, uses his strength in a temper and, with a fierce groan, forces his way up, launching the humanoid across bar. The old man bounces off a table and lands on the ground at Cas's feet.

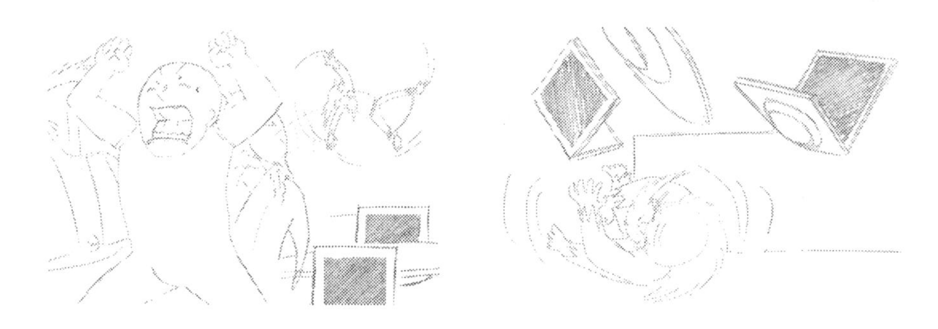

Sivad, frozen, still in the intense karma spin and trying to process the information, does not see what is happening around him. Coming around, he slowly takes off the steagora device, almost in a drunken state from the information flow, to see everyone in the bar standing and looking at Cas, tears streaming down her face as she yells,

"FATHER?"

At the same moment, the door opens from behind Sivad and Chorn, and Galleon, with his band of security drones, enters into Ganda with a commanding presence. All in the bar turn from Cas in anger and look at Sivad and Chorn, thinking that they are the cause of their adored Cas's father's death and of the entrance of the Shobo Order into their place of sanctuary.

Sivad says to Chorn, almost heartlessly, with the rest listening and staring at them, "Can you believe he was *just* a slave? A brilliant slave, but a slave. Time for a new one, I guess."

Out from behind Sivad and Chorn, a low, powerful voice originates.

"He was my SLAVE!" Galleon said, standing with his security drones and the intention of capturing Sivad and Chorn. "You shall now take his place as my servants," Galleon boasted.

Sivad began to lecture Galleon, "Don't you realize that it is against interstellar law to possess slaves who are not cybernetic in nature?" Chorn, looking behind Sivad, bumps him with his elbow as Sivad began to talk more.

The Ganda customers and loyalists to Cas began to approach the two, with weapons drawn and anger in their faces, when **"GET THEM!"** rang out from all directions— the Ganda patrons yell and Galleon orders to his security drones pointing at Sivad and Chorn.

Chorn grabs Sivad by the arm, tugging on him as he continues to provoke, and yanks him aside while the onslaught of angry Ganda customers charge. Chorn barrels into the security drones and Galleon, knocking them aside as the Ganda patrons and security drones collide and trip over one another. Chorn drags Sivad around the commotion and out the door by the back of his collar. Sivad is prepared to fight, yelling with fists in the air while being dragged,

"COME BACK HERE YOU FERBO'S DUNG I'LL TAKE YOU ALL ON".

Realizing that they are both outside, Sivad stands and looks at Chorn as Chorn says, "Let's get the heck out of here!"

"Done," Sivad replies as they flee down the stairs and past the Clark chef who continues to mumbling a random story.

Gen Planet Excursion

Sivad and Chorn board their space vessel and take off from Miniloc's MEP City. Sivad sits down and begins adjusting the navigation systems to head to their next location.

"We're going to the Gen Planet," Sivad says with excitement.

"What's there?" Chorn asks.

"We were successful in our information-gathering mission, and this little toy of ours came in handy," he says, continuing the enthusiasm and holding up the steagora device.

"How were we successful? We almost got our butts kicked off that moon because of you," Chorn says with a bit of contempt.

Sivad moves closer, as if he is going to tell Chorn a secret, and continues with a casual voice, "Check this out, from the old man's head." Sivad grabs Chorn's head from both sides. "I saw in his buffer that Galleon's ship found something from the Blue Planet that has a unique technological *value*. The object is a space probe that disrupts navigation, AND when used with our technology, Galleon's slaves found that it might be able to stabilize navigation in a radiated tackyon environment ... like a wormhole!" Sivad says with excitement.

"This is exciting because, think about it, if we can navigate through a wormhole, then we can travel to other galaxies and universes. That would be a tremendous gain and would make everything much more exciting for us!

"Imagine the value. Because of the Blue Planet and their basic original thinking, we will once again have great technological gains. Thus changing ... something. Evolution requires CHAOS!"

Sivad can hardly contain himself through his explanation to Chorn.

"What? Why would the Blue Planet send out a weapon such as a navigation disruption device?" Chorn asks with doubt but odd curiosity, because he does not always understand how Sivad derives certain answers; he just does.

"I don't know. Maybe it had a higher function, like redirecting oncoming space vessels to the Blue Planet to be conquered and steal their technology. Maybe they aren't as barbaric as our research has shown. Maybe they're aggressive and dangerous creatures with big fangs and claws, looking to take advantage of different species. They might even do anal probing on their victims or something.

"The way they are breeding and expanding so fast, they could quickly overtake many solar systems out there. Our studies have shown that they are aggressive, learn fast, *and*—since their technology is growing as well—it makes you wonder how much they are capable of and how fast they will surpass other species who have been in the galaxy for thousands of years."

Chorn, not sure whether to laugh or be completely perplexed at this level of extrapolation, responds, "That would be absurd. Even with their dense populations, what would happen if their probe came across a more advanced and aggressive species than Galleon's, who would be forced to go to their planet and wipe them out before they could become a threat. The Blue Planet beings would be in grave trouble, would they not?"

"I don't know how barbarians think. Maybe they're a short-sighted species like the Miniloc outlanders," Sivad says, not wanting to lose momentum for his theory.

"No, I think the space probe only had the purpose to relay messages with no malicious intent," Chorn begins, defining his conclusions. He puts his hand to his chin, grasping it with his thumb and forefinger. "Did you get any images from the old man of the Blue Planet's object being damaged or how the navigation disruption took place?"

"Yes. There were some radiation lockdowns before they took it into their possession," Sivad said.

"Well then, there you have it. The damage must have had something to do with the disruption," Chorn defines and then continues, self-satisfied, "So Galleon was at Ganda to retrieve his smelly slave. The stinky slave fell on ME—which I can still smell, by the way—and Galleon may think the stinky guy told you the plan. If he did escape, then there would be an information breach with whomever he told. That would mean that you got us into trouble AGAIN!" Chorn says, shouting at Sivad.

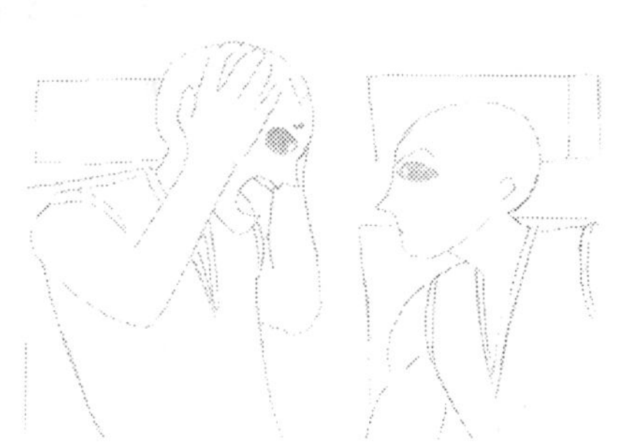

"Right. That's why we're going to the Gen Planet. That will be his next stop," Sivad replies, not even showing that he heard the last sentence.

Chorn takes a deep breath and says all at once, "But if Galleon thinks we know what he knows because his smelly slave knew, and we think he's going to do what we think he'll do, then he'll now be after us too. So why would we go to where he is going if we don't want to be where he is? And how do you know we need to go to the Gen Planet?"

Sivad stiffens up and with a bold voice says, "We have to secure that technology and bring it before the science board for their research and approval. Imagine the potential danger of what Galleon and Shobo could do with the technology and how they'll try to control intergalactic transportation. So we're off to the Gen Planet.

That's where Galleon's going, so we'll go too!" Sivad points out the window, ready to go and trying to motivate Chorn.

"I do *not* have a good feeling about this. I think you just want to cause trouble," Chorn says, acting like Sivad is crazy.

"It is exciting, isn't it?" Sivad says with a smile.

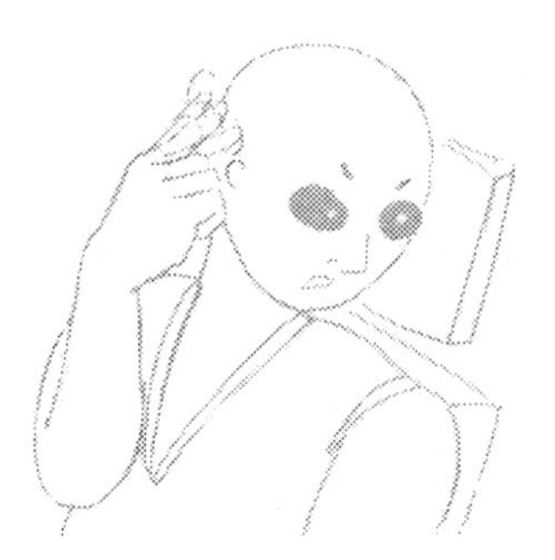

"Uh, I still think you're nuts. But you know me, let's go! What are you waiting for?" Chorn says as he smirks, knowing they are in for another unexpected time.

"Okay, push the engage button," Sivad says.

"You're closer. You do it," Chorn replies.

*****

Sivad and Chorn's shuttle lands just over some trees outside an old, abandoned Gen village destroyed by battle years before, leaving it a desolate ruin. After their shuttle disappears beyond the tree line and the sound of their shuttle fades away, an aura of cold silence overcomes the forest. The wind sends a lone maple leaf gracefully dancing down an overgrown pathway. The sound of the breeze whispers as if it is the last voice of ghosts from the aged Gen battlefield.

A single muffled voice from the dense forest disrupts the silence. "I'm always forgetting to bring what we need. I should have brought a laser machete to cut through this growth. Ouch!" rings Sivad's voice.

"Hey, genius boy, I think the path goes this way," Chorn's says as the bushes rattle and shake. There is no other sound except the voices of the two Akanians.

"UUCH, OW. DAM!" Sivad's voice cries out against the cracking branches.

The restful peace of the village and sound of the wind vanish, and the whispers seem to go into hiding from the oncoming visitors. The bushes shake on the edge of the ruins as the vanguard Sivad pops up over the last step of an eroded stone staircase exiting the dense, overgrown path. Sivad looks back at the trail as he stumbles from fighting his way out, watching Chorn pass him, gracefully walking up the stairs of the freshly used path.

"Next time, you can lead the way," Sivad says as he brushes himself off.

"When do I ever lead the way? I sit back and relax and let the shorter, bulkier ones do the work," Chorn replies, laughing as they look around the desolate ruins with mouths dropped open. "Whoa, what is this place?" Chorn asks.

"It looks like these boys were in a bit of a battle," Sivad says as they begin to walk down the center path of the ruins.

"What were they doing? Fighting over a graveyard?" Chorn says, a bit spooked by the wind howling through.

"Maybe," Sivad says, looking around.

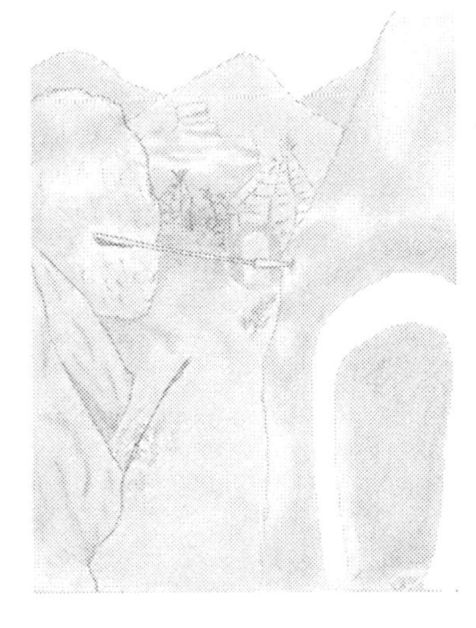

"Maybe," Chorn replies as he steps over the skeleton of a spear-stricken Gen. "I wonder who won?"

Sivad looks back at Chorn in a double take, as if it was a dumb question.

Chorn smiles as Sivad stops, bends over, and takes a closer look at one of the skeletons, saying, "Hey, I didn't know the Gens had battles. We were always taught that they are peaceful creatures who just innately seemed to reject evolution."

"Do you think this could be a significant anthropological discovery? If the Gens are to show that they are evolving after over three thousand years of stagnant growth, then—" Chorn says with academic curiosity.

Sivad intervenes, "Chaos makes the grass grow, I guess, huh?"

"This is so interesting. I didn't know information-gathering missions were so much fun," Chorn says as he raises his arms and looks around in a circle at the captivating sight and continues his rant. "The Gens were the most evolved species on the planet, and they stopped. If they are now evolving, then we should evacuate all the colonies that have settled here. Maybe their primitive language is evolving as well. War means movement and discontentment with the environment of each village. WOW!"

"You're going to be popular with the colonists. What's this?" Sivad says as he disappears into a dark opening.

"What's what?" Chorn says as he turns, his smile quickly fading when he sees that Sivad is no longer next to him. Sivad has disappeared. Chorn finds he is alone in the deserted burial ground and calls out, "SIVAD?"

The wind begins to howl past him, giving him a cold chill. Chorn sees an entrance that is pitch black behind him. Thoughts began to race through his mind that Sivad was somehow snatched by ghosts.

"Wow!" echoes Sivad's voice from the dark passageway, with a curious tone.

"Hey!" Chorn says, as he is a bit frightened and much relieved to hear Sivad's voice. He quickly ducks to enter the short, dark entrance.

"This must be some kind of old ceremonial room for the Gens. What a party they must've had," Sivad says. Chorn becomes used to the dim light and takes a look around from the entrance.

Sivad begins to walk around the raised stage area where drums, bells, and other primitive instruments are located. Dusty and worn, the instruments have not been used in years. Sivad looks at a Gen skeleton hanging off a spear and says to Chorn, "Did you know him?"

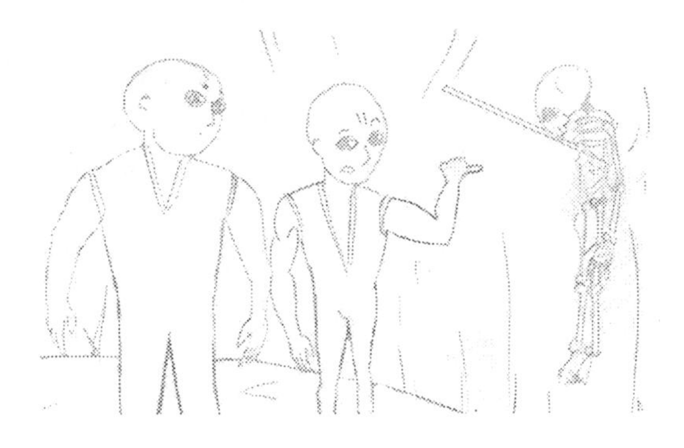

"We used to hang out together," Chorn says as he begins to walk up the stairs onto the staging area. Sivad jumps up onto the stage when he sees some big drums and becomes energized.

"All right!" Sivad says as he picks up some dusty large-tipped drumsticks off the floor.

Chorn starts to protest, saying, "NO! Don't disturb this stuff."

Sivad raises the drumsticks high into the air with a mischievous grin.

Then he starts to beat one of the larger dust-covered drums.

"Yeah!" Sivad's voice sings as the drum booms with a loud, heart-thumping sound, and a cloud of dust rises up around him. Sivad throws the drumsticks to Chorn and grabs another pair off the floor.

"Play, me man. This is the gig!" Sivad says.

Chorn has an unsure smile but starts to beat another large drum anyway. Chorn, beginning to be immersed by the music, dances around to beat a variety of drums. The rhythmic sound echoes as the dust cloud rises. Sivad and Chorn play back and forth as a battle of the drums. Chorn dances through the dust cloud and starts playing the dust-covered bells while Sivad shakes his hips, hands, and drumsticks in the air, dancing around.

"*Spoils of war,*" Sivad sings before he starts to beat his drum again.

Sivad and Chorn stop for a few minutes to allow the dust cloud to settle down as they move away, laughing and coughing from the good time.

Suddenly, there is a foreign drum sound entering into the room through the large hole in the ceiling, echoing off the walls.

Chorn moves closer to Sivad, looking up as if he is hearing a ghost. "What? Was that an echo?" Chorn asks.

"I don't know. Let's find out." Sivad turns and beats the drum some more with a rhythmic beat and stops and waits for a possible reply. Before Chorn could speak, Sivad quiets him and sticks his drumstick up his nose to stop him from speaking while Sivad looks up and waits. "Shhh! This could be some kind of jungle communications room."

The beat reply echoes off the walls in the old communications room. Chorn turns to Sivad, quickly stepping back, slaps him with the back of his hand on his shoulder, and says, "Do you know what this means?"

"If this is a communications room, then the Gens are remotely communicating between villages."

"Hey, wireless communication," Sivad says as he laughs. "This is extremely significant. Don't you see? If the Gens are remotely communicating, then they're evolving! Once again, chaos has begun." Both pause for a moment, knowing that chaos is the motivation for evolution.

"Chaos could lead to more chaos, more chaos could lead to war between Gens, and war between Gens could eventually lead to war with the colonists," Chorn says.

"Whoa! Do you realize what you're saying? If the Gens are evolving and start to conquer each other to show dominance as we have seen here, then ..." Sivad says and pauses.

"The colonists would really hate you for suggesting it," Chorn continues with his analytical tone.

"Then, if it did happen, the colonists would dominate them once the Gens attacked the cities. That would be an unnatural disaster for evolution on this planet."

"We would have to evacuate all the colonies," Chorn says.

"EVACUATE all the colonies? We can't do that. You're talking about generations of highly evolved cities that have been here for centuries," Sivad exclaims.

"This is not the colonists' planet. If the Gens begin evolving again, should we continue to disrupt them?" Chorn replies.

"No, but we should conduct campaigns to work with them. We cannot move the colonists. And besides, the destruction of this village might have been an isolated event and not necessarily indicate that the Gens are becoming more aggressive. It is non-conclusive," Sivad explains.

Chorn says with his arms wide open, "This could be a unique discovery, thus succeeding in our information-gathering mission."

"We'll let the politicians handle this one. And our mission is not only about information gathering; we have to explore as well and find new—" Sivad says as he is cut off.

"HEY! Order us some food," Chorn interrupts and taps Sivad on the back as he points to the drum for Sivad to send a message to order food on the drum.

Sivad begins to beat the drum with his so-called food-beating rhythm.

"And some drinks," Chorn says

Sivad's drink-ordering rhythm sounds.

"Don't forget dessert. And ask them directions to where the most civilized path is located to go to space port," Chorn says while still tapping Sivad on the shoulder annoyingly.

Chorn, satisfied with the find, starts to beat the drum, and they start to have a good time, excitedly pounding away in what they think is musical harmony once again.

Deeper in the jungle, on the other end of the communications link, one of the Gen villages hears the fast tempo of drum music and interprets it as aggressive. Screams sound as all the Gen males grab spears and head down a trail, ready to attack whomever is sending this absurd communiqué.

The faint echo of native screams bounce through the walls of the communications room.

"Hey, do you hear that?" Chorn asks as they both look up.

"Yeah, I don't know. We must be on the wrong wavelength or something. Here, you try it," Sivad says and steps aside.

"Better let them know we want separate bills," Sivad says as Chorn starts to beat the drum.

Up from over a hill, through the bushes, the Gen villagers gather outside the communications room, with spears readied, waiting for their chief to lead them in. The drum music echoes out the entrance of the node as the anxious Gens start to enter the compound.

The Gens enter the node and surround the lower path below the raised stage. They are upset and confused by these two species playing their drums. Not knowing if these intruders are dangerous, they hesitate to strike. Some Gen villages have seen the colonists and their huge, towering cities and flying machines and have been amazed at some of the things they've witnessed. Other tribes stick to their own territory and have never seen or heard of any colonies. This is one of those tribes. They stare in awe at the two bald creatures using their property.

Since Gens are largely pacifists, they watch and wait for the intruders to make the first aggressive move.

"I'll play one of the smaller drums and get some higher-pitched sounds."

"Yeah, get a different tone,"

Chorn says.

Sivad turns and looks up through the settling dust to see the Gens looking down at him from above, on top of the broken clay roof. Then, looking lower, he sees a swarm of Gen heads gathered around, popping out just above the stage floor, standing on the lower path with spears at attention. Sivad tilts his head sideways in a nonaggressive, curious manor then reaches back and taps Chorn on the shoulder as he is playing recklessly and shaking his hips, having fun.

"You should play the bells," Sivad says with a startled voice.

"*Okay!*" Chorn turns in a dancing motion, jumps in shock, and lets out a small, high-pitched, girly scream when he sees all the Gens gathered around.

"Uh, the party crashers are here," Sivad says as they back up into each other.

"You must have played the wrong message," Chorn says as they both gently put down the drumsticks and smile with mischievous grins.

"I hope they're not hungry," Sivad says, reaching out and touching the tip of one of the spears pointed directly at them.

"This is great. Look! We're right. They're carrying spears and being more aggressive. Chaos begins again!" Chorn says, grabbing Sivad's arm in his satisfaction.

"Yep, our boys are all grown up!" Sivad says.

The Gens, confused by Chorn's erratic movements, identify that these two are not aggressive. They tilt their heads to one side then the other looking for any kind of weapon and marveling at the strange clothes and bald skin.

The chief speaks to Sivad, who has not lost sight that there are more than thirty spears pointing at them. Sivad remembers his old lessons that the Gen language is motion based. He tilts his head to show that he does not understand what they are saying.

The chief climbs the stairs and walks over to look at Chorn and says something. Chorn, not understanding, becomes apprehensive and starts to hide a bit behind Sivad. Sivad, seeing that this is the leader, calmly sits down, crosses his legs below him to show nonaggression, and bows his head.

"Ah, placing your head below his to communicate and show intent. Good thinking," Chorn says.

Sivad grabs Chorn and pulls him down a bit hard, smiling at the chief. Chorn falls with a grunt, looks at Sivad, who is smiling, and joins him with a big cheesy smile, staring at the chief.

Chorn looks around, with only his eyes keeping his head pointed at the chief, and says to Sivad through his teeth, "How long do we do this?"

"Shut up and let them make the first move," Sivad says, also talking through his teeth and smiling.

A skinny, discontent Gen climbs onto the stages, wearing a colorful hairpiece, bamboo gators on his ankles and seemingly sharper teeth than the rest of his tribe.

"Let's kill them. If they're sent from the gods, then they will not die. They obviously don't belong here," he says, almost whispering to the chief in their ancient language.

The chief turns his head, looking at the colorful hairpiece, and calls one of his lead soldiers, "What do you think?"

"I think they're harmless idiots who wandered in here by accident," he replies with a lot of bodily gestures and limited language.

"Simple outlanders?" the chief asks as a rhetorical question.

The other Gen shows his discontentment as they all discuss what to do.

Sivad and Chorn become a bit nervous listening to the foreign conversation. Sivad closely watches the movements, gestures, tones, and voices, trying to process the language and define a pattern or rule set. After a moment, he tires of the deliberation from the Gens and suddenly stands up saying, "We're wasting time."

The Gens are confused and anticipate a fifty-fifty chance of following one adviser over the other.

"What are you doing?" Chorn says, surprised.

All the Gens jump back as Sivad walks over to the chief and puts his hand out as a friendly greeting. Sivad expects this will force the chief to make his own decision and give the advisors no time to make his call for him.

The chief, half the size of Sivad, as expected, follows and places his hand out, mimicking Sivad, who gently grabs his hand, holds it, and says, "I am pleased to meet you. I am Sivad," while using a lot of bodily gestures with his other hand.

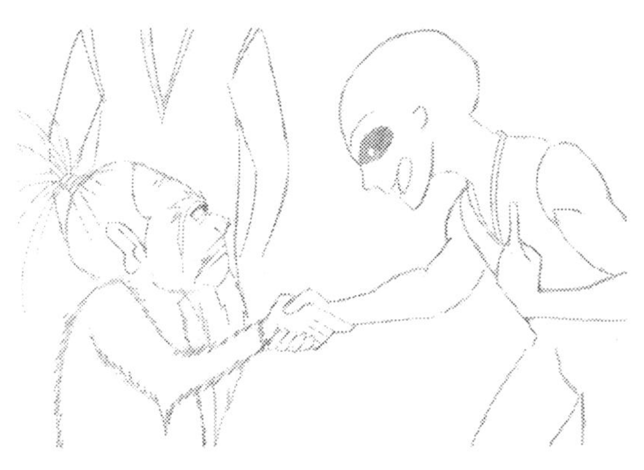

"Just don't turn and bitch slap him on his face with that rogue hand," Chorn jokes, watching Sivad's other hand wave around.

The chief, a peaceful-minded Gen, says out loud, holding his hands in the air with Sivad's, "Ariba!"

Sivad, seeing the response of the soldiers, repeats the chief's words and also says, "Ariba!" with the understanding that it must be a friendly word, possibly meaning "*friends*."

The surrounding soldiers reply in happiness, "Ariba!"

Chorn jumps in, looking at Sivad, and also says, "Ariba! I hope it doesn't mean attack."

The crowd again yells, "Ariba!" in cheer.

"How many times do we have to do this?" Chorn asks Sivad while the soldiers are cheering.

Still smiling, Sivad grabs Chorn's hand and raises it with the chief's. "Ariba!"

The crowd again yells, "Ariba!"

The Gen with the colorful hairpiece stands with arms crossed and a frown on his face. Chorn turns to him and, seeing that everything is friendly, pulls out from his pocket a small box the size of a sugar cube with a red button on the top.

"Hey, oh, no you're not. I gave that to you," Sivad exclaims, knowing Chorn's plan.

Chorn holds out the box and pushes the button, with his arms extended in front of the unhappy Gen. The box begins to play music that begins echoing throughout the node room.

The chief looks at the unsatisfied advisor, pleased that he made the right decision and did not listen to him. "Take it. I think it is a gift for you."

Chorn holds the box out with his hands and repeats what the chief said, in a truncated form. Instead of using the pronunciation the chief used, Chorn unknowingly said, *"Eat it. Rocks are for constipation."* The other Gens began to laugh at the miss-pronounced words.

Chorn smiles and looks around, unsure why they are laughing, when the skinny, little colorful Gen finally smiles and takes the box. He pulls it close to his body, holding it tight, and pushes the button with delight in his eyes, listening to the harmony.

The chief calls out, and two soldiers come forward onto the stage and hold out two necklaces laced with teeth, bones, and a giant jewel in the middle. Sivad smiles, though Chorn is a bit disgusted by the dead pieces being placed around his neck as they bow their heads.

"How come your jewel is bigger than mine?" Chorn asks Sivad.

"Gem-etics, my old friend. Gem-etics," Sivad replies and laughs.

Chorn holds up two of the sharp teeth on the necklace and places them in front of his mouth, grinning as if they were his own fangs hanging down. Laughter erupts among the Gens. The chief grabs Sivad's hand, turns, and starts to walk toward the stage steps, waving his arms to all the soldiers to leave the complex.

The Gen chief wishes Sivad and Chorn good luck in their journeys as his warriors depart. Since Sivad and Chorn could not understand what the chief had said, they just shook their heads, agreeing with the chief.

"The Gens are definitely evolving," Sivad says, watching them leave and marveling at his new necklace.

"Trade, aggression, wars, territorialistic behavior, and reasoning. The senior chancellor will be impressed," Chorn says. As they prepare to continue their journey to the colony where they believe Galleon has landed.

The closest colony from where Sivad and Chorn landed their shuttle is about a half-day's journey by foot. It is one of the more civilized colonies on the planet and has the largest spaceport and trade station.

*****

In the dusk of night, Galleon's shuttle, transporting the Blue Planet's probe from the Gigil Pain to Shobo's 2D City, the headquarters of the Shobo order, hovers down into the colony and lands at a private docking station. The shuttle door opens as the resident security drones gather around the vessel, ready to conduct maintenance and ensure local security. The security drones have already emptied the docking station of all extraneous personnel to ensure isolation so that the science slaves can begin work and test the technology before it is delivered to Shobo. Galleon exits the shuttle first, walking out onto the docking station, with his hands behind his back. He stops and looks around. The chip of power and glory is shown in his every arrogant move.

Following Galleon are four drones with a prisoner behind them, followed by two more drones at the rear. The four drones force the hooded prisoner down the exit ramp, where she falls to her knees. The hood falls back. Looking up at Galleon with large, shiny, sad eyes, the prisoner's face is revealed. It is Cas, the singer from Ganda. Galleon and his drones decided to take her after they ransacked the bar and interrogated the regulars. Galleon learned during his examinations of the bar patrons that Cas was the leader of the *Miniloc Guerilla Pack*, or the *MGP*. He thought she may have insight as to who the two Akanians were, what they were doing in that bar, and what the device on the one's head was. Many questions had to be answered.

Galleon turns toward the shuttle and barks an orders to his drones, "Post two guards on the entrance of the shuttle. Protect. No one goes in or OUT!"

The drones around Cas kick her legs out and forced her to her knees as Galleon looks at her through his gasmask glasses.

"My boys do not like it when their prisoner's head is not lower than theirs."

With a cracking voice, Cas exclaims to Galleon, "You destroyed the Ganda! You hurt my friends! You let those two Akanians go free! It's your fault!"

"Ah, with that, you are right; it is my fault. Take her to the holding chambers," Galleon replies. "Wait!" he says as he turns around again. Galleon bends down and looks closely at Cas, pauses, and says, "What do you know about those two Akanians?"

He proceeds to drill her with a quick interrogation, "Why were they in Miniloc? Why Ganda? What were they doing there? What was the device they had?"

In fear of the questioning and dismayed that Galleon does not know these answers, Cas cries out, "I don't know! I've told you; I do not know!"

One drone, not liking the answer, forces her down to the ground while another grabs her and forces her back up to her knees.

Galleon moves closer. Cas looks up and sees her reflection in his gasmask glasses, a tear rolling down her cheek.

"What did the old man tell you?" Galleon growls at Cas.

"That was my father!" Cas yells in an exhausted, angry voice.

Galleon, surprised by the new information, thinks to himself, *Hmm, that explains why the old man went to Ganda: his daughter and the leader of the MGP.*

"Your father? Hmmmmm," he mumbles as he thinks. "What did the Akanians want with him?" Galleon asks, still probing for more information as the drones push her forward to ensure she complies with his questioning.

"They killed him! They killed my father, and you let them go! You bastard!" Cas replies, emotional and exhausted.

"NO, they did not! I killed him. Ha-ha," Galleon replies and laughs while Cas, who was trying to be strong, begins to sob. Galleon would not let another take credit for anything he has done. He is far too proud and would be offended if another was able to kill one of his slaves rather than him.

Galleon continues with the questions. "What did the old man want with the Akanians? Answer me!"

Rather frustrated from not obtaining satisfactory answers, Galleon shouts, "You are useless to me like this. I hate it when chicks cry; their infectious brains just seem to shut down when emotion takes over."

He clutches his fists and orders, "Extract any information you can out of her. Use any methods necessary. Take her away!" He turns to another drone after six drones drag the prisoner away as she tries to kick and scream.

"Find out what you can about the two Akanians. I need to know if the old man told them anything, if they know about our *Blue Planet probe project*, and if they're trying to report back to the science board. If they do, then we could have a problem with the federation. Stop them any way you can!"

Before the drone turns to go to work, Galleon interrupts, commanding, "Also, find out where they were destined for and why they're so far away from their own solar system."

An image displayed on the drone's mirrored face of Sivad and Chorn in ball and chains as slaves. Words ticker-taping across the bottom spelled out,

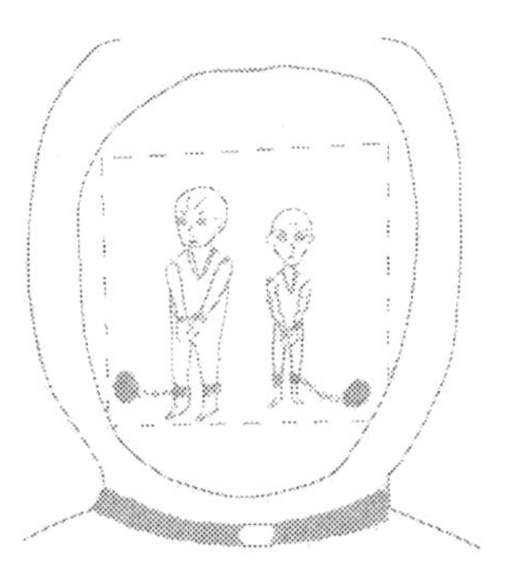

"**They would make good slaves for us.**"

"I like the way you think. Yes, yes, they would make good slaves," Galleon says, satisfied in his drone. "Find what planet they've gone to. Locate their ship," he orders.

The drone turns while two other drones immediately pull out and set up a control panel at the base of the exit ramp. The lead drone enters information into the console and presses a big red command button.

In orbit, a hatch door opens on the Gigil Pain. From the bay door, sounds of screams call out as small peanut-shaped probes, with doglike search instincts programmed into them, sniff the galaxy, hunting for the Akanian spacecraft. The probes jump and launch themselves one after another from the Gigil Pain. The rockets of the peanut-shaped probes fire as they take off to other solar systems, common traffic routes, and inhabitable planets and moons hunting for their targets.

Unknown to the lead drone, Sivad and Chorn are not where the probes are destined. Instead, they are on the Gen planet, right under the drones' mirrored faces. All the probes are launched, leaving none to search the planet below.

*****

Back in the node room, Sivad and Chorn finish philosophizing about the Gens' evolution and decide to continue their journey.

"Let's leave this party," Sivad says as they walk down the stage staircase.

"Yeah, let's go find some other ruins with more dead things in them. We can put them around our necks." Chorn cringes as he looks down and shakes his necklace, then he turns and grabs the hand of one of the Gen skeletons stuck to the wall by a spear. "No, you can't come with us. You must stay here and protect this place," he says as he jokingly reasons with the skeleton. Sivad walks out. Chorn, still talking to the skeleton, gives a slight whistle and says to the Gen skeleton while pointing a finger at it, "Stay!"

Taking one final look around, satisfied with the results, Chorn starts to hear the ghostly whispers and howl of the wind again, giving him a spooky sensation. He turns and starts running for the door, saying, "Send me a communiqué!" as he hurries out the door to catch up with Sivad.

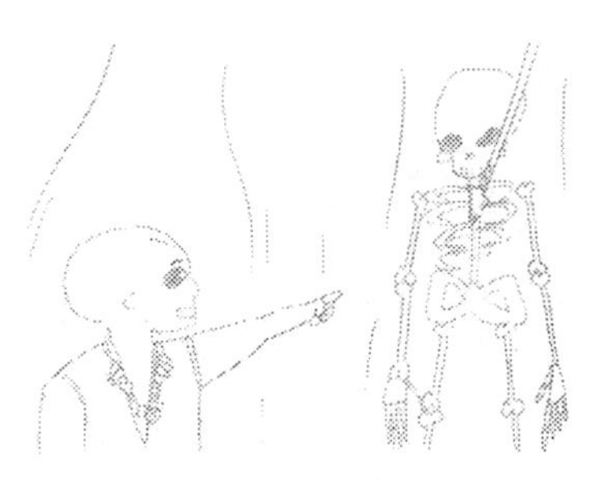

Gen Village

Walking through the dense forest, heading toward the nearest colony, Sivad, as usual, is out in front. Unlike his last painful experience, before they found the ruins, this time, he gracefully bends the branches to slither through the jungle with animal-like instincts, or so he thinks to himself as he starts to imagine that he is a fierce animal stalking through the undergrowth.

Chorn, close behind, casually gets slapped in the face with branch after branch. He tries to duck and swerve from each whip with no luck.

Sivad, almost lost in thought and immersed in his imagination, gets interrupted when a painful "Ouch!" and slapping noise comes from Chorn. Sivad turns. "What did you do?"

"What did I do?" Chorn says, not happy and rubbing his face from where a branch struck.

"This jungle's so dense YOUR LAUNCHING twigs at me."

"THIS TIME, I am going to lead the way for a change," Chorn says as he forces himself by Sivad.

"Lead on, sport. You're the vanguard," Sivad says, accommodating Chorn with a slight bow.

"Hey, look, there's a trail!" Chorn says, looking over some bushes as he starts to walk over to it. "You see?

That's what leadership is all about. It's about finding the trails," Chorn says with a smug smile as he looks back at Sivad.

Once Chorn turns forward again, he runs into a spider's web and raises his hands to his face to remove the sticky silk. "YUCK!" he gasps, trying to wipe it off. At the same time, he stumbles out onto the trail from the thick bush.

Suddenly, there is a snap from the ground, and Chorn's feet are whisked out from under him with a rough swoop.

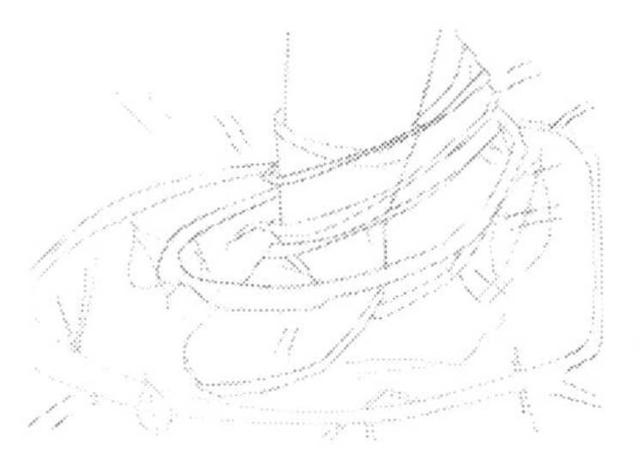

"What the—" Chorn screams as his body slams against the ground before being dragged into the air by his feet. He comes to a rest hanging upside down from a tree, with his head one meter from the ground.

"**WOW!** I don't like that trail," Sivad says, shaking his head and starting to giggle at the upside down Chorn. Seeing Chorn this way, Sivad starts to laugh almost uncontrollably at the sight while Chorn hangs by the vine.

"Ya know, there is a philosophy about leadership," Sivad says, laughing as Chorn bobs up and down on the branch. "Leadership is not something to play with. Sometimes it can leave you hanging in precarious, submissive spots. An animal snare, for example," Sivad says as he laughs with his arms open, embracing the scene.

Chorn growls in frustration.

"Down, boy!" Sivad says, still laughing. "You shouldn't let leadership go to your head now, ya see," Sivad continues, slapping himself on the knee, seeing Chorn's head turning red. "Gravity SUCKS, huh?" he continues, laughing

"The only thing going to my head is all my blood. HURRY up and get me down from HERE!" Chorn exclaims.

"I don't know. Maybe I should leave you hanging there for a while simply because Y-O-U got caught up in such a simple, primitive trap," Sivad says, pointing at Chorn and stepping up onto a rock, arms open and ready to grab the tree branch above Chorn's feet.

"SHUT-UP!" Chorn says briskly

"You call yourself a genius? Brainpan of a Gen, I tell ya," Sivad says, still laughing, and slips off the rock.

"SHUT-UP!" Chorn exclaims again.

"Oh, ferbo pellet! I think I pissed myself," Sivad says, still laughing, almost dropping down to a roll while Chorn squirms helplessly in the trap.

Sivad climbs back up on to the rock, reaches up, and grabs Chorn's foot and holds it like the catch of the day.

"Oh, I think I need a picture of this. The boys back home will never believe I caught the GREAT Chorn. We're going to eat well tonight!"

"Come on! Shut up!" Chorn says again, but he can't help but start to break a smile from Sivad's laughter.

Due to the heavy gravity on Akan, Akanians are very strong when they want to be. Sivad grabs the branch and starts to pull it down. "I tell you, Chorn, the fruit on this planet is very strange."

"Stop joking. This is not funny! Hurry up and get me down," Chorn says impatiently as he laughs as well.

"Don't worry; you'll fall off when you're good and ripe," Sivad says, still amused, while he struggles to bend the tree and fight off the branches, having to sweep them aside as they brush his face.

Chorn hits the ground with an "Umph!" as Sivad jumps on the tree, giving it its final bend and holding it down. Branches and leaves fly everywhere as Sivad crawls down the tree over Chorn to keep the weight on the treetop and get to Chorn's feet that are secured in the trap. Chorn swings his weight around to stand up and rest on top of the bent treetop to help keep it down for Sivad. The flex of the tree quivers at maximum threshold, waiting to recoil. It takes both Sivad and Chorn to hold it steady so Sivad can untie Chorn's feet.

"I didn't know you were into bondage," Sivad says while getting to Chorn's feet. "Rather kinky."

"Just get me untied, you dork. This tree doesn't seem to be very stable," Chorn says

Sivad steps on the end of the tree while Chorn sits on the top half, holding the tree in position as he begins to have his feet untied.

"Well, it looks like you've been pardoned from a hanging. I guess that means if you're hung and live, then it's a sign that you're to be set free," Sivad says with a deep, slow voice, working on the knot.

Chorn moves his head back and forth, looking at the tree and the positioning while Sivad is preoccupied by teasing him and untying his feet. Chorn suddenly realizes something about their positioning on the tree, but it is too late.

"Well, that should do it. Time to throw you back." Sivad steps off the treetop that Chorn was holding down.

The tree recoils with such power that it catapults Chorn along with it, launching him into the air.

Chorn lets out a scream and flies upward and off the branch with enough force to send him over the large bolder just behind the primitive trap setting.

"Oops! Bottoms up, Chorn!" Sivad says as he watches Chorn take off.

Sivad stands up and starts to hurry around the rock when he stops, realizing there may be more traps around, and begins to walk gingerly around the rock, tiptoeing to ensure he would not get caught up in a similar trap. He knew it would be the end of him if Chorn caught him in the same type of trap.

"Once burned, you're a fool; twice is a fool's practice. Better get him a bandage," Sivad says, disappearing around to the other side of the rock to fetch his friend.

Chorn's continuous scream is heard like an incoming bomb as he descends upon his unsuspecting targets. Below is another small Gen village, where the inhabitants are gathered around their ceremonial pond located in the center.

The pond has a large log resting on boulders spanning across the surface and is surrounded by straw and stick-frame huts.

The villagers watch as two Gen males battle on top of the ritual log. The fight is for who will be qualified and strong enough to marry the chief's daughter. The battle sound echoes to the drum beat as the Gens combat each other.

They begin to attack, grabbing and pushing each other, trying to knock the other off the log and into the water below. Both Gens are strong males striving to show they are more masculine than the other, thus receiving the honor of marrying the chief's daughter. As the villagers watch intently, they hear a terrifying noise screaming over the ceremonial drumbeat, becoming louder and louder. One log warrior looks up, points, and yells an expletive in their language.

But before anyone can look up to see what is coming, Chorn lands on top of the battle-driven Gens, knocking them both into the water. Chorn crashes onto the top of the log, bounces hard, flips backward, and lands in the water with flop, causing a large splash extending like a tidal wave over the chief, his daughter, and other Gen spectators close to the pond, watching the battle. All that is heard is the "Ahhhhh! Oooooo!" from the crowd and Chorn grunting as he hits the log and lands flat backed in the water.

Sivad startles the villagers when he jumps out from an overgrown trail, running around the bolder into the Gen camp to ensure Chorn is okay. He sees his friend in the water and the chief and villagers all wet.

"That boy loves to travel!" Sivad says to himself as he starts walking around the water.

The entire village turns and looks at the chief as the water soaks into his fur and drips off his limbs and brow. The villagers' attention quickly diverts to Chorn sitting up in the pond, trying to catch his breath from the impact, while Sivad walks in a casual stroll through the village, holding a big, nervous smile on his face. The two prospective husbands continue to soak in the ceremonial pond.

Chorn, not realizing what he has just done and still delirious from the impact, starts to talk to himself, splashing his hands once in the water as he sits waist deep. "Damn it, Sivad! Why did you let go? I had a bad feeling about this since we were on the dune at Miniloc." Chorn stops when he notices that he landed in the middle of a Gen village and has about thirty Gens standing and staring at him with unhappy expressions on their faces.

Chorn sees Sivad walk around the log very gently, with the nervous smile on his face. A still-upset and sore Chorn says to Sivad as he stands up, "Now what did you get me into? Help me out of here!"

Sivad, feeling a bit guilty, gracefully walks over to Chorn to help him out of the pond in front of the chief. He looks back and forth at Chorn and the chief, ensuring neither side will attack him.

"Ah, so you're upset, huh?" Sivad says with apologetic grin.

Sivad, not knowing what else to say to Chorn as he holds his hand out for Chorn to grab, says, "Haven't I seen you **hanging** around somewhere before?"

"Yeah, get me my rubber duck, catapult boy," Chorn says as his dripping hand grasps Sivad's. He goes to step out while securing his foot on a rock.

Sivad says, "Wow, you REALLY took off. That was so COOL! Wish I could of—"

Still upset, Chorn grips Sivad's arm tight, gives a brisk tug, and uses his Akanian strength to launch Sivad into the water, splashing the two already soaked battling Gens.

Chorn laughs, not paying attention to the possible trouble around them and having some fun at the satisfaction of getting Sivad wet as well. "Ha! Catch me some dinner while you're in there!" Chorn says.

"Oh, the dangler strikes back," Sivad says from the water as he rolls under the log, sits between the two soaked Gens in the water, and puts his arms around them as they sit in shock. He awaits the Gen chief's reaction and the consequences, trying to not show any aggression.

The wet chief is surprised, upset, and confused by Chorn's disruption of his sacred ceremony, not to mention the intrusion into the village by the two foreigners. He can barely hold himself while he pauses momentarily, watching and thinking, as he can only halfway hold back a smile from the craziest thing he has ever seen. He also feels the tension and dead silence from his villagers.

The chief begins to laugh jollily and is happy that the two comical intruders appeared to be no threat, and he is dismayed. He is a traditional chief and upholds respect for their rituals.

The chief walks over to Chorn, holds his wrist, raises it as high as he can in the air, and says in his own language, "Winner!"

Chorn, baffled by this, plays along, smiling and waving to the crowd.

"This stranger was the last to fall off the log," the chief says, looking at the villagers then back at Chorn with a disappointed face, squinting one eye. The chief, looking back at the crowd, drops Chorn's hand. "No way!" he says as he shakes his head, mumbles, and walks into one of the huts.

The villagers, unsure about the chief's decision, gather around Chorn with curiosity. Sivad is still sitting patiently in the pond, watching Chorn while the villager's approach.

"Hey! Hey, what do I do?" Chorn asks Sivad nervously, with his head looking back and forth at the villagers.

"Run with it. I think they're harmless, and you're now a hero of some kind," Sivad says after watching the chief.

"They don't eat heroes here, do they?" Chorn says.

"I don't know. They do look a bit hungry," Sivad replies jokingly.

"Hey, hey. Don't touch!" Chorn says when the crowd opens in one direction to a young Gen girl standing alone with a shy smile on her face and a homemade straw ribbon in her hair.

"Uh, a prize for the hero?" Sivad, says laughing as he stands up in the water.

The young Gen girl holds Chorn's hand and snuggles her soaked fur into Chorn's leg, looking up at him with infatuated eyes.

"You want to trade? You're the one always leading us into trouble," Chorn says.

"Nope, you gave away my music box, *and* it was you who led us into this one. He-he!" Sivad says to Chorn, who is taking a second look, knowing that Sivad is not going to help and is enjoying this too much.

The chief, after disappearing in his discontent into the stick-frame hut, returns holding an elaborate mask. The mask is a colorful headdress with two eye slots, a mouth opening, and a big nose made for Gens. It has long straw eyebrows, grass hair, and what looked to be a straw mustache.

The chief walks directly over to the nervous Chorn, reaches up, and places the headdress over Chorn's face. Chorn, insecure about what the chief's intentions are, begins to raise his hands when Sivad jumps in, quickly saying, "Better let him do it," in a long, drawn-out tone.

Once the chief secures the mask on Chorn, he turns to his tribe and begins to say something in their language. Chorn cannot understand when the chief was saying, "Winner of the log-fighting competition!"

The chief wanted no chance for this outlander to marry his daughter, so he completely refrained from speaking any further. All the villagers let out a cheer, with understanding and relief in the chief's quick decision.

All were happy, except one, the daughter who became rather attached to Chorn's leg and did not want to let go.

"*We will continue the wedding ceremony later,*" the chief says as he gives a scolding look at his daughter for her desire to keep the outlander. "*It is a good omen when the Gods send, umm, guests to our village.*" The peaceful chief says with a pause of uncertainty in his voice.

"What? What just happened? What is this thing on my leg? She's acting like ... we got married or something! Sivad? Sivad, where are you?" Chorn's muffled voice sounds from under the mask. "Damn, did you ditch me again?" he says as he tries to look for Sivad through the grassy eyeholes of the headdress.

"He-he. Can't wait to see your babies," Sivad laughs as he is helped out of the pond by three over-smiling Gen males. "Hey, these guys are a bit goofy." Sivad laughs about the three Gens.

Trouble Brewing

At the Gen spaceport, under a dimly lit aura, Galleon walks down a corridor filled with the sound of a beautiful voice. Cas is held in one of the detention chambers, where Galleon is passing through. Cas's song of sadness and oppression echoes throughout the walls, with all her emotion and heart. Galleon stops to listen, absorbed by the beautiful sound, he recalls an ocean planet he once visited with beautiful amphibious people, where the carnivorous women hummed a song like sirens on the shore, hypnotizing their prey to draw them nearer.

As Galleon turns forward, gazing at the ground and shaking his head for being drawn in by the charm, he raises his head and, with quick steps, walks directly into a large column, banging his head.

"GASP! I am having a bad day," Galleon mutters to himself, bouncing off the column and moving on.

He arrives at a darkened communications room, leans over a flashing monitor, presses a button, and begins to speak,

"Shobo, Galleon here. I take it you have received my report, theories, and plan of action? I am awaiting your reply," Galleon says with a strong voice, showing Shobo that he is confident and loyal.

A holographic image appears in front of Galleon about one-third the actual size. As the image clears, Galleon greets with a bow the most feared individual in the galaxy, an older male of an unknown species looking similar to that of an Akanian but taller and more worn, with an attitude like a walking corpse. Shobo, the leader of 2D City and a strong order in the galaxy, appears with his head hung low, as if the knowledge he possesses weighs him down and sways him side to side. His deceivingly slender, mummified-looking body is cloaked in a robe, appearing as if he has been dead a thousand years.

Galleon's excitement to test the new theory of the navigation tool and possibly be the first ship to travel from one galaxy to another and back again showed in his ambition and rush to gain approval by Shobo. Galleon's goal was to present Shobo with his ship, *the Gigil Pain*, to be the test source, integrating the new systems. Shobo knows that the first one to travel to another galaxy will develop a big name for himself, gaining power and fame. Thus, seeing into Galleon's motivation, he must maintain discipline and control of one of his most trusted loose cannons. Shobo knows that Galleon can be overaggressive; therefore, he is careful to not lose power by a reckless mistake. Galleon's temptation to jump into the new navigation tool can be dangerous; in turn, Shobo must attempt to balance Galleon's ambition with his leadership and subservient behaviors in order to maximize his usefulness to the order.

"Yes, YOUR findings ARE very interesting," Shobo replies, showing no interest in either direction, to allow Galleon to test it or not. His voice changing tone every few words.

"I have begun development and integration of the new technology into the Gigil Pain's navigation systems in anticipation of your approval, sir," Galleon says, confident in his actions.

"Does anyone ELSE know what YOU have discovered?" Shobo asks, evading his authorization to go ahead with the plans.

"No, sir, we have secured the technology and the Blue Planet's probe and are ridding ourselves of any extraneous persons." Galleon refers to Sivad and Chorn but does not want to say anything just yet, as he does not know if they have any knowledge of the plan.

"Where IS the probe NOW?" Shobo asks with his fluctuating voice.

"It is in route to 2D City and with me now in a secure docking station," Galleon answers.

"Hmmmm. WHEN will you ARRIVE in 2D City?" Shobo asks.

"Tomorrow, sir."

Pausing for a moment, Shobo jumps in with his decision, his slow voice telling the ambitious Galleon the logical steps, "Do NOT be overly ANXIOUS to integrate your systems YET with this navigation device. We do NOT yet know THE consequences and HAVE not emulated or fully TESTED it yet. It would be bad to RUSH in without the RIGHT amount of research and consistent results."

"Research? My team is ready now, sir. My science slaves have done the research," Galleon says with a more curt tone.

"KNOW your place, Galleon. Do NOT be fooled by YOUR drive. By exploiting THIS technology now, we COULD lose control of it, as WE do not KNOW the risks, the variances, AND the vulnerabilities OF it yet," Shobo strongly states, annoyed by his minion's haste.

After a moment's pause and with a calmer voice, Shobo asks, "Are YOUR loyalties congruent WITH the goals of the order, Galleon?"

"Yes, sir, they have never left your side," Galleon replies, with his head hung low in respect and disappointment.

"WELL done then. Bring THE object and YOUR findings before ME tomorrow. We CAN discuss the objectives MORE at that time." Shobo signs off. The holographic image disappears down into the viewer.

Galleon, not happy with the conversation, turns and sees a can on the floor. Out of frustration, he decides to kick it to let out some steam. He swings his leg back, and with a powerful kick, he misses the can. His other foot slips out from under him, forcing him to fly through the air, landing hard on his back.

Galleon springs back up and lets out a *growl*. He brushes himself off and crushes the can under his foot as he walks to the exit.

"I'm really having a bad day!"

*****

Dusk settles at the Gen village where Sivad and Chorn are gathered around a campfire with many of the villagers. Dinner is roasting on a skewer over a fire pit. It is a relaxing time for the village while they sit awaiting the feast, enjoying the drum music and smoking tobacco. Some Gens sit in front of their huts and a few on the ceremonial log, dangling their feet. Others sit on rocks and logs used as chairs, all staring at their strange guests.

A few males approach Chorn, who is still wearing the mask and Gem-tooth necklace, and poke him in the nose, mumbling something in their language and laughing.

"Sivad, they're laughing at me. I need to take this thing off," Chorn says. "Plus, it's getting hot under here, and I can hardly see."

Sivad, starting to smell the aroma of the cooking bird, looks over at Chorn and his snuggle bear, who is still attached to Chorn's arm. "I think you should leave it on. We don't want to upset the villagers or be impolite."

The chief yells out in the Gen language at his daughter, "Why are you holding that outlander still? Stop wasting your time. We're only postponing your marriage one day. He is not it."

She grips tighter to Chorn's arm and, in a smug voice, talks back to her father,

"I want him! He makes me laugh. See, he is still wearing the stupid mask you gave him for winning the log contest. He won, and now he is mine, mine, mine!"

The chief and daughter continue to go at it while Sivad talks to Chorn. "How romantic. I'm pretty sure you're married now *and* the in-laws don't like you. It's because you're bald, ya know," Sivad says.

Chorn comes back with a quick defensive response. "At least my crush is a cute girl ... or something," he says, looking down at her, not knowing how to call the female.

Sivad looks next to him with a double take. Standing at his side are three smiling Gens, staring at him.

"I didn't know you were so kinky," Chorn says.

"They're male Gens," Sivad says, pointing his thumb at them.

"Oh, I think they like you."

"What, these guys? I ... I think I adopted them," Sivad says.

"Well, you make sure you feed them and give them some baths as well," Chorn says, wrinkling his nose, sensitive to the smell.

Sivad looks at the roasting bird, takes his hand, and wipes his mouth in hunger. "Speaking of smells!"

The chief walks over to Chorn and starts talking to him, pointing at the mask.

"I think he's saying it looks good on me," Chorn says.

"What looks good on you, his daughter?" Sivad jokes.

"No, the mask!" Chorn replies.

"What mask? I thought you always looked that way," Sivad says while gazing at the roast.

Chorn, with the mask on, takes a second look at Sivad. "Do you think it's okay to take it off now?" Chorn asks Sivad.

"Well, you have had it on since we arrived, and the chief is talking about one of the two, the mask or his daughter. Just turn it around so the face is on the back of your head. That would be a good compromise."

"I don't think she'll let go to turn around," Chorn says, referring to the chief's daughter, as he turns the mask around to the back of his head.

The three Gens smiling at Sivad as the food comes around watch him intently, with eyes wide open. Sivad grabs a drumstick, tears it off the carcass, and tries his first bite.

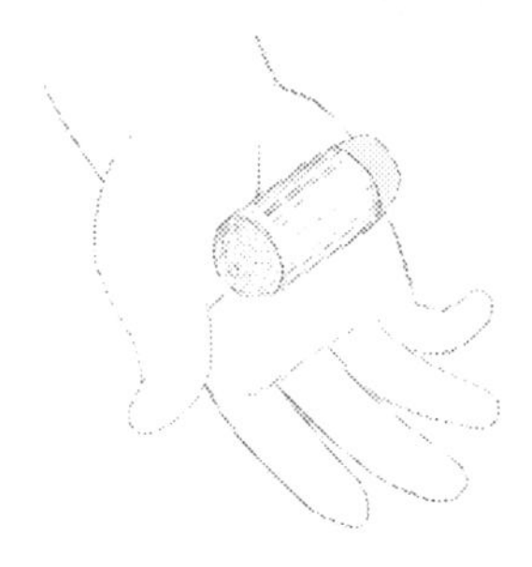

"The way they're looking at you makes me wonder what you're eating, or where it came from. I have in my pocket a meal all on its own," Chorn says as he reaches into his pocket and pulls out a vitamin capsule, tosses it into his mouth, and swallows harshly.

"You must be on a diet. Can't you smell this? Mmmm-mm, after having food like this, how can I go back to swallowing food tablets?" Sivad says, digging into the feast with both hands.

The three Gens start to mimic Sivad's eating habits and begin downing food right and left as Sivad speaks to Chorn with his mouth half full, "Are you sure you don't want any of this? This is good," Sivad comments, pointing a drumstick at him.

Chorn looks at the great party going on around him and says, "No. This is what I like, the cultural behaviors, so primitive, so exuberant! Listen to that music." The music is a fast-paced drumbeat with flutes and a guitar that fills the forest with the Gen songs.

Next to Sivad, food starts to fly up into the air. The three Gens started a small food fight between each other. Sivad glances and chooses to ignore what is happening and continues on with his meal, looking at the fire.

In the middle of the food fight, the three Gens begin to wrestle around, quarreling likes cats in a pile.

"Better tend to your boys. Looks like they need a leash," Chorn says as he relaxes.

Sivad slowly turns his head and looks at the Gens with his mouth full of food, chewing away. They instantly stop wrestling, and the dust cloud quickly settles. All three Gens sit still in a row, smiling at Sivad with mischievous grins as if they were in trouble by him. Sivad, not saying a word or showing any interest to intervene, chews calmly on his drumstick and looks back toward the village.

Chorn, head tilted, watching, is amused that Sivad is too preoccupied or has no interest to stop them, yet the Gens strangely complied. However, once Sivad looks away, they begin to wrestle around again.

"Ah, kids will be kids," Chorn says as Sivad grunts in agreement with a full mouth.

"Yeah, I'm going to be a good dad someday." He says sarcastically.

During dinner, while Sivad thoroughly enjoys the food, Chorn is passed a smoking pipe from one of the Gens. Not to be impolite, Chorn takes a small puff off the pipe and begins to hand it back when he pulls it back for another puff and turns to Sivad, still holding the pipe. "Hey, this tastes, oh, not bad," he says as he takes another puff.

A Gen says something to Chorn, pointing at the pipe. Chorn looks perplexed, trying to understand what he is saying, when Sivad jumps in nonchalantly. "He said it's herbal tobacco."

Chorn is even more confused by how Sivad knew this. "What? How do you—" Chorn starts to say when Sivad interrupts.

"It's easy. The language is really quite basic," Sivad says, mimicking the Gen who gave Chorn the pipe and waves his hands in the air as if he is hovering them over a plant, "herbal," then points to the pipe and says, "tobacco," in a higher voice.

The Gen who handed Chorn the pipe is impressed at the quick understanding and becomes exited talking more to Sivad to learn more.

"I have been watching them move while they speak," Sivad says while moving his hands around a lot so that the Gens can understand what he is saying. "They also tend to exaggerate the noun with a higher voice," Sivad continues.

The music stops as all the Gens are amazed that this outlander can understand them to a degree so fast. The chief, not realizing that the Akanian customs are different from their own, comes over and starts to plea to Sivad using his hands and body, telling him how his companion interrupted the ceremony, that he is not going to marry his daughter, and that the head dressing is a token for a sporting event.

Sivad shows he understands and starts to communicate in the same fashion while using a few Gen words he has picked up already, explaining that they appreciate the hospitality, apologize for the disruption, and understand, but he does not want to tell his friend. "So let's keep it a secret, huh?" Sivad says to the chief as he smiles mischievously, placing his finger over his mouth. The chief smiles back with relief and agrees to continue the charade.

"Let's keep what a secret? And how did you learn the language so fast? You were just eating," Chorn says, not entirely amazed, as Sivad always did have a knack for languages.

"Oh, the chief was telling me something funny about these three Gens over here," Sivad replies as he makes up an excuse.

"*You are welcome to stay!*" the chief boasts to Sivad as the party continues on.

Sivad turns and smiles at Chorn, who is still puffing on the pipe, looking at Sivad from the corner of his eye, knowing something is up. "Very intuitive. It must be something in the food," Chorn says with an eyebrow raised, talking out the corner of his mouth while smoking the pipe.

"Ah, admit it; you may be one IQ point smarter than me, but I am better with languages," Sivad says as he is given another pipe from a Gen who lights it for him to try the tobacco also. Sivad looks around at other Gens, smoking around the campfire and enjoying the party under the night sky.

On his first puff, his nose uncontrollably crinkles. "Ugh! Do *not* inhale this stuff," Sivad says to Chorn.

"*What*? *Why*? What happens if I inhale it?" Chorn says with some worry.

"This stuff has a kick," Sivad says on his second puff.

Sivad looks up, blows out the smoke he just puffed, and watches the smoke rise, covering the stars then dissipating into a shape of the voyager satellite he saw in the old man at Ganda.

Sivad begins to feel the calm surrender of the night as the moon rises higher, shinning down onto the village. The silhouette of the trees gently moves in the breeze, framing the night sky, and the music becomes a mellow drumbeat with just a guitar playing slow, relaxing music, while crickets chirp in the background.

The party had settled down, and most of the Gens had retired to their huts, leaving Sivad and Chorn now sitting almost alone on the ground, leaning against the log they sat on earlier. They feel the glow of the campfire on their faces, the moon's blue light surrounding the camp as Sivad and Chorn reflect on the tranquility of the easy life,

"You know, it's no wonder the Gens stopped evolving long ago," Chorn says, smoking on his pipe.

"What do you mean?" Sivad replies while blowing a smoke ring.

"Look at this," Chorn says, pointing around at the peaceful village. "Their environment is tranquil and unchanging. I could do this every night. If I lived here, I wouldn't want to evolve either. I mean, listen, isn't that beautiful," Chorn says as his smoke turns into the shape of a grasshopper chirping away into the night. After a short pause, Chorn continues, "Yeah, this is the life."

"Chorn, this village does not show any signs of evolution. It is still primitive and ritualistic," Sivad says with a distinguished puff.

"That could be a problem," Chorn replies, head popping up, as he does not want his piece of paradise disturbed.

"The more aggressive villages will become dominant and look to expand, forcing all villages to submit or evolve. It is the nature of things. *Chaos* forces evolution," Sivad says.

"Maybe they will begin peaceful trade between villages and not be like the rest of the universe and submit to gluttony and greed," Chorn says, being the devil's advocate.

Out from the darkness, a high-pitched, nagging voice cries out,

"Chorn, pupuptana nagy."

"That's your old lady calling you," Sivad says with a smile, knowing that Chorn still does not realize he is not married.

The chief's daughter yells again in her high voice, a bit louder, with her head sticking out of the hut, "Chorn, pupuptana!"

Chorn starts to get up, almost as if a reflex takes over. "Oops, got to go. The bird calls. Time to hit the sack anyway," Chorn says.

Sivad laughs. "You're already housebroken, how pathetic. Just make sure you keep your pants on, huh? We don't want to go starting anything you can't finish," Sivad says as he points his pipe stem at Chorn.

Chorn stops then sits back down. "You can be so gross sometimes!" he says, then pauses. "No, no!" He shakes his head, denying that a female would try to control him.

"Choooooooorn!" the voice, now softer, echoes, and giggles are heard from the surrounding huts.

"Chooooooooorn, Chooooooooorn, Choooooorn!" is heard with giggles from the other Gens in their huts as they mock the chief's daughter by saying his name too.

"Okay, okay," Chorn says as he gets up. "Got to go now. You better not be too long; she scares me."

"He-he, I knew you liked the domineering types," Sivad says, watching Chorn get up and puffing on his pipe.

"So much for the peaceful life. Now I know why we evolved; it was not to dominate and conquer other villages, but rather to get away from our own women," Chorn says and laughs on the way to the hut.

"Now you're thinking like a Gen. Ah, me boy's all grown up," Sivad says as Chorn walks away, looking back at him.

The villagers are now settled into bed. Sivad is alone around the final flames of the campfire, enjoying the moment with the sounds of nature. Chorn rustles around in the hut, saying, "Stop it. Stop it. That tickles!"

Sivad smiles, takes a deep, satisfied breath, pats his satiated belly, and places the pipe on the log. Sivad reaches down and pulls out the steagora device and starts to look at it under the remaining glow of a few flames from the fire.

In the shadows, the small rustle of a creature came from the grass near the pond in front of him. Sivad decided to see how the steagora device would interpret this creature, so once more, Sivad places the device on his head. The fire's crackle and the cricket's chirp become louder and louder as the steagora device enhances the sounds. Sivad looks at the grass move again and walks closer to the pond to find what kind of creature is hiding there. When Sivad bends over, there is a brief moment when the moon's light reflects off the pond, and suddenly, an exotic-looking fish with fins like arms and legs slowly begins to emerge out of the water and grass, looking straight up at Sivad. Sivad falls back onto his butt, startled by the strange fish. The creature, with half his body in the water and half on the shore, props his elbow on the dirt and his head on the lower part of his fin, raises an eyebrow, and looks directly at Sivad. Sivad, blinking faster, not sure if what he sees is real, because he is wearing the steagora device, continues to stare at the peculiar fish. The fish changes fins, moving his head from one fin to the other, and speaks to Sivad.

"Yo, Whatz up, big daddy?

"Yoa off-beat for this dwelling, Whatz-up with dat?"

Sivad, surprised at this jive-talking, intelligent fish, leans forward, curious. "Interesting. What is your name?"

"yu'z call me Bubble, short for Bubbleishious! Mmmm-mm. He-he."

Sivad sits on the ground and starts to talk to Bubble. "Bubble? You can speak?"

"Bubble. Bubble Port. Bubble Bee. Bubble Bum. Raining Gens off logs, colonies, and venturerererers—the Rs are the hardest," Bubble says.

"What have you been doing?" Sivad asks with curiosity.

"Oooooh, just been hangin' around, riddin' my way through these enthrallin' times. Yippee! Yousa has things to do, places to go, plans to thwart. Get movin', get goin', get on de way, lallygaggin' alien. He-he-he."

Bubble goes into a talkative ramble, wagging his dorsal fin out of the water like an excited dog's tail, babbling about nothing or something as he launches himself from the shore back into the water, galloping around the surface, acting like he's riding a horse, slapping his butt, then diving into the center of the pond, disappearing from Sivad's sight.

Sivad, completely entertained by what he saw, walks back to the campfire, where there is more light, and takes the steagora device off his head to look at it.

"This thing is fun. What strange results ... talking fish," he says to himself.

He looks down at the device and notices that the device is not switched on. Surprised, he looks back toward the pond, back over to the pipe sitting on the log, and at the device, scratching his head, not quite sure about what just happened.

"It's been a long day," he says to himself.

Sitting down on the log to catch the last light and warmth from the fire, Sivad has a revelation. "Bubble Port. Colony. Venturererers? Oh, my! We have to leave tomorrow to catch up with Galleon and the probe. I almost forgot." Sivad grabs his stuff as the campfire light fades away and enters the hut where Chorn is sleeping.

Dawn of a New Day

The sun rises and beats its way through the jungle roof and into the village. A gentle mist reflects in the dawn's sunlight, rises up from the pond, and flows like a gentle river through the camp, hovering just above the ground. The sun peeks through a hole in the thick grass hut, shining like a target into sleeping Sivad's eyes. Sivad shuts his eyes hard to block out the light, as Akanians are more sensitive to bright lights. He awakes.

Becoming more lucid, he opens his eyes and looks out the door toward the camp's courtyard. The village is still in a state of peace and quiet as the first morning bird sings his song. The party and celebration from the night before is over, and a new day has begun.

Sivad sits up and looks over at Chorn, who is sleeping soundly, snuggled into the chief's daughter like a big teddy bear, blowing her fur from tickling his nose. Sivad smiles as he looks at Chorn sleeping so soundly, because he still doesn't know that he is not married. They are guests in the village, and Chorn is being a good sport, as he does not want to be impolite to the chief.

Sivad bends over and slaps Chorn on the foot, breaking his restful peace, "Yo, snuggle buns, time to get up. We've got to get to the spaceport."

Chorn rolls over, lifts his head, and cracks his eyes open, groaning, "Oooohh! Five more minutes."

"Come on, meathead! Get up," Sivad says as he hits Chorn again.

"I had such a strange dream. These monkey people were—" Chorn says with a quick jerk of shock as he looks next to him. "Ah, Gen crap. It wasn't a dream," Chorn says, disappointed.

Sivad gets up and walks outside into the settling mist. He looks at the pond, trying to find the peculiar but insightful fish from the night before, still wondering if it was real or not.

Chorn gets up with a big morning stretch, arms high in the air, reaching up as he lets out a big yawn. The chief's daughter is still deep in sleep, with a happy look on her face. Chorn looks back at her. "Ahhh! What did I do last night?" His face looks perplexed.

Chorn walks out of the hut and into the courtyard when he sees Sivad lying down on the ground by the pond, looking into the water. Chorn scratches his lower back and stretches as he walks toward the jungle.

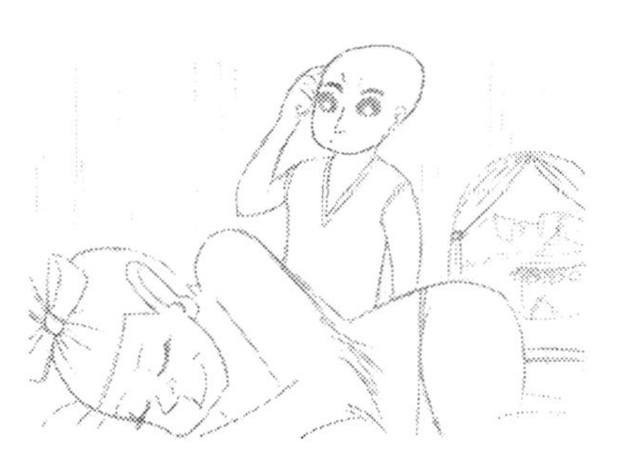

"Sivad, what the cosmos are you doing? Hey, where is the, uh, bathroom?"

Sivad, immersed in searching the pond for any sign of the fish, grunts and points in the direction of a large bush.

"Oooh! Roughing it, huh?" Chorn says as he walks to the other side of the bush.

Hearing Sivad and Chorn's voices, in the entrance of another hut, three Gens pop their heads out, one above the other. With excited smiles on their faces, they look at Sivad.

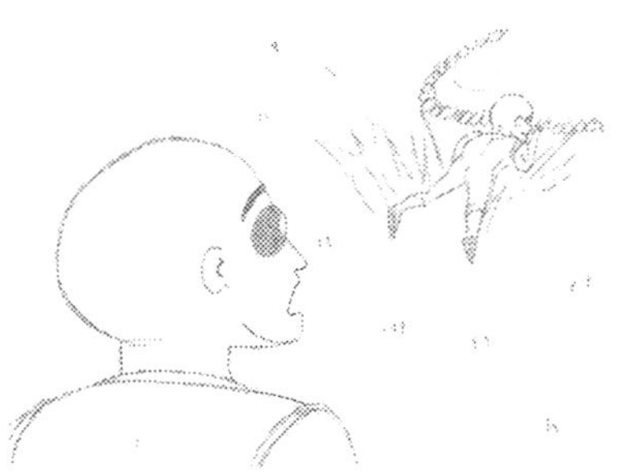

"Oh, shoot!" Sivad gets up and turns to walk in the other direction when all three Gens are suddenly at his side, holding his hands and smiling up at him.

Sivad bends down and lines them up.

"If you are going to be all over me, then you need names YOU are Kenzo," he says to the smaller one on the left as the Gen nods.

"YOU are Kenpo," he says to the one in the middle, again receiving a nod.

"And You're ..." Sivad places his hand on his chin, trying to think of another name. "Ah, Kento," Sivad says with his hand in the air, thinking that it does not matter anyway since they were leaving soon.

"Together, you are Ken," he says to make communication easy with them.

The Gen villagers begin to arise, coming out of their huts as the morning mist settles into the ground and dissipates completely. The Gens, groggy from the night's sleep, walk out and disappear into the bushes to do the same duty as Chorn.

Chorn, returning from his morning hike, watches the Gens walk by. "Look out for that tree. It's messy over there. Doesn't smell too good either, but it has lots of fertilizer," he says, pointing behind him as he walks over to Sivad and knowing that the Gens have no idea what he is saying.

Chorn turns and sees Sivad and the three Gens lined up at attention.

"Good morning. What are you doing? Setting up the first Gen military camp?" Chorn says, smiling

"Nope, naming them," Sivad replies.

"Naming them? You shouldn't do that. That's how you become attached to objects."

"They're not objects. This one is Kenzo, and Kenpo, and Kento, and together they're Ken. The first Ken Club," Sivad says, holding his arms out and smiling as though he is proud of his task.

The chief enters the village from the bushes, walks over to the fire pit, and kicks the ashes to find the ones still smoldering underneath. He calls out to one of his Gen men and orders him to build the fire for breakfast. More villagers start to gather around and wait for the chief to speak. He looks around and begins to give the day's tasks to each of his tribesmen. "You pick fruit. You get roots and vegetables. You get wood." You do this. You do that. Finally, he turns to the three Gens by Sivad, points at them, then points at Sivad. "And you three take care of those two. Keep them out of our way." All three Gens nod their heads and turn to Sivad.

Chorn, observing all of this, says to Sivad, "Hey, Gen hierarchy. Order and unity are the building blocks of structure."

Suddenly, from one of the huts, a boisterous voice is heard. The chief cringes and cowers down with teeth grinding and eyes squinting to the sound as he turns and walks back to the hut.

"Now we know who's in charge," Chorn says, leaning over to Sivad.

"Yeah, we should get out of here while we can, or at least before they give us work to do," Sivad replies.

Sivad and Chorn start to back out of the village. "Thank you. Thank you for your hospitality. Thank you. We will be going now," Sivad says in the Gen language as they both nod their heads, when out from the hut comes a taller, fat, old Gen female followed closely behind by the chief.

The Gen female yells and screams at the chief as she exits then walks over to Sivad and Chorn, looking them up and down as if she is interrogating them. From behind the large female Gen, the chief makes gestures at Sivad, pointing at the female and mouths, "Wife," without using his voice.

Chorn mumbles out the side of his mouth, "Where was she last night?"

"Why, fond of her too? That's the chief's wife," Sivad mumbles as he nods his understanding to the chief. "At least we know who the bitch is in this relationship," Sivad mumbles.

The Gen mama barks at Sivad for speaking then turns to the chief as he shrinks, waiting to be scolded. The daughter peeks out the side of the hut from where the Gen mama came, blinking her eyes at Chorn and smiling at him as the Gen mama and the chief talk.

"What is she saying?" Chorn leans over and asks Sivad.

"I don't know. Stop talking. You're going to get us in trouble with her," Sivad replies.

"Well, I thought you knew how to speak their language."

"I don't speak screaming, irate Gen," Sivad says.

"I've figured out basic gestures and speech, but that's different. This is a chick. Heck, I don't even know what the females on our planet are saying half the time," Sivad mumbles.

"Yeah. They're called the anti-logic. He-he," Chorn giggles. The Gen mama turns to him, and he jumps back a few centimeters, standing at attention. The Gen mama reaches up and pinches his cheeks, smiling and boastfully laughing, showing her missing teeth and a very large mouth.

"I'm not food," Chorn says while is face is being pulled.

The chief walks over to Sivad and starts quietly talking as the Gen mama babbles at Chorn, deforming his face as she pulls and tugs on his big cheeks while Chorn tries to maintain a smile not to be disruptive.

The chief tells Sivad that he just told her that their arrival is a good omen for the daughter's wedding day, as it has a meaning of change and prosperity.

Sivad and the chief exchange a low five, slapping hands, both knowing that it is not true. But the Gen Mama is superstitious and will believe that these two outlanders are a positive sign from their gods and that their visit is a gift of good fortune.

"Good man. Good man," Sivad says to the chief.

The daughter, seeing her father, ducks back into the hut with a "humph" of disappointment.

The Gen mama yells out to some of the Gen females, and they line up one by one. She begins to order them to prepare some food for their journey to the outlander's colony.

"Hey, what is she saying?" Chorn asks Sivad again.

"She said that you can have your pick of these Gen females lined up," Sivad says, having no idea.

"But am I not already supposed to be married to ... one of them?" Chorn asks as he points his finger around the camp.

"No, you're not," Sivad says.

"NO, I am NOT?" Chorn steps aside and looks at Sivad. "You've been messing with me this whole time, haven't you?" Chorn continues.

"Why, are you disappointed? He-he," Sivad says, walking over to pick up the pipe still on the log. "Look at the bright side; you got a lot of sleep last night. Frankly, I have not seen you get that much sleep in a long, long time." Sivad is still confused about the night before and analyses the pipe.

"All you needed was your big teddy bear, or teddy monkey person."

Chorn stretches and slaps his chest. "No argument there. I did sleep well. But the dreams were *weird*." Chorn looks over to the line of female Gens. "Yeah, my brain does feel recycled. Of course, so does my funny bone," he says with a hint of sarcasm, turning his head toward Sivad. "So then, I'm not married, and I can pick," Chorn says while pointing at the Gen girls with a smile on his face.

"Whoa! Whoa, big daddy! Slow down," Sivad says, turning and placing his hand on Chorn's chest, because he was joking about the females. "And you said I was gross?"

The Gen mama finishes giving her motivational speech to the females, and they go off to do their duties and chores.

The chief walks back over to Sivad. "Wait and we will help you prepare for your journey. It is only a half-day's walk from here," said the chief.

Sivad, hearing this, crackles and pops. "Half day? Chorn, why did you want to park so far away?" Sivad asks Chorn.

"Why, what did he say?" Chorn says.

"He said that the colony is a half-day's walk."

"Wait a minute. So you understand the chief but not the wife?"

"Yeah, I can relate to him," Sivad says.

"You really have a double standard, huh? Se-lec-tive listening," Chorn says as he rolls his eyes back.

For Gens, even a half-day's walk is a journey, as they do not stray too far away from their villages.

"Ken Club, come here," the chief turns and calls out to the three Gens. They all line up, smile, and nod their heads in excitement as the chief referred to them by the name Sivad had given them, and they are surprised the chief knew so fast.

"I shall send these three with you. I would like to learn more about the outlanders. Will there be more of you coming to our village, and what are they like?" the chief asks Sivad.

Sivad, with a disappointed look on his face, knows that they may get in the way, but he sees that this is a very big step for the Gens. Although completely unexpected, he nods his head with understanding to the chief.

"Chorn, the Kens will be accompanying us to the colony," Sivad says so Chorn understands.

Chorn whispers to Sivad, "In your beloved chaos theory, curiosity in society leads to exploration, exploration leads to experience and education, and education, well, that leads to higher evolution. This is indeed a big step and honor for you. You can show the Gens the new world outside the village. And we can show others that the Gens, after five thousand years of stagnant evolution, are becoming curious and beginning to show signs of evolving once again. But they're only going to the colony with us, no farther. I told you NOT to name them."

Chorn understands to some degree, while Sivad is still debating in his mind about the usefulness or inconvenience that the Kens could cause.

"This is great. Evolution in motion. *You* have the responsibility to feed and babysit them ... *and* bathe them," Chorn says, sniffing over them.

The Kens look up at Sivad, smiling and latching onto him. They look forward to the journey. Sivad turns and gives Chorn a worrisome look.

The Gen mama walks away in the background, laughing jollily as Sivad and Chorn sit down on the log and look around at the village of Gens all going back to their chores.

Sivad says, "You know, we're starting something that we'll have a hard time maintaining control of here."

"Don't you mean *you*? He-he. You're the one who named them. Told you it breeds attachment. Besides, if they have to learn, then you would be a ... well, somewhat of a ... I guess, role model. Ha-ha! If they are evolving, then this is a great opportunity," Chorn says, trying to distance himself from the hassle of taking care of the Kens.

Sivad, not sharing Chorn's optimism, states, "We have no procedures for this. Bad events can happen."

"Good things can happen also, and we and the Gens will have to take the responsibility for both. That's how experience works; we take the good from the bad and learn from our mistakes. And I feel they may come in handy on our journey." Chorn stops and absorbs his own insight. "I got married, and you got the kids. He-he," Chorn continues, joking sarcastically.

Sivad looks up to see a bird fly over against a blue sky and into a fig tree, where the bird delivers food into the nest, feeding the young chicks. The bird embarks from the nest, flying off to gather more food. "Well, the boys have to figure it out sometime," he says, knowing that going to the colony could start an unstoppable change for the Gens.

Some Gen females approach, giving the Kens supplies for their journey. The Gen mama chuckles as she stands next to a primitive instrument with something like xylophone keys built from bones and an animal skull on the top as a decoration. Wind chimes dangle from one of the horns. The post marks the beginning of a dark entrance into the jungle. The Gen mama points to the dark hole in the bushes, still laughing in her thunderous tone; it is the path to the colony. The jungle trees and brush darken the trail like a portal to the unknown, and the last remnants of the morning mist seem drawn to this particular shadowed route.

The Kens look down the path as their anxiety builds. They hide behind Sivad, who bows his head to the Gen mama and vanishes into the mist, with the Kens clinging to their guide.

Chorn follows, bowing his head to the Gen mama as he passes, and is absorbed by the shadows. A wicked, low-toned roar is felt in the village as Chorn vanishes, with a wake of mist swirling around behind him then settling into the earth.

Once Sivad and Chorn leave, the Gen mama walks over to the chief, grabs him on both shoulders, and, with a big smile says,

"YIPPEEE! We are finally rid of those three troublemakers!" Referring to the Kens.

The chief lets out a big grin, and the village starts to party again, with drums, dancing, and instruments.

Colony's Trek

A bird sits on a flower, bouncing on the stem, in a wide meadow of lush mountain flora enclosed by the dense jungle wall dividing the wild chaos from the peaceful calm. The wind carries faint voices, causing the bird to take flight as the flower bounces up from the weight being released. Bushes start to rustle from the overgrown jungle wall as Sivad's voice becomes louder,

"Ya know, you've got to stop referring to these three as Gens or the monkey people; they have names now. They are Kenzo, Kenpo, and Kento, and they are part of an exclusive organization called the Ken Club," Sivad says as the Kens look up with sour faces at Chorn, nodding their heads in agreement.

Chorn steps high over a fallen branch and ducks through some over brush. "I told you not to name them. Now look at you; you're becoming attached to - Zo, Po, and To," Chorn says as Sivad emerges out into the lush meadow and bright light of the sun.

"Ouch. This planet is bright," Sivad says, squinting and adjusting his eyes to the change, followed by Chorn exiting the jungle and blocking the light with his arm.

"Wow, it's daytime. That jungle was dark," Chorn says as he looks back to where they came from.

The Kens see the meadow and take off into the flowers, running and bouncing through them, hopping on top of each other as the flowers fly into the air and birds take off from their morning feeding.

"Wow, these guys don't get out much. First time seeing a meadow or something?" Sivad says, amazed how hyper the Kens are.

"This is actually a beautiful planet," Chorn says as his eyes adjust to the bright meadow.

"Sure, if you like dense jungles, bright planets, dry air, and mosquitoes," Sivad says as he slaps his arm. The mosquito grunts with a high pitched, **"Umph!"**

Sivad looks at the dazed mosquito and flicks the bug off his arm. The mosquito arcs in the air, squealing, then regains control and flies back in front of Sivad's face and shakes its fist, yelling in squeaky voice, then flies off.

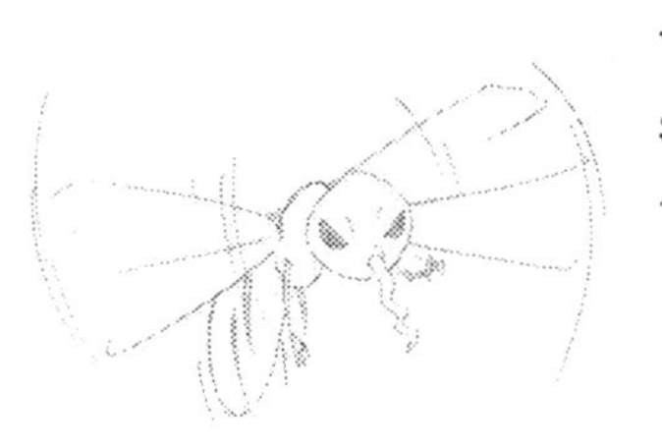

"Damn I hate mosquitoes. Resilient little bastards," Sivad says, cringing.

Chorn walks forward, looking at the wall of jungle ahead. "How much farther do you think the colonies docking station is?"

Sivad catches up to Chorn at the crest of the meadow's small hill as the Kens roll down and run around.

"It's just through those trees. It looks like it drops down over there. We might be able to find a decent path."

"Why did we park so far away this time?" Chorn says. We parked as per our procedures. A bit further because there was no where to land, big parking lot," Sivad contends.

"This field would have been a great spot," Chorn says holding out his amrs.

"Well, think of it this way, look at the fun we had getting here: you were a drummer, a piece of fruit, you learned to fly, and you went swimming. Plus, I did't see it." Sivad says knowing that the meadow would of been a great place to park. Sivad starts walking down the hill towards the jungle ahead.

Chorn looks at Sivad with a loss of words still on the hill. "And, and you, uh, HELPED!"

Sivad looks back and smiles. "Let's go."

"I did have fun! But you're still a DORK." Chorn smiles and moves on.

Crossing through the meadow, Sivad finds an animal trail, where Chorn and the Kens regroup and enter the next jungle cavity.

Sivad walks down a beaten path, leading the way, with the Kens just behind him, playing with the leaves and brushing their hands along the ones growing out into the trail, and Chorn following in the rear, when Sivad stops, holds his hands out and says, "Shhhhhhh!"

Chorn moves up next to Sivad and whispers, "What is it?"

Just then, a large gorilla came out from the bush directly ahead in the middle of the path.

"Woooow! Oh, shi—" Chorn gasps.

The three Kens are nowhere to be seen, having disappeared into the brush for safety. Only their wide-open eyes, big ears, and chattering teeth are seen from behind the leaves.

"It's a silverback gorilla. Look at it. Isn't it magnificent? Look at that back, the thick brow ridges, and those arms! Wow, I want arms like that!" Sivad says as he admires the animal.

"Is it dangerous?" Chorn asks, knowing that Sivad has studied this animal before.

"I don't believe it has interpreted us as a threat. Just stand very still, and make no sudden moves. It can charge and rip us into Akanian pieces, but that's only if we show aggressive signs to it. Otherwise it's in its nature to prove its dominance and force us to submit. That's the responsibility of the silverback. He is the leader of the gorilla family and has the sole objective to protect the sanctum of the family any way he can," Sivad says, slowly turning his head to Chorn.

Seeing that Chorn is no longer there. Sivad looks in both directions, trying to find him. "Chorn?" Then, from a bush, he hears a sound.

"Psssssst, you can do it!" Chorn says, hidden behind the bush with his thumb in the air as a vote of confidence in whatever Sivad has planned.

"Glad you got my back!" Sivad says, now standing alone in the middle of the path, as he makes direct eye contact with the gorilla and experiences a sensation of electricity running up his spine, triggering his senses, leaving only anxiety and a little fear. He had studied these mammals before and knew they could be dangerous.

Showing no signs of fear, Sivad gently walked forward a few steps, moving closer to the beast and confronting his own fears.

The gorilla glances down the path at Sivad with no expression on his face, turns, and walks back into the thick jungle brush.

Not breathing for the past minute, Sivad takes a deep breath and sighs. "That was beautiful!"

When the gorilla moved into the overgrown brush, a light at the end of the trail appeared.

"We're here, my dear possums," Sivad says with a slow accent and walks forward.

"That's because we're smarter than you," Chorn says as he gets up from the brush, wiping himself off.

The Kens look at Chorn and then each other and nod their heads in agreement. Kenzo looks at the other Kens and raises his finger next to his ear in a circular pattern. "Crazy," he says.

"Yeah, he's crazy, but you'll get used to it," Chorn says with an obvious understanding. "The light. The light. Go to the light. The light is the key to your freedom, if you don't get mauled by a smelly gorilla," Chorn says in a low, restrained voice, joking to Sivad.

Colony Station

The five adventurers exit the jungle and enter a clearing in front of a large rock wall built by the colony to ensure they maintain their laws of non-interaction and non-intervention with the local indigenous natives. Directly in front of them, at the end of the path, constructed into the wall is a large arched doorway. The doorway is made of old, thick wood and has a rectangle peephole closed off by an iron shutter toward the top of the door.

"Ahhh, back to civilization. Our camping trip is over, and I'm not only hungry, but in need of a shower as well," Sivad says, smelling his armpit. The Kens shake their heads and wrinkle their noses, agreeing. Sivad looks at the Kens. "I didn't ask *you.*"

"Akanians have not been here in a very long time, Sivad. These sapien colonists may be surprised to see us," Chorn says while he leans over and sniffs Sivad. "It's the meat you've been eating that makes you emit a smell," Chorn says.

"This wall is huge. After being in the Gen villages, I see that the pilgrims here have been doing a good job following the law not disturb the locals," Sivad says.

"How do we get in?" Chorn asks, analyzing the entrance.

"Just knock on the door and see who's home," Sivad says to Chorn.

"Knock on the door? But it won't make a sound. The door is at least fourteen hundred millimeters thick. If I knock, it would be logical to say that it wouldn't make any type of resonance or reverberation. What good would that do?" Chorn says. The Kens look up at him, not having any idea what he is saying.

"It's just a theory. I think you should try anyway," Sivad says while knocking on air.

Chorn begins to tap on the door with his finger, looking at Sivad, just to entertain his theory of knocking,

"Sivad, if the colonists built this wall to keep from interacting with the Gens and it is illegal for the colonists to have any contact with the Gens, then who are these guys going to be?" Chorn says as he continues the tapping and points at the three Gens tagging along with them.

"We're outlaws! Somebody spank us. He-he," Sivad says, smiling and shrugging his shoulders.

Chorn jumps back from his tapping when there is a sudden thump and some faint, high-pitched voices on the other side of the door. Sivad, Chorn, and the Kens all place their ears against the door to listen and hear,

"I'll get it."

"Out of the way. I got it."

"No, ouch!"

"You can't get to it!"

"Humph."

"I got it! Get off!"

"It's my turn!"

Then the small peep crack with a sliding door on it begins to rattle and shake. A faint, high-pitched scream comes from the other side, followed by a thump on the ground as the Kens jump back at the sounds and look up at the peephole.

The peep crack opens abruptly as it becomes unstuck.

Sivad and Chorn step back to see better while the Kens try to look under the door to see what is happening on the other side.

"Who goes there?" The speaker says in a high pitch then clears his throat and follows up in a lower-pitched voice, "I mean, who goes there?" Two of the most bloodshot, stressed-out eyes Sivad has ever seen peer through the peephole.

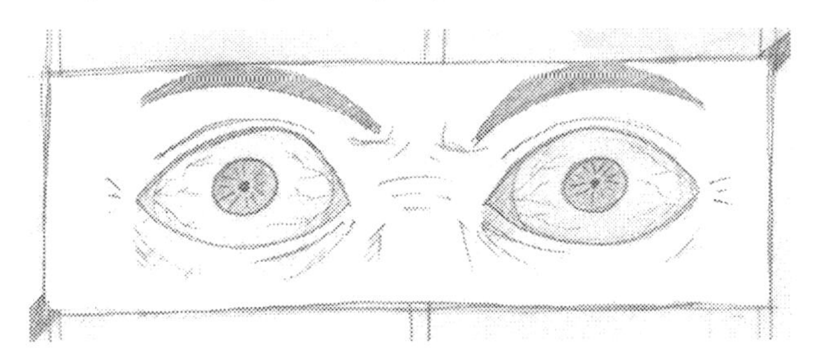

Sivad and Chorn look at each other and back at the eyes, perplexed by how to answer the question.

"Us," Sivad jumps in, still using the Kens' body language, and says in a loud voice, "We would like passage into your colony." Sivad's arms open wide.

The other voice is heard from behind the door in almost a whisper,

"Ask them why. Ask them where they are from. Ask them why are they out there. Ask them why they look funny. Ask them if they know the password. He-he. Ask them. Ask them."

"Shut up and get down!" The stressed eyes look away for a moment.

"Ouch! Dang!" and a thud of one falling is heard.

The eyes from behind the door look back at Sivad and Chorn, and in a low slower voice, the speaker says, "What is your purpose?"

"Good, good. He-he-he. That's a good one." The other voice is heard followed by, "Ouch! STOP kicking me!"

"What is our purpose?" Chorn says to Sivad. "That's a personal question." Sivad listens to the rustling behind the door and becomes amused at the strange characters.

"Wait!" the voice orders to Sivad and Chorn as the sliding door slams closed. A rustling sound is heard behind the door as if cats were fighting.

The sliding peep door opens again, and a different pair of eyes stares down at the group. "What? What do you want here?" asks a fast-paced voice.

"Obviously, the victor," Chorn says to Sivad as he continues to negotiate with the doorman.

"We want in ... now!" Sivad orders with confidence.

"Oooooooooh. Well, why didn't you say so? Okay!" The sliding door closes then opens back up again. "Who are those others with you?"

"They're our druids, and they want in too," Sivad orders again.

"Yeah, good one. Is that the best you can come up with?" Chorn says in a quiet, sarcastic voice, not satisfied with the statement.

The sliding door closes.

"Obviously, they're complete morons with the brainpan of a ferbo. Thus it won't matter what we say," Sivad says, shrugging his shoulders.

A loud, low-tone sound of a metal latch sliding open, as if it has not been greased in a very long time, is heard when the door squeaks and chirps from being pulled millimeter by millimeter, forcing it to open from the tight doorframe.

The three Kens who had begun digging a hole to bore under the door stop as the door opens, look up, and grin at Sivad then, with mischievous actions, start covering the hole they dug, shuffling the dirt with their feet, with their hands crossed behind their backs, looking around and whistling as if they would get into trouble for digging the hole.

"Strange. I wonder if our species was ever like that," Sivad says to Chorn with his eyebrows lowered, watching the Kens.

The door cracks open, and two small men push and struggle to open it all the way. As the door opens, the colonist city begins to appear down a sloped hill. Just inside the door, on the hill, a flea market is set up in the open space between the city and the wall. The city towers above the ragged tin-roofed market, where local transportation and multistoried buildings are alive with activity. Once the door is pushed all the way open,, forming a cloud of dust, the two small men turn around with a "Gasp!" and "Umph!" Completely out of breath, they bend over and put their hands on their knees and lean back against the door, looking up at their new guests.

"WOW! What *big* heads you have."

"We are Akanian," Chorn say with pride.

"You're a carnival what? He-he." The two men giggle.

Chorn walks through. "I don't appreciate you mini-sapiens mocking my cranium."

The Kens pop their head around the wall through the door one on top of the other, looking inside for the first time. Mouths and eyes wide open, curious about everything.

"Hey, those are Gens!" one small sapien says, followed by the other to close the sentence, "They can't be here!"

"No, they are not. They are the exclusive Ken Club and are with us," Sivad says with confidence, looking around inside. H e turns toward Chorn, disregarding what the two sapiens said. "We don't need to tell them anything, as they would not understand," Sivad says to Chorn in a quiet voice as he walks by.

"No kidding. I'm just wondering which is the more dominant species on this planet, the Gens or these colonists?" Chorn replies.

The two small sapiens and the Kens approach each other, about the same height, look at each other nose to nose, looking up and down, making a full evaluation of one another.

Up the hill with quick, small steps, a jolly fat man wearing robes with arms held high comes toward Sivad and Chorn, yelling, "Welcome! Welcome, strangers! It's strange that you came in from this entrance. This entrance has never been used, that I know of," the fat mans says, losing some enthusiasm when he looks at the three Gens, who are gazing around.

"We are Akanians, and they are with us," Chorn says.

Obviously, there would be no fooling this fat jolly guy. As he looks around, Sivad nonchalantly says,

"We are on a secret mission for the Gen mama and seek passage and accommodations. Can you assist us?" Sivad turns around and looks at the fat man almost with arrogance.

Chorn, enjoying this play continues on. "Which way is the largest docking station?"

The fat man became nervous, twiddling his fingers together. "Akanians? We don't see too many Akanians in these parts. In fact, I have never seen them before. I actually thought you might be a myth or something. Oh, well, it is jolly good you are here," the fat man says cheerfully.

"We are real, and we are tired," Sivad says.

The fat man leans over to Sivad and says, "You know, we have certain policies about interacting with the, uh, natives, ya know?" He points his finger at the Kens.

"Please do not concern yourself with them. They are with us, and we shall take full responsibility for them," Sivad replies.

"Well, that's good enough for me, as long as you feed them and bathe them," the fat man says and begins to walk.

Chorn laughs because he said the same thing. "Hey, I think I like this guy."

The fat man turns toward Chorn and smiles then abruptly stops. "Hey, are you guys actually spies? I am Wollabee. I can help, yeah? That is so fascinating. Anything you need, just ask me."

Sivad elbows Chorn, pushing him forward. "Your turn. You take care of this one," he says while they start walking down the slop to the market place. Chorn and Wollabee talk on the way down and Sivad turns to the Kens points his finger and says, "You guys be good huh?"

The Kens respond with innocent looking faces shaking their heads in agreement.

While walking through the flea market, the Kens cannot seem to keep their hands off the merchandise for sale, touching and feeling everything they pass by. Chorn steps in each time and puts the products back, smiling at the merchant. He turns to the Kens. "I need to get a leash for you."

One of the merchants replies hastily, trying his best to sell. "I have some leashes! You want? You buy! You buy! Keep your pets on a leash; it's the law. You buy! You buy!" Chorn grabs the Kens and walks by.

Sivad walks with Wollabee in front, asking questions about the colony. "How long have you been here?"

"Oh, the colony has been here for over three hundred years or so," Wollabee replies, skipping along, excited to have guests.

"Do you ever interact with the Gens on this planet?"

"No, no, it's against our laws."

"Do you have any people conducting anthropological studies on them?" Sivad asks.

"Oh, no, the federation should be. We don't concern ourselves with them. They're a bit strange. They remind me of bulldogs eating custard or peanut butter," Wollabee concludes, looking back at the Gens.

"Yes, I KNOW," Sivad says, when Kenzo kicks him in the butt.

"Hey, hey! Be nice!" Sivad says to the Ken gang as they give him the evil eye.

"So, hey, is it true that Akanians can lift ten times their body weight? Is it true that you can see in the dark? Is it true that you have IQs of over three hundred?" the fat man inquires, excited to meet Akanians.

"Yes," Sivad replies, holding his butt, blocking it from another possible Ken gang attack.

"I have heard many things. Are you here for the same excitement as the Shobo Order?" Wollabee asks

Sivad stops and turns. "What excitement?"

"Yeah, there are security drones everywhere, and one of Shobo's men has completely cleared out one of the hangers. He is a bad one, a bad man, indeed," Wollabee says fidgeting his fingers.

"Do you know why?" Sivad asks the fat man while looking at Chorn, who has somehow acquired three leashes and is struggling with the Ken gang to put them on and get them under control so they will stop touching everything.

"Ah-ha! Mess with me, will you? Umph! Ahhhh! Get in! Damn, you little—" Chorn struggles with the Kens as they fight back.

Finally, Chorn gains control, and the commotion settles. Out of the dust, with all the flea market clerks watching, Chorn drags the Kens in an orderly fashion, with them finally under control and on leashes.

Sivad and Wollabee look back as Chorn smiles followed by the unhappy Kens.

"No, no one does, but he did make mention of you or, at least, Akanians. I think?" Wollabee said as Sivad jumped in attention,

"What do you mean, made mention of us? Does Galleon know we're here?" Sivad inquires.

"No. Rumor has it he's looking all over the galaxy for two Akanians. Oooooh, that Galleon, hey, he's dangerous," Wollabee says, becoming more nervous.

"I also hear he had a girl with him as well," Wollabee says, leaning closer to Sivad as if he was telling a secret.

Chorn, listening, jumps in. "Cas from Ganda?" he asks Sivad. "Why would he want her?"

"I think the old slave was her father, and since she thinks we killed him, well, that would mean she's teamed up with Galleon and is also after us," Sivad replies.

"But why would Galleon be after us?" Chorn asks with surprise as they reach the end of the flea market.

"Au contraire, my friend, does he know we're after him? And what he doesn't know, he cannot find. So in attempting to find us, we will find him," Sivad says as he generously unties the Kens from the leashes.

Chorn gives Sivad the leashes and says, "Your turn," referring to watching the Kens.

"Wow, Wollabee is full of information. He must get around a lot."

"Be good, no hands, no touching," Sivad orders to the Kens as they look up and smile with innocent faces.

"I have to hand it to you, Chorn; you do know how to herd cats. That is management." Sivad tosses the leashes back to Chorn. "Might want to try duct tape next time."

"Hey, if it works! I'll use these later. Sivad, I don't think we should go after him," Chorn says, grabbing Sivad's arm. "I have that feeling again that something is not right," Chorn continues.

Sivad looks up, closes his eyes, and takes a big whiff. "Everything smells fine and the adventure continues." He becomes distracted. "Mmm. What's that smell?"

Wollabee points over to the barbeque sticks. "Oh, yes, they're good too."

"Oooh, that looks good. Is it safe?" Sivad asks.

"Yes, it is quite popular and tastes very good," Wollabee says as he hands Sivad a stick.

"Sivad, its *meat*," Chorn says. "He eats when he's nervous," Chorn comments, looking down at the Kens and watching them line up, salivating at the smell and watching Sivad start to eat the kabob.

Wollabee gives the two Akanians directions to the docking station where Galleon has parked his shuttle. Sivad, after eating a couple cubes, flings the last three steak cubes off the stick and into the air at the Kens. Kento and Kempo jump one by one, catching each piece in their mouths as they fly over. Kenzo, who is the tallest, reaches up and grabs his piece and tosses it into his mouth.

"Ah, phooey. I'll just go with you. It's on my way home anyway. Let's go this way. Let's go. Let's go," Wollabee says with excitement as he shakes his hands.

The group crosses over to the local transit path to the base of a building.

"This is where we will catch the local transport to the station," Wollabee says.

Chorn leans forward and looks both directions down the street. "Will it be long? I don't know if Sivad can sustain his life without eating again in the next ten minutes. He could BLOW up or something."

"Oh, my! Really? That's terrible," Wollabee says, believing everything Chorn says, because he does not know too much about Akanians.

Sivad turns to Wollabee and begins to correct his friend and stop the onset of a rumor about Akanians blowing up if they don't eat or eat meat, when from around the corner walks a single security drone.

The security drone stops in the middle of the sidewalk when he sees Sivad and Chorn talking to the fat colonist. Their body language shows that what Chorn says is taking some convincing. Chorn acting with his arms Sivad Blowing up and Sivad trying to correct him waving his hands in a *no no* manor.

The Kens see the security drone and become curious about his mirrored face. They walk over to the drone, unsure about this creature who is not too much taller than they are. They walk around it, smell it, stand on their tiptoes to look at their reflections in the drone's face and jump back, as they have never seen their own reflections before. They are not sure if they see another Gen inside the mirror or if the reflection is their own.

During their analysis, the Kens start to climb on the security drone. The drone holds himself solid and does not budge.

The Kens tap on the glass, lick it, smell it, scratch on it, everything they can do to try to see what is inside and identify what it is.

The word "**Akanians**" displays inside the drone's shield.

At that moment, Sivad looks over to see the Kens climbing on the security drone as he finishes talking to Wollabee. The drone, just standing, waiting, and staring at Sivad and Chorn, does nothing.

"Oh, my, it's one of those drone thingies. I think your friends like him," Wollabee says and starts to wave. "Will he want to join us also?"

"I highly doubt it," Chorn says as the local transport arrives. Sivad whistles at the Kens to join them and stop playing with the drone.

"Hurry," Sivad says as he grabs the fat man and lifts him up off the ground, into the air, and onto the transport.

"Oooooooh! Weeeeeeeeee!" Wollabee yells with shock.

"He is undoubtedly looking for us," Sivad says as the transport's doors close and it begins to move.

They walk to the back, take some seats, and watch the security drone become farther away, then seven more drones charge around the corner to join the solo drone, and they all watch the transport leave.

"Wow, there are so many of them," Wollabee says. "Oh, I have never been manhandled like that before. That was fun," he continues, excited about being picked up and thrown onto the transport.

"That's what they do. When they're alone, they're harmless. But when they're all together, *then* they become full of madness, pouncing on you like a deranged family of blitzkrieg-driven jungle cats," Chorn says to the fat colonist, imitating a jungle cat pouncing, causing the poor man to become nervous.

"Well, I think they're creepy little things, aren't they?" Wollabee says, looking at the three Kens as each one shakes his head in all different directions, showing no understanding of what he just said. The Kens, doing their own thing, begin to quarrel, slap fighting each other for a window seat.

"Don't worry. I think you're creepy little things too," Wollabee says to the Kens. "How do those ... thingies communicate?" Wollabee adds point back at the drones.

"They're cybernetic machines that have communications chips imbedded in their biological minds. They are organic, but we're not sure how much of them is machine," Sivad explains to Wollabee.

"Oooh, well, that's not so bad. I could use a memory upgrade. I just can't seem to remember so many things nowadays: where I put my keys, my wallet, even my head. It's this hot summer air. Makes the mind ... loopy," Wollabee says

"Well, then *you* would be a slave too," Sivad says.

"Oh, that's not good," Wollabee replies.

"Sivad, what do you think they want? Obviously, since they regrouped once the single drone saw us, that would indicate they're truly after us. But why?" Chorn asks while Sivad leans toward the window, watching to see if the security drones are following them in any way.

Sivad sits quietly for a bit to think about the question, looking out the window, watching a thunderstorm begin as the raindrops start to gently fall to the ground. The colonists' buildings pass, and Sivad watches the locals run from the rain as they cruise by on the local transport. He finally says, "I don't know."

"What?" Chorn says since there was a long pause.

"I do not know. They can't possibly know that I saw everything the slave knew about the Blue Planet's probe. Nor do they know about the steagora device we made and what it can do. As far as their understanding should be, we are of no threat to them," Sivad finishes.

"Maybe they want to cut our heads off for the old man dying," Chorn says, grabbing his throat, with the Kens feeling their own throats, worried about what Chorn is saying.

"Or maybe they want to make us slaves," Chorn continues.

"Slaves!" Sivad says, raising an eyebrow and looking at Chorn, taking a break from watching the rain. "Na, they wouldn't go to all this effort just to make us slaves. I'm sure it has something to do with the Blue Planet's probe. They must think we know more than we should, but in actuality, we know more than they think we know. Therefore, since we know more than what they think we know, they are after us for what we know," Sivad says.

"But how could they know what we actually do know?" Chorn asks as the transport arrives at the docking station's shopping mall.

"They think they can stabilize navigation through a tackyon wormhole. Maybe they figured out how to and are going to try to use it," Sivad says, standing to offload from the transport.

"But what actually would be wrong with that? We do it all the time, and if we found it, then you *know* we would try it," Chorn replies as he walks off the transport.

"*Well,* IF they *can* control the wormhole navigation, then they will most likely monopolize the technology and seize any new advancements they find in other galaxies, not to mention the ability to monopolize the trade routes. We may end up not being the smartest species out there any longer. Plus, this kind of discovery should be tested and approved by the science board before anyone makes this kind of space or time jump. There are so many variables that could go wrong, and there are so many dangers," Sivad says, walking with the group over to the shopping mall to an escalator.

"True. Then we must report this as soon as we can. It is our process," Chorn says, getting onto the escalator.

"I'm not sure we have enough time. If those drones are after us, then the *order* is worried. They will surely be waiting for us at each stop," Sivad says.

"The Gens' communications room would be handy now. Where are drums when we need them, huh?" Chorn replies.

"Damn them! They didn't even bring the pizza I ordered," Sivad sarcastically jokes.

"Hey, how did they get a hold of the satellite in the first place do you think?" Chorn queries.

Since Sivad and Chorn are walking slowly, immersed in their conversation, Wollabee takes the Kens down a shopping corridor where they have a great time. When they come back from playing, the Kens jump on Sivad, very excited, and start telling him about what they saw.

"Okay, okay, one at a time."

Wollabee smiles and says, "This is the local connect to my train. You need to just go up the stairs ahead, in front of the train station and follow the signs to the space dock. Its easy, even these cute little guys can do it." He shows some signs that he is becoming attached to the Kens.

"Thank you, Wollabee, for showing us the way. We appreciate your support," Chorn says.

"Certainly, it's not every day that we see Akanians around here and especially ones who are ... fugitive spies. It's been fun. *Bye-bye.*" The friendly fat colonist waves as he enters the train ticketing area.

"What a nice sapien," Chorn says.

"Uh, yeah. Up the stairs, he said. Let's go boys!" Sivad shouts as he marches the Kens forward.

Systems Ready

On the dock, Galleon prepares his shuttle for takeoff, receiving its final maintenance check and loading the necessary supplies for the transport of the *Blue Planet's* satellite to 2D City. Galleon stands next to the docking station's main hanger doors, his shuttle behind him as he talks to one of his loading drones holding the cargo.

"Is everything prepared? I want no delays. Make sure the ship is ready to go *on* schedule in two hours." The mirror-faced drone nods his head, showing that he understands orders.

Galleon turns to a security drone, who appears just behind him. There is a slight pause as he looks at the drone's emotionless reflection, then Galleon speaks.

"The two Akanians have been found *where*? They are here on Gen? Why haven't you subdued them yet? They were found on a local transport. Where were they going? Which direction?" Galleon pauses then growls, "Mmmm, ensure all security drones are on full alert and recall the space search probes."

The security drone turns and leaves to expedite the commands. Galleon looks at his ship with the *Blue* Planet's probe in the cargo hold and begins to talk to himself as the loading drone listens, believing that his fearless master is talking to him. "This is unexpected. They definitely know something. Akanians always have a plan of attack. They are always prepared and never do anything without quadratically equating each option and variable. So what's their plan? How do they think they're going to manage stopping me? What will they do?"

Galleon places his hand on his chin, thinking of things he has to do before he leaves. He continues to talk to himself. "Turn on the alert command systems in my quarters and prepare the girl. I think I should leave early."

The loading drone, hearing all the orders and questions, is unsure which part, if not all, is for him. In turn, thinking that his master is talking to him, the drone displays on his mirror, "**Leaving early. Engage command launch sequence on shuttle.**" Galleon turns and leaves. Immersed by his self-directed questions, he ignores the loading drone's display.

The loading drone's adaptive programming has become accustomed to making an assumption based on vague commands by their master. Galleon is not always clear with his commands, and when miss-interpreted or unfulfilled, the drones understand that the penalty is decommissioning. In turn, the loading drone interprets Galleon's lack of confirmation as a command. He turns and activates the shuttle's navigation command and the engine's start-up cycle.

"**Systems online. Ready for early departure**," the drone displays.

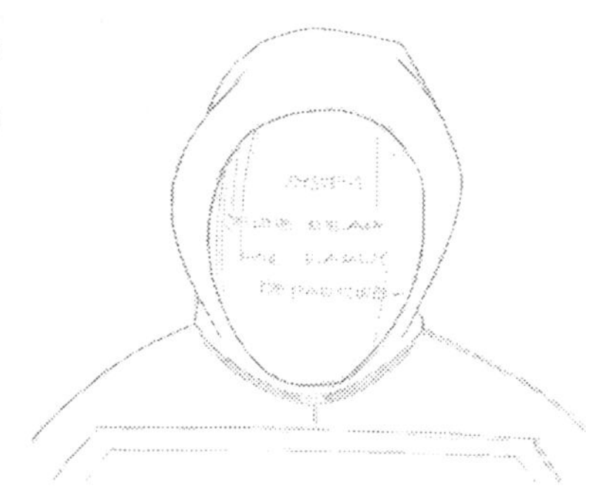

*****

After ascending what seemed to be an endless rise of escalators going up through the shopping mall to the space docks on the top floor, Chorn asks, "Hey, Sivad, where are we going, and what are we going to do? Do you have a plan, or are you just winging it?" Chorn smiles because he already knows the answer to his last question.

"I don't know. I haven't thought that far ahead yet. I figure, if we keep going up, we'll hit a space dock eventually, *or* at least a cloud," Sivad replies.

"Have you noticed that everyone is looking at us very strangely? I wonder if Galleon has been alerted to our presence yet. What will he do? He is an insightful sapien. What scrupulous traps will he prepare for us?" Chorn wonders aloud as he moves his hands in a melodramatic manner and closes them like jaws taking a bite out of a victim. The Kens, seeing the intensity, jump back and huddle into each other.

"I suppose they're looking at us because we are Akanians. I'm certain that. Like the fat guy, they most likely have never seen our species before. Or it could be our primitive Ken Club members here. Or it could be these native dead-animal tooth necklaces we're wearing," Sivad says in analysis of a single point of Chorn's questions.

"You shouldn't keep referring to him as *'that fat guy.'* Wollabee was nice. There's nothing wrong with a little fluff," Chorn says, patting his belly.

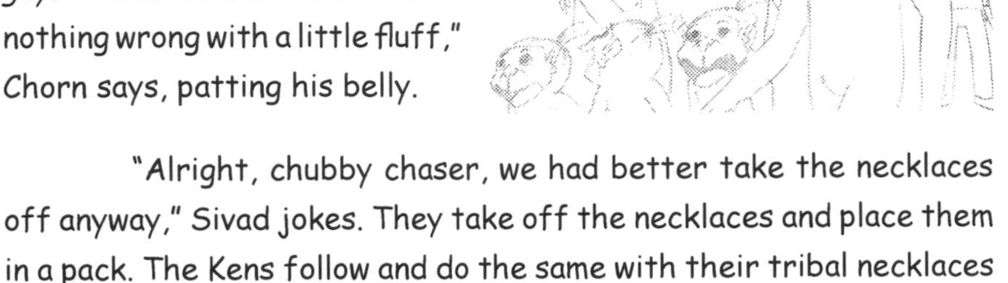

"Alright, chubby chaser, we had better take the necklaces off anyway," Sivad jokes. They take off the necklaces and place them in a pack. The Kens follow and do the same with their tribal necklaces as well.

"Hey, hey, be nice!" Chorn says as he drops his necklace into the pack.

The Kens start to tap and tug on Sivad as he is closing the backpack then begin to push him, jumping up and down.

"Boy! When they have to go to the bathroom, they are feisty little buggers, aren't they?" Chorn says.

Sivad bends over, asking Kenzo if they have to go by the limited vocal language and body language of holding his index finger and moving it side to side, but all three Kens start pointing in excitement in front of them through the crowd at a mirror-faced security drone heading right toward them. Sivad grabs Chorn and pulls him down as well.

"What the—" Chorn says, falling downward.

"Shhhhhh. Look! Stay low," Sivad says.

"I hate it when you *shush* me. It always means something bad is near or, even worse, something bad is going to happen," Chorn says.

"Let's go. Follow me," Sivad says in a quiet voice as all five of them start to duck-walk across the mall floor, with their knees fully bent, waddling to the nearest store. The crowd stares at them for doing such a strange act.

They quickly enter the store and dive under a clothing rack, watching to see if the security drone spotted them.

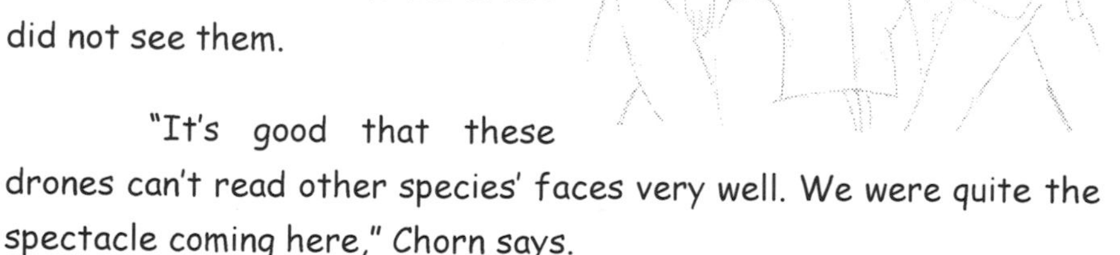

The security drone walks by them, pausing every few seconds to monitor the crowd. Sivad and Chorn watch with relief; the drone did not see them.

"It's good that these drones can't read other species' faces very well. We were quite the spectacle coming here," Chorn says.

"Yeah, do you think we drew enough attention?" Sivad smiles.

"Let's try to be less conspicuous from now on, shall we?" Chorn says. He looks over and sees Sivad and himself reflected in a mirror bright as day and shakes his head.

"*Not* a chance," he says to himself.

"Good idea, if we can -. Hey where did—" Sivad says then cringes, knowing something is happening behind him.

Behind the clothes rack, a ruckus begins. Sivad and Chorn stand up and turn to notice that they are in a lingerie store for females, and the Kens are playing with the undergarments.

Kenpo straps a brazier to his head, tying down his ponytail hair. Kenzo uses T-back underwear as a slingshot, examining it and testing the elasticity. Kento rubs a soft, silk teddy on his cheek and walks into a dressing room.

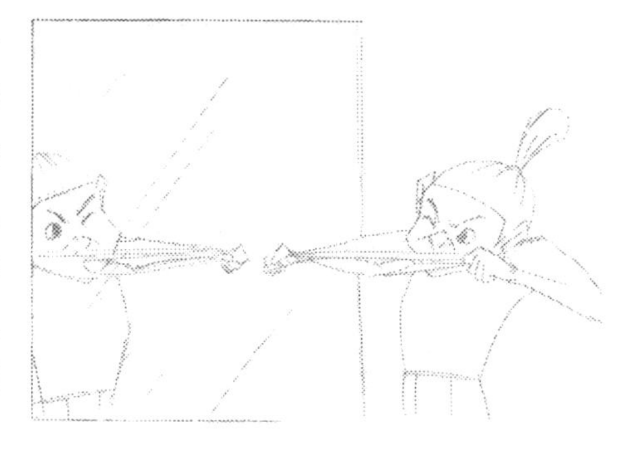

"Inconspicuous? You take care of this, and I'll keep watch. I still have the leashes if you need them," Chorn jokes.

Sivad grabs the T-back underwear from Kenzo, and he grips on even tighter, forcing a tug-of-war, with both pulling at the thong, stretching it to its limits. Kenzo, laughing, having fun with his new slingshot, does not want to let go.

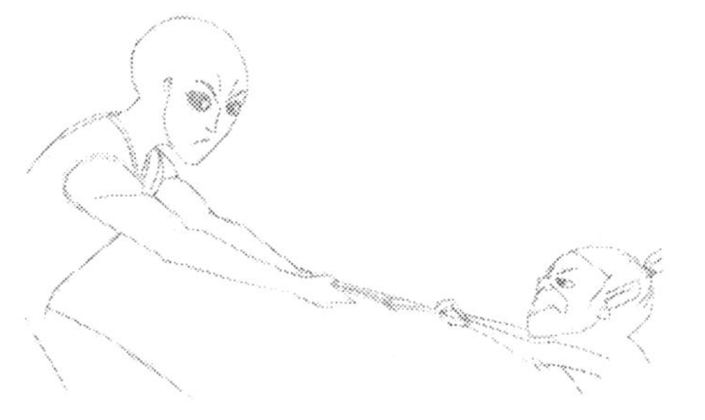

"*Let it go! Now!*" Sivad orders.

Finally, Kenzo releases the thong, sending Sivad flying backward onto his butt.

Next to where Kento disappeared into a dressing room, a door opens, and out walks a security drone wearing female lingerie. He walks over to a mirror next to Kenpo, admiring the silk nightie he is trying on.

Kenzo looks at Sivad with one hand on his knee and the other across his mouth, laughing. Sivad tries to hold in a smile. "Funny, real funny! I should slingshot you back to your village with this thing," Sivad says standing up. Sivad stretches the T-back underwear a few times and continues his sarcasm. "It might just make it as well." Looking at the underwear then over at Kenzo.

Sivad looks at a large humanoid female as she walks into the store between he and Kenzo, looks down at the underwear, and says to himself with a low voice, stretching the thong,

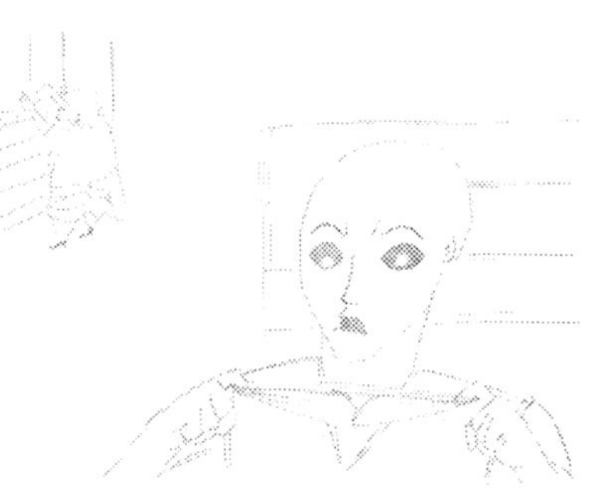

"I wonder if it's one size fits all?"

At the mirror, not yet noticed by the rest of the gang, the dressed-in-drag security drone poses next to Kenpo. Kenpo reaches over and feels the lace undergarment, admiring the outfit and talking to the security drone's nightie as he models. The security drone tilts his head in flattery, as if he blushed by the small Gen's compliments, even though he could not understand what the little guy was saying.

Kento finally came out of the dressing room, no longer holding the silk teddy, with a satisfied grin on his face, walking with a bounce, as if he had lost two pounds.

Kenpo finally looks up at the security drone's face and sees a second security drone in the mirror. He looks back at the drone's mirrored face, then back the mirror again, and then back to the mirrored face.

His mouth drops, and nothing comes out when he realizes that these are the drones they are trying to avoid. Kenpo does not realize there is only one drone rather than two, because in his panic, he sees both the drone in drag and the reflection, looking as if there are two drones. The security drone bows elegantly to Kenpo, who has helped him to decide whether to purchase the garment or not. He had not yet realized who this Gen was and who he was traveling with. His search and monitor program had been paused while he shopped.

Sivad and Kenzo are still playing with the T-back underwear when Chorn notices the dressed-in-drag security drone and his newfound Gen friend trying to conjure up a scream.

Kenpo is too scared to move but finally develops a low shriek that becomes louder and louder.

Sivad looks up. "Oooh, no!"

At the same time, the large women Sivad was looking at earlier, holding a very small thong and brazier, went into the dressing where Kento had just come from with a satisfied look on his face. As Kento walks away, suddenly, the women screamed loudly, "Uh-, YUCK!"

The women screamed at the entrance of the dressing room, Kenpo screamed at the sight of the security drone, and Kento stopped in his tracks with an innocent look on his face of "*who me?*" while he pointed questionably to himself and looked around at the ceiling.

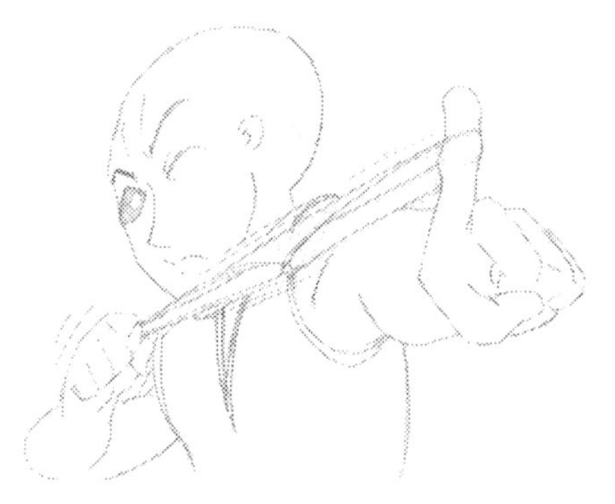

In a reflex motion, using the underwear, Sivad pulls back, aims, stretches the elastic limits, and snaps it like a giant rubber band at the security drone, hitting him with a direct shot in his mirrored face. The security drone, surprised by this, jumps backward, loses his footing, and falls to his back, with the thong undergarment still on his head.

Sivad runs over and grabs the air toward the exit. Kenpo, while passing Kento, grabs his ponytail, yanking him along. Kento, floating along by his hair, grabs Kenzo with his feet, forming a four-man train, with Sivad dragging all behind. Kenzo brings up the rear and enjoys the ride, quickly grabbing a silk nightie from a table on the way out.

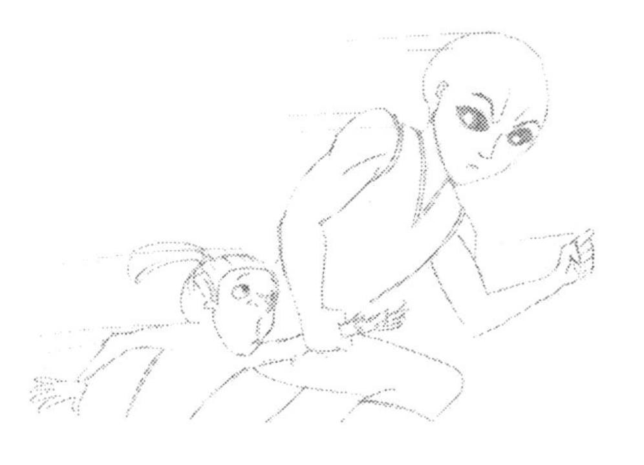

Chorn leads the way down the mall's corridors, forcing a hole in the crowd for Sivad and his caravan behind. In front of him are a small gathering of security drones who have been in touch with the drag drone, ready to pounce on

Sivad and Chorn. Chorn, using his strength, leans over while running and puts his arm in front of him, busting his way through the drones, launching them backward into the crowd and out of Sivad's way.

Sivad, Chorn, and the Kens flee down the corridor and up the final escalator toward the heart of the space station as the shopkeeper, an androgynous sapien much like Wollabee but dressed in brilliant colors, jumps and yells at them in a feminine voice for shoplifting the merchandise. "*Hey*, get back here! *Help! Help!* Those ... those thingies stole from me!" Then the shopkeeper looks at the displeased security drones getting up off the ground. "Oh, my," he says and runs back into the store in fear.

The dressed-in-drag drone emerges from the shop, angry, and pushes the shopkeeper out of the way while he tries to run back into the store. The drag drone, who is the head drone of his squad, looks at the other drones who gathered quickly and aggressively points toward the fugitives in a "*get them or else*" manner.

After recovering from Chorn's aggressive blocking, the squad of drones stop and stare at the lead security drone, ogling at his lingerie with all their heads tilted to one side. The drag drone's image reflects off of the mirrored faces of his squad, and he again moves his arm in a command to get the fugitives.

Sivad, Chorn, and the Kens race down the large, high-ceiling corridor, entering into the docking station's computer operations center, attempting to get away. A large gang of security drones, already alerted to their presence, are in close pursuit.

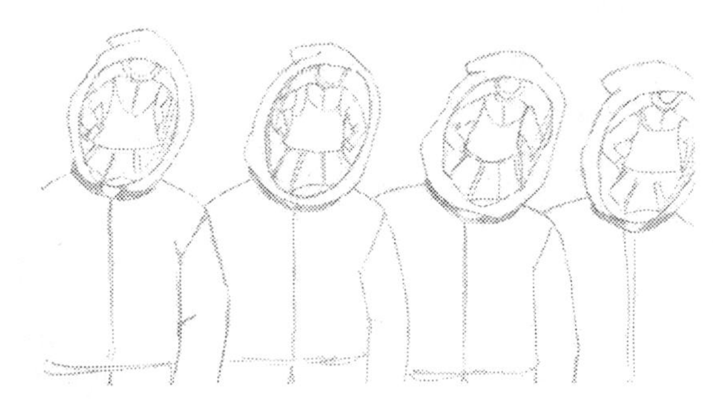

Entering into what appears to be a closed-off operations room, Sivad and Chorn realize that they have just trapped themselves.

"Shoot!" Sivad says, holding the Kens' hands.

"Trapped!" Chorn follows.

Chorn analyzes the computer equipment and searches for any type of leverage while Sivad looks at a large closed docking station door made of metal.

"Where does this go?" Sivad asks as he looks around for a button or doorknob to open the door. The Kens, seeing his hands feel around the door as if he were trying to open it, also begin to feel around.

"Ah! I've locked them out," Chorn says as he successfully finds the locking mechanism for the entrance, and the entrance slams shut.

"And locked us in?" Sivad says.

"Give me time. Give me time," Chorn says.

"*Go, go*, mechanical man, Chorn! *Go, go*!" Sivad says. There is a large thud on the main door, followed by a laser blast.

"*Go, go*! Go, faster, faster!" Sivad smiles to make Chorn calmer but still stresses the urgency.

"If we can open this door, then we can get away," Chorn says, pointing briefly at the large hanger door Sivad had been feeling, searching for an open button.

"Yeah, but what's on the other side, and how many more drones are there?" Sivad says.

"Well, we don't know what's behind door number two, and we do know what's behind door number one, so let's take our chances," Chorn says while he works in haste.

Suddenly, the security drones blast through the locked door, and six drones come blitzing through.

The Kens hide behind Sivad's leg, and they all start backing up from the blast and the security drones entering the room. Chorn backs up fast into the computer panel as the drones come closer. The security drones pause for the lead drone to say attack and ensure they have their prey in checkmate, backed into a corner, before they subdue the two Akanians and take them to Galleon.

Chorn, backing up against the computer panel, holds his hands out and leans forward, ready to defensively attack, when his butt makes contact with a lever, inadvertently forcing it up. Suddenly, the large bay door opens from the middle, the bottom half opening down and the top opening upward.

Sivad, seeing this, immediately makes a reflex decision and uses his strength to toss the three Kens over the opening wall. The Kens fly into the docking station with the thrust of a catapult then roll with smooth grace on their landing.

"Oops! A little too hard," Sivad says, watching the Kens fly up and over the last piece of the opening door.

Chorn delays for a moment, allowing them to get farther away as he holds back the drone force from charging. The drones begin their attack and reach for Chorn as he makes his way through the bay doors and onto the dock. After a few lunging steps out onto the docking station's platform, Chorn slips as the security drones grab and reach at his feet.

Chorn tries to gain speed, but the drones continue getting enough of a grip on him to slow him down as they slip off from the strength of the Akanian. Unfortunately, as one drone slips off, another grabs hold, then two, then three. With each step, more drones are able to get a hold of him, gripping him and climbing higher. Chorn feels as though he is in quicksand, and it is overtaking him as he struggles. The security drones finally overcome him and drag him to the ground.

By this time, over twenty drones blitz the dock's platform, piling onto Chorn to ensure that he cannot use his Akanian strength to get free. The Kens jump onboard the only vessel on the platform to hide. The shuttle's hatch door was wide open, and the turbines from the engine purr as they have already been stated and warmed up and all systems ready for departure.

"Go! Go!" Chorn yells looking at them.

Sivad, distressed, looks back to see Chorn subdued by the drones when he becomes confused, as he does not want to leave his friend to the mercy of these hideous creatures. Sivad stops just outside the shuttle's hatch door and turns, ready to go back and attack with all his power and defend his friend.

Chorn, when getting enough leverage to launch one security drone across the floor, crashing him into some large, cylindrical supply containers, was able to get a glimpse at the shuttle and the open hatch door. He saw the Blue Planet's satellite loaded and ready to go. Seeing this and seeing Sivad start to turn and come back, Chorn begins to yell,

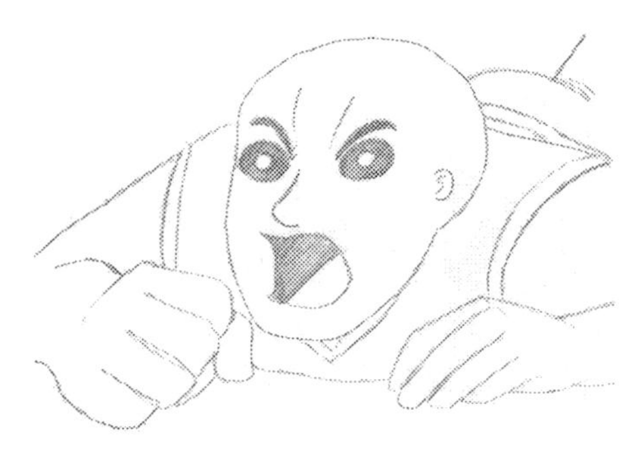

"NO, NO, GO GO GO!"

From behind Sivad in the shuttle, all three Kens grab him, yanking him up into the ship, knowing that their only chance for escape is with Sivad.

The Kens look at Sivad and point to the controllers while chattering their teeth and mumbling in hysterics. They close the hatch door before the security drones can get there.

Sivad yells, "I'LL BE BACK!" jumps into the pilot's seat, and, with the engines already warmed up as if the ship was waiting for him, takes control and begins to hover the shuttle, turning it toward the mob of security drones.

"DAMN, WHERE ARE THE WEAPONS!" Sivad yells. The ship directly faces Chorn, who now has fifteen drones holding him down. Sivad says in an uncommon, angry Akanian voice, "I WILL be back, I WILL BE BACK MY FRIEND!" Sivad, not finding any weapons, reluctantly turns the ship and takes off from the colonists' space port.

Stuck to the side window from the thrust of turning and taking off, the Kens are not only frightened, but also amazed that they're flying. The fear soon disappears, and the excitement takes over. They look at each other, smile, then move their heads forward, trying to put them out the window. Their heads bounce off the porthole, hitting the glass barrier, while trying to see the jungle below becoming more distant.

*****

Ready to depart to see Shobo at 2D City, Galleon enters the space dock, where he finds twenty of his security drones in chaos, trying to maintain control of an upset Akanian. Galleon becomes angered that his ship is no longer on the dock.

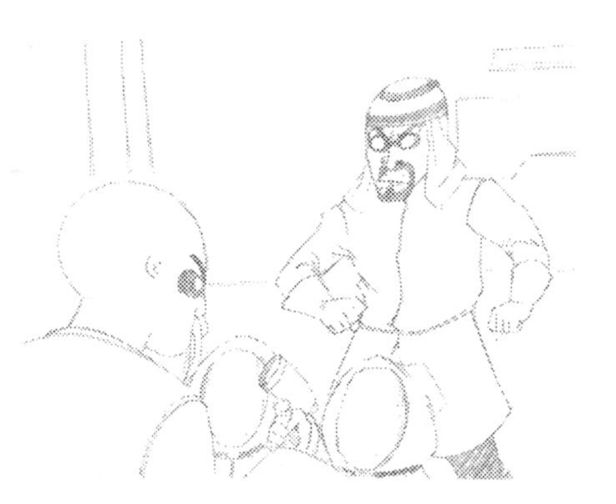

"Where is my *SHIP?*" he yells. One of his head drones hesitates then rushes over to give their master an update.

"It has been what? STOLEN?" he reads on the security drone's display. Galleon represses his emotions, gritting his teeth, then let's loose an outraged swing, knocks the security drone onto his back, and walks over to the defenseless Chorn.

"Where is your friend?" Galleon asks as calmly as he can.

Chorn struggles on the floor and refuses to answer.

The security drones force him up to his knees, trying to please their master.

"Where is my *cargo*?" Galleon begins to show his anger, speaking louder and spitting his words in Chorn's face.

"WHERE IS MY VESSEL?"

Chorn, regaining his confidence, replies, "Far away by now. You will never catch Sivad. He is too smart and too powerful for the likes of *you*!"

"You cannot intimidate me. Your Akanian friend shall be found and brought before me, where both of you will become my slaves!" Galleon pauses. "This *Sivad*, he will be back for you, will he *not*? We *will* get him," Galleon says as he turns to his head security drone, who is apprehensive at his master's side from being knocked over.

"Take this *slave* to the detention center and have him wait to be processed," Galleon orders.

Chorn still tries to intimidate Galleon as the drones take him away, with his hands tight behind his back. "Sivad will be back for me, and I will be gone, and you will *never* see it happen."

Galleon looks up and searches the skies for the shuttle. He sees a small flash in space just off the moon's horizon. The flash is similar to that of a ship jumping to light speed. The hijackers are now far away, and he has to wait for another shuttle to come down from his ship to pick up his crew.

Ganda Reunion

Sivad leaves the atmosphere of the planet and looks back, still distressed and confused that Chorn is not with him. "Why would you tell me to GO Chorn, WHY?

Sorry, old buddy. I *will* rescue you, be a slave with you, or *die* with you. I will be back *no* matter what it takes."

While talking to himself, Sivad looks back to see if the Kens are okay. Seeing that they are unharmed and already preoccupied, swinging from the cargo, Sivad turns and faces forward. He snaps his head back again to see that the cargo the Kens are playing on is the Blue Planet's space probe. Sivad smiles and lets out a laugh while putting the ship on autopilot.

"Chorn, YOU Romallian hound!" he says, getting up from his seat to take a closer look at it, understanding that Chorn was quick enough to see the space probe. YES! I knew there was a reason you said *go*. You saw this too, you leg-humping hound! You knew we would get the upper hand if we had the Blue Planet's probe. He-he!"

Two of the Kens look at Sivad talking to himself. They tilt their heads and look around for who he is talking to when Kenzo suddenly starts to yell and scream, pointing forward. Sivad looks up to see that Kenzo is yelling about crashing. The ship is on a direct collision course for the Gen Planet's moon, and approaching fast.

"OH CRAP!" Sivad says while rushing back to the pilot's seat and increasing power, swerving hard to just miss one of the moon's large crater-made mountain ranges. They fly over and duck down into the crater's core.

"Damn gravity belt! Need more power," Sivad says as the ship begins to rise up, forcing the Kens to the floor from the pressure of the G-force. They just miss the mountain range encapsulating the other side of the crater.

"*Whew!* That was close," Sivad says, looking over at three upset Kens with their arms crossed. Scolding glares are pasted on their faces since Sivad became preoccupied with the probe and did not watch where he was going.

Sivad turns his head forward and thinks that all is clear as they fly over the dark surface of the moon. He begins to prepare the ship for light speed when a small asteroid orbiting in the moon's low gravity sails over the horizon and impacts the ships tail section, damaging one of the two engines and starboard mobility thrusters.

"*Noooo! Darn it!* Where did that come from?" Sivad says, feeling the impact and adjusting controls very quickly to regain control of the spinning ship.

"Ooooh!" Sivad gasps again as he takes control and sails the ship into deep space. "*Hey-*, minor details. Didn't see that one coming, huh?" he says, smiling at the upset and now very scared Kens.

Sivad conducts a quick diagnostic, and the Kens faces are glued to a window fogged-over from their intense panting. They are on the lookout for more space debris.

"Oh, ferbo nuts! We lost the starboard thrusters and engine, which means that, unless we fly upside down, we can only turn left."

Sivad pulls up the star navigation systems to search for a location where they can repair the ship. "Hmmm. Judging by the arrangement of the stars, there is a planet, Farthe, a few light years away, but I don't think we'll make it there in less than a few light years by the looks of the engine's damage. Hmm, *or* even closer, the three planets of Ciab."

Sivad looks at the planet arrangement and starts to point his finger at the three planets of Ciab. "Eeny, meeny, miny, moe. Ah, the only one even semi-hospitable is Ciab Prime, and it is still barbaric and

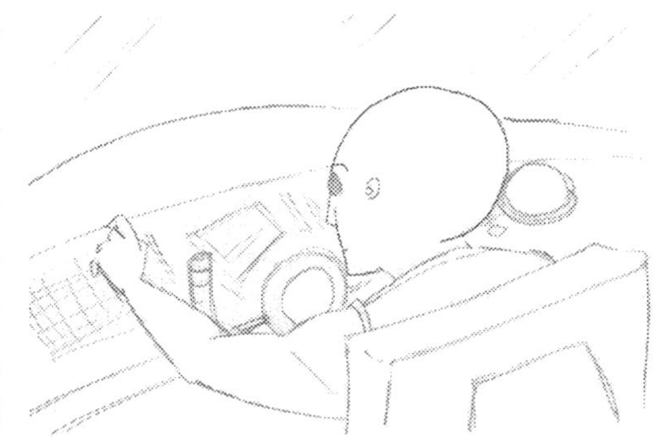

cold. They have a strange culture there. Should be interesting. What do you guys think?" Sivad asks the Kens, who are still looking out the window. "I really hate the cold, and you guys have never even seen snow." A red-alert buzzer begins to sound while Sivad talks to himself. "It looks like the decision has been made for us. Cold Ciab Prime it is. I hope the landing gear still works," Sivad says, looking back at the Kens.

Sivad adjusts the navigation systems and sets the course.

The Kens do not understand what Sivad is doing or mumbling about as they stare out into space.

"We have a few hours before we reach our next obstacle, which is landing this primitive heap of junk. Chorn could have built something better in his sleep. So let's take a closer look at what Galleon has found, shall we?"

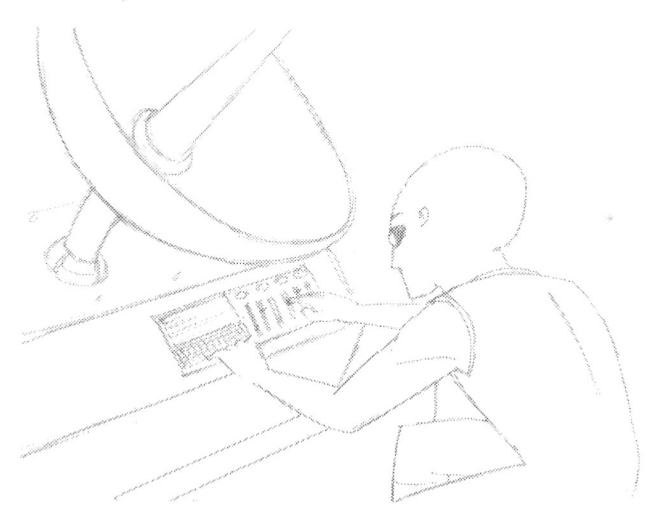

Sivad inspects the probe and the shuttle's database and finds that the data, research, mechanical findings, and plan of use have all been prepared, ready to present to Shobo.

"*Wow!* This is great. We have everything. That old slave guy in Ganda was working on this project. *Wow!* Plus, there is so much information from Galleon's personal database, and—*WOW*—he is ambitious! We got everything! This must have been Galleon's private shuttle. *Wow!*" Sivad expresses excitement as he makes a backup of all the research Galleon's slave teams discovered.

"We now have hard evidence. That is one of the drawbacks of the steagora device, no evidence, just insight." Sivad talks while working on the computer, with his mind multitasking. "I had better make two copies just in case." Sivad smiles and nods his head at the Kens, who watch him walk around with one hand in the air saying, "*Wow! Wow! Wow!*" as he downloads the information from the shuttle and the probes' docking station. Once completed, he places both copies into their pack next to the tooth and gem necklaces.

*****

Back on the Gen Planet, the detention center's door opens, and the drones powerfully thrust Chorn into the dimly lit room. Chorn stands and turns quickly, with arms out, ready to fight, looking at the small army of drones while the door slides closed, locking him in.

Chorn hears a sound of something moving behind him. He turns to see Cas sitting up on the bench where she was resting. In a one-eighty emotional turnaround from the intense moment, Chorn smiles and says in a calm voice,

"Hey, you're the singer from Ganda? It's a bit far away to have a gig out here, isn't it? Business must be pretty bad, huh?" Chorn turns to look around to see if there is a way out or anything he can work with or make tools out of.

Cas, surprised and offended at the insensitive statement, replies, "No thanks to you and your *buddy!* You Akanians are the cause! They destroyed our bar and killed my father because of YOU!" She stands and pushes his shoulder, provoking a fight.

Chorn looks at her and, with a defensive voice, says, "*No, no*, we didn't kill anyone. He was an escaped slave who led Galleon to Ganda. Sivad and I were just having some fun. Then you, *you*—do you think we started the fight?" Chorn asks, waving his hands in front of his chest, confused and looking around again.

"*Look at me when we're talking! Jeez!* Do all Akanians have such a short attention span? You're all arrogant troublemakers!" Cas says, still offended.

"Well, there's no use arguing about it now. We need to get out of here," Chorn says, having no luck finding anything in the empty, dark detention cell.

"That's the first sensible thing you've said so far," Cas replies in a sarcastic voice.

"Besides, we wouldn't be in this mess if your father didn't—" Chorn pauses in a quick thought. "Then again, we wouldn't have found out about the—" Chorn stops midstream, trying to keep the probe a secret. "The ... *thingy!*" Chorn turns and squats to look at something while mumbling to himself. "We wouldn't have found out about the Gens showing signs of evolving either," he says, shaking his head sideways.

"You, you are ... *errrrr!* You're so insensitive," Cas says, frustrated in talking with Chorn. "So are you a girl Akanian or a boy Akanian? I can't tell you apart," Cas says, trying to evoke an argument by insulting Chorn.

"I am a *male*, thank you," Chorn snaps back. After a slight pause while Cas sulks, he says, "I guess meeting you can be construed as positive. Outside being stuck in this smelly room together, we can entertain ourselves by arguing. I just hope Sivad is okay."

"Positive?" Cas stands up on the bench, towering from above, looking down at Chorn, with her hands on her hips, ready to pick a fight again. "Positive? My father is dead, Ganda is gone, and we're going to become slaves or worse! *Wait!* It is worse—*I'm stuck here with you!*" Cas yells.

Chorn turns to sit down, trying to calm the tempers. He closes his eyes, thinks and feels for a moment, then says in a higher-pitched, calmer voice, with a gentle smile, "Everything will be okay! You'll see."

"Who is your short friend anyway, this Sivad?" Cas inquires with sarcasm as she abruptly sits down on the bench with Chorn.

"Sivad? Well, he's not normal for an Akanian," Chorn says, looking up at the ceiling.

"What do you mean, *not* normal? Don't you Akanians believe that harmony, conformity, and discipline are the elements for your so-called *perfection* and think that all other species are barbaric? Heck, no one ever even sees your species traveling out in the galaxy. You just keep to yourselves, like, just because you're the first species to travel the galaxy makes you better than the rest. What were you doing at Ganda anyway?"

Chorn replies as calmly as he can, "No, not better, but more evolved. And Sivad tends to find trouble, or cause it, whichever comes first. And it is not of your concern, *but* we are on an important mission."

"Oh, well, excuse me, Mr. Smug on a *mission*. So is the *mission* goal to destroy and disrupt?" Cas responds in a calmer, almost joking tone.

"No, that's just Sivad. He's good at that," Chorn says as they both crack a smile.

"So, is Sivad a girl or boy?" Cas says jokingly as Chorn opens his mouth to retort, but he then realizes she is just pushing him. "Well, I think you're both strange," Cas finishes and sits back against the wall.

"By the way, I'm Chorn," he says when the detention cell door suddenly slides open and six drones line up inside, with more waiting outside. The drones nod their heads in the direction of the door to herd Chorn and Cas together for transport.

"I'm Cas," Cas says quickly.

"Everything will be okay," Chorn says.

"Like this is *okay*? It doesn't look okay," Cas says to Chorn as she walks by and out first.

Chorn looks closer at one drone's mirrored face to see his reflection and a dirt smudge on his face. He spits on his hand and starts to wipe it off, still looking closely at the mirror, when the drone pushes him toward the door in an attitude that he took offense to the action.

"Okay, okay. Don't get so pushy. Hygiene is important, you know. You guys should really learn to communicate better. Get a mechanical voice or something. I could make one for you? *Ouch*, grow a sense of humor, huh?" Chorn says as he is pushed out the door. "Violence is not a good way to express your emotions. My professor always says, when—"

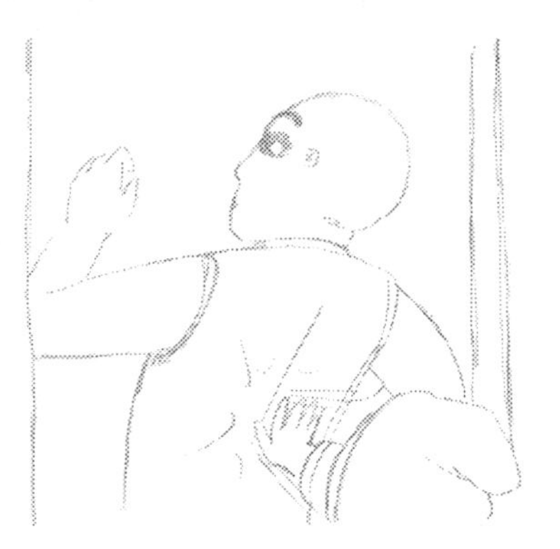

A drone pushes Chorn again to shut him up.

"Easy there, ya little munchkin!" Chorn snaps at the drone.

Chorn and Cas are herded onto another prepared shuttle.

"Where are they taking us?" Cas asks with some concern, though pleased that she is no longer alone.

"Well, wherever it is, there will be one heck of a party later and, most likely, an uninvited bald part-Akanian fellow as well," Chorn says, referring to Shobo.

"Shobo?" Cas says with concern as she boards the ship.

*****

Galleon watches them being loaded onto the ship from a distance.

"Shobo is not going to be happy, not happy at all," he mutters to himself.

Crash Landing

Not too far away, in a nearby solar system, Sivad and his gang prepare to enter the orbit of Ciab Prime. The shuttle, with damaged engines, is becoming more difficult for Sivad to control. It begins to shutter and shake while entering orbit. Outside the vessel, the friction of reentry starts to cause the nose of the ship to glow, and the atmospheric gasses engulf the ship as it enters the upper atmosphere of the jet stream.

"We're coming in too steep, and no power to pull up! Ooooooh, I was afraid of this," Sivad says in a panic as the ship violently shakes.

"OH, NO! Let's go. Let's go. Let's get out of here," Sivad says to the Kens as he jumps up from the pilot seat, grabs the Kens and the pack, and prepares to disembark mid reentry.

The noise grows, and the cargo containers of cylinders and boxes are tumbling and rolling across the ship's deck.

"LOOK OUT!" Sivad says and grabs Kento.

"We have to bail out. To the back of the ship, escape hatch," Sivad points and yells to be heard over the noise.

The Kens are confused as to what is going on around them, with Kenzo moving his arms as if he was a bird landing smoothly as they run to the back.

"No, no, no wings, dead thrusters. We are dropping like a rock and have zero control! Let's get out of here!" Sivad yells, running to the back of the ship. They just pass a porthole when it breaks in an inward explosion, spraying the transparent carbon fragments into the ship and allowing in clouds from the upper atmosphere.

Sivad runs past the Blue Planet's space probe. "Bummer to lose you. See ya!" he says as he pats the probe and heads to the escape pod in the back.

Sivad, entering into the escape pod, notices that the door to the pod is missing. "*What the? Where's the door?* We have to eject," Sivad says, looking back at the nose of the ship and watching the ground approaching fast.

In the escape pod, Sivad does some quick calculations in his head and hopes he is correct.

"Okay, everyone hang on tight. We need to slow our fall and eject the pod. Remember, if I say eject three times and you're still here, then you are the captain!" Sivad yells to get his voice over the noise, with a lot of hand motions for the Kens, preparing them to eject from the shuttle.

"Ready!" Sivad says, watching the ground come closer."Set! I hope this works. GO! EJECT!" Sivad yells as he pulls the lever to eject and braces himself.

The pod launches from the back of the shuttle moments before the shuttle crashes and ignites in an explosion on the snowy cliffs of Ciab. Sparks fly from the shuttle and pod separation. The thrusters of the escape pod fire and launch it into the air. Sivad's calculations are that the speed of the descent and the launch of the thrusters from the pod will counter one another to minimize the total velocity of descent.

The pod launches into the air and flips over. The thrusters finish their burst. Sivad pops his head out of the doorless entrance to take a look around and accidentally touches the thruster valves. With a reflex motion, he pulls back.

"Ouch! That's hot!" he says as the Kens rapidly nod up and down to agree, seeing Sivad's red fingers.

The Kens tap Sivad on the shoulder while they all look down through the portal they are standing on. The ground is approaching fast.

"Oops! Over-calculation of thrusters. Let's get out of here." Sivad and the Kens jump just a few meters before the pod impacted into the ground.

Sivad lands on the top edge of the cliff with a hard impact into the snowy ground and a loud "*Umph!*"

The Kens each land with grace and precision, one after the other, landing in a warrior's pose of one knee down, one fist down, and the other hand raised into the air, looking down at the landing with focus then up at Sivad.

With a determined growl, Sivad sits up and pulls his one foot from a sunken hole in the snow, shakes off the hit and ice on top of him, and places his right hand down next to the cliff edge to get up. "YES! We made – IT!-"

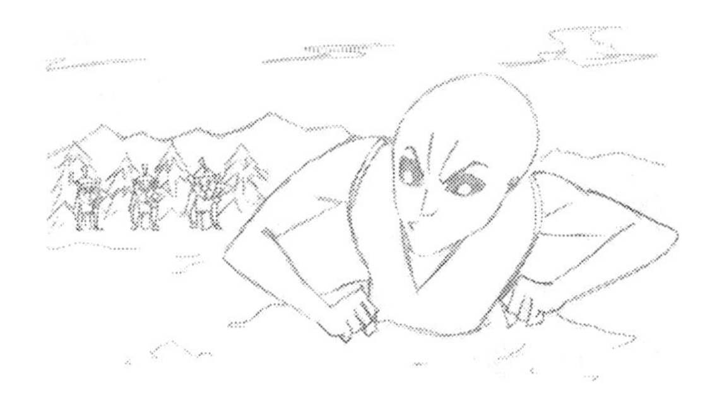

When he leans to push on his right hand, to his surprise, there is no ground under his hand as it slides through the snow, not supported by anything underneath. The snow quickly cracks around him, and he rolls off the cliff, giving the Kens a surprised look. "Oh, craaaaaaap!" he yells as he falls off the cliff wall.

The Kens look down and watch him fall, yelling all the way. Sivad bounces off a soft, snowy edge, muffling his voice, then lands a meter deep in the soft snow below. He groans from the frustration and cold of the snow going into his shirt.

The three Kens look at each other, and one after the other, they yell and jump off the cliff wall to follow Sivad.

At the bottom, they land one on top of another and become buried in a deep snow hole, as deep as they are tall. For a moment, no one moves. Sivad rests silently in his body-shaped snow cutout, listening to the quiet serene of the mountainside, the wind blowing, and the muffled sounds of ice cracking on the cliff wall. Sivad can hear the Kens rustling about and wonders how they got down so fast.

"At least it was a soft landing this time. I think I will just lay here for a moment. The cold will keep the swelling down. Ouch! - I hope Chorn is okay. Where is the next town? Damn, we have no ship now. How do we get off this ice cube?" Sivad mumbles to himself while lying comfortably in the snow.

Outside Sivad's snug burrow, snow falls off a nearby tree. The Kens pop their heads out of their den one after the other, looking around, seeing that there is no danger. They are finally safe on the ground, but they have never seen or felt this type of ground before.

One sticks his tongue out and licks the snow. His eyes light up, and they all disappear back into the hole only to reappear by popping out to start playing on top of the snow.

Kenzo makes a snowball and throws it at Kenpo, hitting him in the head. Kenpo picks it up and starts to eat it while Kento builds a snow Gen and lies down and starts burying himself in the snow.

While the Kens have fun in the snow, Sivad groans and finally sits up, this time watching where his hand is going down and making sure he is not going to fall again.

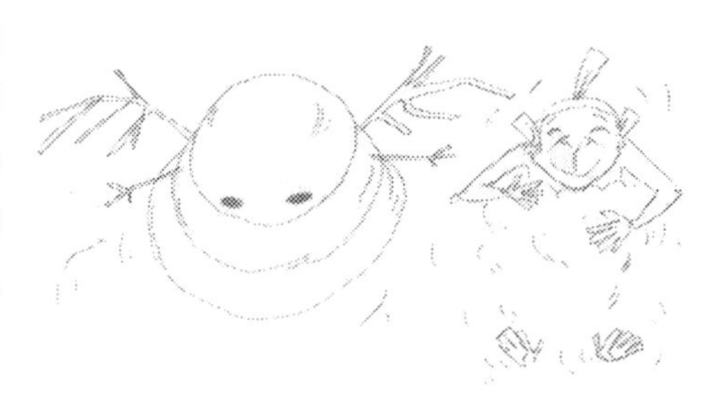

"Good, ground!" he moans as he picks his battered body up from the hole.

Sivad reaches back into the hole to grab the pack and puts it on, looking at the destroyed ship not too far away.

"If Chorn were here, he could probably make us a snow vehicle out of that heap of junk," Sivad says, looking at the ship then around at the vast snow-covered mountain peaks.

Suddenly, three consecutive snowballs from each of the Kens hit Sivad, two in the body and one on the side of his head.

"Yeah, I probably deserve that from the terrible landing but …" Sivad says as he wipes the snow away and reaches down to make a snowball.

"Now it is time that you feel the true *wrath* of the Akanians," Sivad says in a low, constricted voice. Sivad throws snowballs back at the Kens to be met by three more snowballs. A snowball fight ensued.

*****

Cas looks out the shuttle window and is amazed at the sight below as the vessel cruises over 2D City, heading to its docking bay.

The dark city with glimmering lights has two long, flat, wide, rectangle-shaped planes gyrating around in opposite directions. Both planes are connected through a single axis for gravity. The center is a sphere-shaped axis that looks like a small moon.

"Where is this?" Cas asks Chorn.

"This is 2D City, the headquarters of the Shobo Order."

"What do you know about Shobo?"

"Well, by his looks, he is obviously part Akanian. I have heard that he is the product of some kind of experiment we did over four hundred years ago. I don't know the details, as it was before my time, and no one will talk about it. But now he is the leader of a city he created. Most of what he does is not bad, it's just good business and infrastructure, but he does tend to bend, if not break, the intergalactic rules quite a bit. He surrounds himself with a dark aura and these midget drones, which makes him scary," Chorn replies.

"Have you ever met him?" Cas asks.

"Nope, and I don't know anyone who has either. He doesn't meet with anyone, *ever*. Frankly, with all the strange things I hear, I wouldn't want to meet him," Chorn says.

"Maybe since he's some part Akanian, it would mean that he is civilized or more evolved as *you* say, and he'll be a good host to other Akanians," Cas says sarcastically, emphasizing the word "evolved" with her fingers in the air, making quotation marks. "Which would mean *you* are doomed to be his buddy," Cas says.

"Or he could be the opposite and hate Akanians and *collaborators*, which would mean we're both doomed. It is perplexing," Chorn replies looking at Cas and rolling his eyes.

"At least I can take comfort that, either way, *you* are doomed," Cas says with a smile.

"That's not very comforting," Chorn adds, smirking.

"You're not much on sensitivity, are you?" Cas replies and looks out the window.

"Sorry, I'll practice on this drone." Chorn turns to the drone standing at attention next to him.

"Hey, Mr. Reflected Manifestation, when you take your mirrored face off and look in the mirror, do you scare yourself? I think you should go practice." Chorn continues to heckle the drone as Cas shakes her head, smiling. She is beginning to like this strange Akanian, finally warming up to him a small amount.

*****

On Ciab Prime, Sivad and the Kens walk down the mountainside and enter into a frozen town. The cleared streets are lined with mounds of slush and ice, piled against the walls of the buildings and edge of the road. Sivad walks down the almost-empty street with the Kens, who now, after their first time playing in the snow, have figured out that snow is not always fun; they begin to feel the chill.

The denizens look at Sivad and the Kens as they run across the street from building to building. A local will run from one door to another, closing it hard and fast, then another local will do the same, and every few seconds, the same loud door opening and closing occurs. The Kens become entertained by the strange behavior as they freeze in the cold.

Due to the cold, the denizens of this town tend to stay indoors, spending all day in the pubs, in the commercial establishments, or at home. When they go anywhere in the town, they run from place to place, opening and closing doors very hard so the doors seal properly against the inner frames.

Sivad and the Kens walk into the town and head for a local trading post to start bartering some of their supplies for transport or a communicator.

"Let's stop in that establishment over there and see if we can buy some transportation or a communicator *and* warm up; it's a bit chilly out here, huh?" Sivad says to the Kens as they all chatter their teeth, arms crossed to stay warm, and nod their heads, waiting to go inside and become warm.

The trading post's music echoes down the street, and the sound of laughter emanates from within, intriguing Sivad.

"Sounds like a lively place," Sivad says when the doors burst open.

A whiney yell originates from inside, "No! I didn't *k-n-o-w-*!"

A grunt is heard, then another, then the sound of a table breaking. The Kens tilt their heads sideways, curious about what is going on inside. They stand behind Sivad just in case. Suddenly, an armored-space-suit-wearing humanoid is thrown out the door into the air, landing and skipping across the icy street. He gives off a loud grunt as he lands headfirst, sliding on his oxygen pack into a slushy snow bank. The trading post doors close hard, and the music becomes muffled.

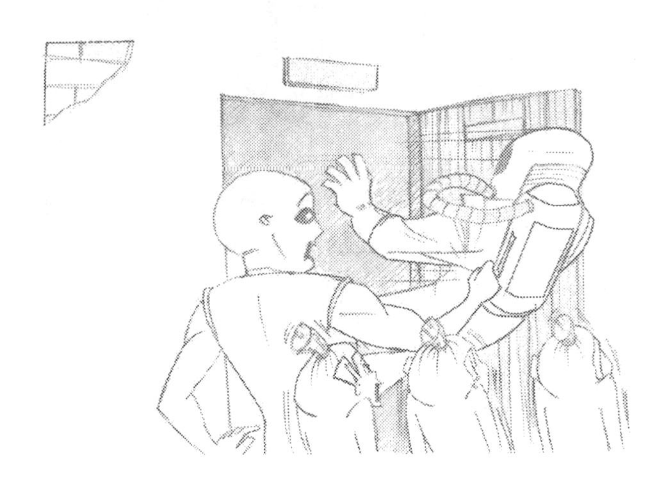

Sivad walks over, looking down at the armored space man, holds out his hand to him, and says, "Prince Grant? How is that, uh, experience-gaining mission coming along? Have you been able to complete anything or satisfy any of, uh-, your requirements?" Sivad says in a bit of a cocky tone. The prince sits up, brushes the wet snow off himself, and grabs Sivad's hand to get up.

The three Kens giggle and start kicking more snow onto the humiliated prince.

As the prince stands, he grabs a pile of snow and underhandedly tosses it in a sissy style at the three Kens who are trying to bury him in slush. The Kens duck, and the snow sails over their heads as they look at each other, ready to get into a snowball fight. Kenzo mimics the sissy throw, and Kento and Kenpo begin to laugh uncontrollably.

The prince growls at them, turns to Sivad, and, as benevolently and as manly as he can, says, "How do you know who I am?"

"Ah! We saw you in Ganda, trying to sell some piece of junk gem that could never be used and has no value on Miniloc. You should know your customers and their needs better," Sivad replies, still being cocky and talking down to the prince as a primitive. "I see you got out from under that table when the fight broke out back at Ganda," Sivad says.

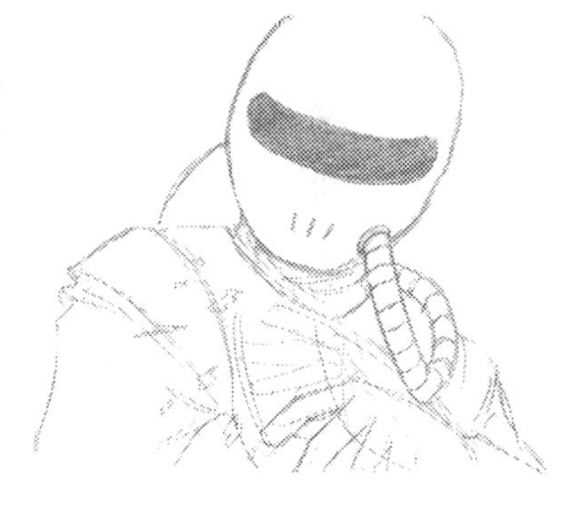

"Table? Uh, I was, uh, checking it." The prince is at a loss for words, embarrassed and brushing snow off his suit.

"So what's happening here?" Sivad asks and points to the pub the prince was thrown out of. The Kens snuggle into Sivad's legs to keep warm and start to nag him to go inside. Ignoring them, Sivad says, "What did you have to gain here?"

Evading Sivad's questions, Prince Grant is irritated by the locals, "The frost seems to give these people a bite. They're *not* very friendly," he says.

"This is Ciab Prime, the most friendly out of all the Ciabs. Have you seen the other Ciab planets yet? Now those places don't just bite, but they will chew you up as well." Sivad makes a joke to lighten the conversation, even though he has never been to the other planets and knows they are uninhabitable.

The Kens, hearing this and anxious to get indoors, take Sivad's hand and start chattering their teeth on his hand and arm to get his attention.

"Whoa! When you get to an elbow, it's mine. Okay, okay, let's get inside before these guys turn into snow Gen, the frosty Gen Ken. Probably hungry too," Sivad says as he wipes the slobber off his hand.

They all go into one building, down from the trading post pub, and enter into a majestic-style general store with a café and sit down at one of the rustic wooden tables near the window. In the background, the locals continue to exit doors and enter other doors, running from place to place, slamming the doors shut.

The Kens, happy to be indoors, sit and slouch as if they are melting into the chairs, absorbing the heat as their fur thaws and the icicles drip onto the floor.

Prince Grant takes off his space helmet and sets it on the table. When he takes off his helmet, two big ears pop out of his head, and the Kens stare, still melting from the warmth.

"Does this chill not affect you? You seem like you are not cold and are not wearing that much," Prince Grant says.

Sivad tosses his head back and explains, "On Akan, the temperature, although warm, changes drastically four to five times daily, falling between 70 and 110 degrees, with intense radiated sunlight and cold shaded times caused by our five moons. We have evolved with extra layers of skin to protect us from these intense changes, and they also help our bodies absorb moisture from the air. I feel the cold, but it would not make sense to dwell on it. Therefore, I can continue with my objectives and not be distracted by the cold."

Prince Grant's eyes, already glossing over from the boring conversation, look around at some of the characters in the store while Kenzo takes some food out of the pack.

"This place is tough! Hey, what's that your pets are eating?" the young prince inquires.

"Some sweets that the Gen mama gave them. And they are my Ken club, not pets," Sivad says as the Kens nod their heads in agreement, not happy with the prince's comment.

"Whatever is a Jen? Anyway, this is a tough place, and them eating sweets like that does not look tough," the wood-be warrior says.

"The crunch is tough," Sivad smiles.

The prince continues, "Ya know, we need to act tough here if we're going to develop respect from these people."

Sivad laughs as he knows that the prince is trying too hard.

"Na, you just need to be wiser than they are, not tougher. Being tougher will just teach you how to fly, as you just did coming out of that door. You need to work on your landing though or get a longer landing strip," Sivad says, joking with confidence.

The Kens, not liking the tone of the comments made by the prince, begin to tease him about his large ears. Kenzo reaches over to Kenpo and pulls his ears up and out, chattering away as Kento laughs, then the other two join in and giggle.

"Your Jen pets are a bit rude, huh?" Prince Grant says, staring at the Kens.

Some hot drinks arrive at the table, and the Kens and Sivad hold the cups close to warm up, taking sips of the hot cider beverage.

"Annoying little things, aren't they? Where did you capture them?" the prince asks.

"We just came from the Gen Planet," Sivad starts to say, taking a drink of cider, when he stops to think about Chorn.

At the same time, he hears Prince Grant ask, "Where is your friend who was with you in Ganda? And hey, what happened to that girl at Ganda? You know the one, the singer, Cas? I heard that Galleon took her and is going to make her his slave. He-he. I'd like to have a slave like *that*," Prince Grant chatters on while Sivad thinks to himself. "Yeah, I would've jumped in on the fight, but you know royalty ..." the young, annoying kid rambles on, still trying to talk tough.

Sivad pauses silently for a moment, looking out the window, and watches a denizen run from one door to another to stay warm. He finishes a sip of cider when he raises one brow and looks at the prince with a strong-minded gaze as the prince babbles on.

"You have a Teflon tongue that won't stop slipping off your teeth," Sivad says to stop the prince from talking, annoyed by what he was saying.

"Huh?" the young prince stops talking.

"Let me offer you some advice, kid. Acting tough does not make you courageous. You need to stop being so annoying and stop trying to push so hard. It's pathetic if you show you're trying too hard. In the end, opportunities will find you," Sivad says, repeating one of his old spiritual wisdom professors from when he was young and thinking to himself that he always thought that course was a waste of time until now.

"I'm not trying to be rude, but seeing you at Ganda and then here, well, you could use some coaching if you want to please dear old dad," Sivad says then leans forward toward the prince, as if he had a secret to tell. "*Hey*, you have a ship, right?" Sivad asks in a low tone.

"Yeah," the prince nods his head, curious to learn more and thinking that the Akanian can give some good advice.

"You're looking to accomplish a benevolent act, right?" Sivad asks.

"Yeah, that would be good," The prince agrees, nodding his head.

"You have vast resources available to you, right?" Sivad is still talking as if he were telling a secret.

"Yeah, well, kind of," the prince answers.

"And your planet is not far away," Sivad says.

"Yeah, so? *Hey*, did your old partner die? Do you need a new partner? *Oh!* That would be *great!* We could have some incredible adventures. I know this place where—" the prince says, leaning forward from his relaxed position in his chair with numerous new ideas when Sivad interrupts him.

Sivad looks side to side to appear as if he is checking for unwanted ears listening in. "*This* could be dangerous," Sivad says to intrigue the prince. The prince's face lights up with curiosity about what Sivad is speaking of. "There is a damsel in distress too," Sivad says, pointing at the prince, eyebrows raised. Sivad sits back and smiles, as he sees that he has sold the adventure to the prince, and continues to think.

"*What*, what? Where is it? Who is the girl? She doesn't look like these guys, does she? I don't know, I mean, your taste in girls may be different than mine," Prince Grant says, pointing to the Kens, who are eating and drinking. He leans forward, intrigued to learn more, and Sivad sits back in his chair.

Sivad quickly leans forward to the prince. "Cas, the singer from Ganda, has been captured by Galleon, and she and my partner are being held, most likely, at 2D City."

The prince, excited about this opportunity, can hardly contain himself. "Cas! The singer! And we will have to rescue them, right?"

"*Yes!*" Sivad says, raising a single eyebrow, surprised that the young prince has caught on so fast.

"And it will be dangerous? And we will be heroes? The excited prince says.

"*Yes!*" Sivad says leaning closer

And Cas will be rescued by *me*, right?" the prince confirms.

Again Sivad answers "*Yes!*" with one eyebrow raised,

"Oh, my father has all the supplies we need. We have a huge army and knights ready to die at my order," the excited prince says.

Sivad, a bit taken back by the comment that he would order his knights to die, says, elongating the answer but not wanting anyone to die or sacrifice themselves, "*Ye-s!*" Sivad nods his head while saying yes then stops and says,

"*No!* No one will die." Then, in a calmer voice, Sivad continues, "This has to be a covert rescue. We don't want to start a war between your planet, Farthe, and the Shobo Order. They are far too strong and vicious. We shall use your father's resources, and we, as a team, will rescue Chorn and the girl. Through this, you will gain the respect you are looking for and become a hero, and Cas, well, she might just like you," Sivad says then looks up at the prince's ears and finishes dropping his head back with a concerned look on his face, knowing that the prince is young and overzealous.

The prince, already dreaming of his glory, sits back and takes a sip from his cup, daydreaming about the plan. The Kens, not showing they were listening, look at Sivad and start slapping each others' hands under the table, low fiving each other, with smiles as if they just suckered the prince into the adventure. Sivad looks at the Kens with surprise that they seemed to understand and puts his hand out under the table for a low five from Kenzo next to him.

Wanting to get his friend back from Shobo, Sivad looks and points directly at the prince and says, "*Heroes.*"

"*Alright!* When do we start? What are we waiting for? Let's go kick some Shobo booty!" Prince Grant stands up, ready to go. "Where's your ship?" Prince Grant asks while standing and grabbing his helmet.

"On the Gen Planet," Sivad says with a strange look. "I think it would be best if we take your ship, less conspicuous. We'll pick ours up later," Sivad says as the Kens nod their heads, smiling, looking at Sivad then over at Prince Grant for the answer.

"Alright, let's go see my father. He should be excited to help us once he sees what good deeds we intend to do. This is better than our historical knight stories," Prince Grant says with excitement.

Prince Grant leads the way out of the café, and Sivad looks down at the Kens and says, with a concerned look on his face, "Do you think this is going to work?"

The Kens shrug their shoulders and tilt their heads with little confidence.

"That's what I thought. This kid could get us in trouble. But the plan is solid." Sivad looks up at the sky when leaving the café. "It's the best I can do, Chorn! Here we come!" Sivad says, nodding to himself as he walks out behind the Kens, grabbing the pack with the Blue Planet's probe information inside.

Sivad and Prince Grant walk by the trading post pub that the prince was previously thrown out of.

"Hey, Grant, this place is tough, huh? I need you to do something before we go; you need to go inside and show them you can handle it," Sivad says, wanting to have some fun before they depart.

"Na, na, let's just go," Prince Grant says, with his head hung low, not to be seen.

"I want to be sure you have what it takes to go on this important, dangerous mission with me. Are you strong enough? Are you fast enough? Are you smart enough?" Sivad says, pushing the intimidated prince.

"Yes, I am, *but* this has nothing to do with our mission plan," the prince pleas, as he does not want to go back in that pub again.

"On the contrary, it has everything to do with our mission. What if, when it comes down to it, you do not have what it takes? Then something bad will happen to one of us. We don't want that to happen. We need to know that you have the courage and loyalty we need and trust. Excuses are for losers," Sivad says convincingly.

"That will not prove anything but me getting my butt kicked again," the prince insists.

"Go in with confidence, be tough, and ask them for a drink and directions to the general store next door. You can do it!" Sivad says, motivating the young man.

"If I go in, then where will you be?" the prince asks with an insecure voice, looking for some kind of backup.

"We will be in just after you enter," Sivad replies. "Now go!"

Prince Grant walks inside, grumbling.

"Hey, head high, shoulders out! Remember, you are the armored spaceman. *Be* tough!" Sivad says the last words to him with a clinched fist then looks down at the Kens and giggles with them.

Prince Grant tosses his shoulders back and struts into the trading post.

Inside, the armored spaceman walks across floor to the bar and orders a glass of iced tea in a low, confident voice. People around him laugh because he ordered a weak drink and one with ice when they are on an ice-cold planet, not to mention he is wearing a helmet. People around him joke, "How can he drink it? What a wuss." Prince Grant laughs with them nervously.

"Extra ice," he orders.

A large nomad-looking character approaches from behind. The prince sees his reflection and says to himself, "Armored spaceman. I am the armored spaceman. Be the armored space man," trying to convince himself that he is tough. The oversized nomad is the same who threw him out before.

In the background, Sivad walks in with the Kens by his side, looking around.

"Hey!" the bartender yells.

"Your animals have to stay outside!"

Sivad glances down at the Kens and says to them, "I guess you still have to evolve more before you will be accepted into the galaxy federation, no matter how primitive and rude some of the accepted species are."

Sivad reaches down, grabs Kenzo's nose, and looks back at the bartender with a low browed glare. "His nose is not wet or cold. It *is* a bit sticky though," Sivad says as he wipes his hand on his pants.

In an aggressive voice, he says, "These are my guests."

Kenzo slaps Sivad's hand off his nose, also trying to be tough. The bartender mumbles something that sounds like "damn Akanians, always causing trouble," and Sivad goes and stands against the wall by the door and watches the nomad approach Prince Grant.

The nomad grabs the prince's shoulder and says, "I thought I told you to leave and not come back!"

Prince Grant looks over at Sivad, takes a deep breath, and says to the nomad in a condescending, Sivad-style tone, "No, you did not say that. Did you imply it by kicking me out before?"

The nomad is disturbed by this comment and has no answer but an angry look on his face. The armored spaceman's confidence grew.

"Do you know where the general store is located? Why don't you run and fetch me some ice?" the prince said with confidence.

Sivad, hearing this overconfident statement, cringes his small nose, and the Kens cover their eyes, peeking through their fingers.

The nomad, at a loss for words, grabs the armored spaceman in anger and throws him onto a table then picks him up over his head. Prince Grant screams, "So that means no to the ice?"

The giant nomad throws him down and kicks him through the door, again launching him outside, sliding across the ice road into a slush pile.

The nomad started to head out to further beat on the armored spaceman when Sivad, standing by the door, stopped him by grabbing the nomad's arm.

"I don't think that would be a good idea. My boys and I will have to throw you around and bounce you off a couple of tables," Sivad says, nodding over at the Gens, who are posed and ready for battle.

The nomad, not impressed and one who is not to be messed with, sizes up the much smaller Sivad and the Kens. Then he grabs Sivad by the shoulders and throws him outside, skipping him across

the icy road and into the same snow bank that Prince Grant rests up against.

Just after, the Kens try their luck and attack one by one, and one after the other, they also fly through the air, out the door, skipping and crashing into the slushy snow bank. Sivad and the Kens, satisfied with the results, give each other a dazed smile.

"Did I learn something from this?" the annoyed Prince Grant asks Sivad as they all rest on the snow embankment.

"No, but it was fun a experience, huh? And you showed the courage to go back in there, and we all got beat together.

Teamwork! He-he." Sivad and the Kens all smile and laugh. "We'd better get out of here before he decides he wants more!" Sivad gets up, and they rush off.

"I don't like you anymore. You give me a bad feeling," Prince Grant says as they run.

Incarceration

On 2D City, Chorn and Cas are caged in a small, round laser-walled jail cell. The cell's high-frequency red and blue lasers stream down from the ceiling to the receivers on a cylindrical floor mount. The laser emitters on the top hang from the ceiling by a single large chain holding up the laser platform. The laser bars are so powerful that one touch would fry the skin or sever an appendage. In the cell, there is only a single chair, where Chorn sits contemplating his next move. Cas rests on the floor.

"Sitting here on my stool of woe. Distressed, you see. An inactive Cas at my feet, with no hope are we," Chorn jokes while he attempts to mull over the situation in poetry. Cas, with her head resting on her arms, smiles and begins to hum in sync with the words.

"Oh, to the despair. Dejected are we. Desolated on my thrown of misery, with no paper to spare. Hopeless are we? Maybe, but you shall see, if we can truly remain to be." The quiet hum begins to fill the room and echo off the walls, offering a feeling of restfulness as Chorn begins to run out of poetry, yet he continues his dirge, "Will our gallant stranger, that noble Sivad, liberate us from oppression? Or are we alone to savor in this moment before we become slaves and are put to work cleaning some smelly cave?" Chorn smiles as he runs out of new words while Cas continues to hum.

"Behind these beams of light, unable to take flight, in deep space at this great height, we are out of mind and out of sight," Chorn stops and listens to Cas's tranquil humming.

"We- are always sear-chin', we are loo-kin' for a new adventure. We are always tra-velin'. We are fly-in' through space and ti-me," Chorn sings a with a low soft tone to Cas's music.

"How do you do that?" Chorn stops and asks Cas.

"Do what?" Cas gently sings in her hum.

"Now, that, like in Ganda. Your voice seems to roam and pulsate, causing a soothing sensation to all who listen. Your voice doesn't just resonate, but it really fills the room. It seems it would take a great deal of skill and practice. I have never heard anything like it," Chorn says.

"That's very nice to say. Thank you. Actually, it is just something I have always been able to do. I guess that is why they made me a partner at Ganda, which *you* destroyed," Cas says with a semi-light tone, as she does not want to argue again. "I didn't know Akanians could do poetry," Cas comments.

"Poetry? Na. We're better at conforming and working together in harmony than being creative. Robotism and perfection. Rather boring if you ask me. Damn, I sound as cynical as Sivad now," Chorn says of his own culture.

"So what happened to you and your friend then? Were you guys also experiments like this Shobo guy?" Cas asks.

Chorn looks at Cas, confused, thinking that he and Sivad are normal, then rethinking it before he answers. The door to their dimly lit dungeon slides open, and four elite security drones, dressed in black and red robes rather than the tradition brown, boldly walk inside, followed by a bald, slow-moving being swaying side to side as he walks. Behind the lumbering creature, dressed in oversized gray robes, two more elite security drones enter while two more wait outside.

One of the drones carries a wooden box and places it on the floor near the incarceration cell.

Chorn says to Cas in a quiet voice before she raises her head to see who entered the room, "Keep your head down and don't move."

The individual who entered the chambers with power slowly climbs onto the wooden box, situates himself standing then stops and stares at Chorn, who is sitting on the stool with a cocky expression, one hand on his knee and the other elbow resting on the other knee as he looks up through the lasers at the side-to-side rocking species.

"Shobo," Chorn says in a quiet voice.

Standing on the box, Shobo raises his hands and arms into the air. His loose-fitting sleeves fall down to his thin, aged elbows, and he begins to speak in a very slow voice.

"YOU are Chorn, and it is unfortunate that YOUR compatriot, Sivad, got away, with MY property! We WILL catch him." Shobo's low-toned, slow, preaching voice shatters the remaining echoes of Cas's hums. When Shobo speaks, Cas feels shivers go down her back. She looks up at Chorn with scared, sparkling eyes, covered from Shobo's sight by the hood from her shawl.

Shobo lowers his hands and continues his speech, scolding Chorn. "WHAT I do not understand is WHY the senior chancellor of Akan would SEND such inexperience as YOU to break into MY shipping dock and steal MY belongings. YOU and YOUR cohort are just young, ignorant, fresh graduates! The ONLY rationale I can imagine IS that this must have been a suicide mission, bound for failure, WITH the sole purpose of making a statement to ME that Akan is watching."

"You sure are full of yourself, or full of something," Chorn says under his breath.

Shobo, hearing this, continues, "Nonetheless, YOU will become MY slave. Now, WHAT is YOUR purpose here?"

Chorn looks down at Cas, knowing that the government of Akan would make a decision for the sole purpose to make a statement such as what Shobo informed, but after a moment of thought, he realizes that it is not true, because they instigated each event that took place.

"Your comments are vain. Our mission initially had nothing to do with you. And the sequence of events began after we departed Akan," Chorn says, trying to maintain his confidence in Shobo's ominous presence.

Shobo, working to break Chorn's self-assurance and have him take the first step of acceptance that he will become a slave, says,

"DO not BE overly shrewd. The senior chancellor KNOWS exactly what HE is doing and WHOM he is sending. HIS insight is strong; HE feels it; HE knows just as I do. But HE is helpless to stop THE progression that WE have forced. In turn, HE is only making a statement by using YOU. What is it about YOU and YOUR associate? Bad grades? Dated his daughter? Different?" Chorn looks down, thinking about what Cas had said about him and Sivad being different and what Shobo just said about the mission.

"Ahhh, different! I can SEE it in your eyes. In an isolated PART of the galaxy, FAR away, in the land OF accord, why are YOU different? The education system DICTATES that ALL must conform. I would SAY that, if YOU are different, then YOU could end up like ME," Shobo says with pride, "or be expendable AND become a slave."

Chorn, surprised at the insight of Shobo, becomes more vexed and confused, because all that he had said could be possible.

An elite security drone walks over to Shobo and helps him off his box. Shobo places his hand on the smaller drones head and steps down, saying, "YOUR acceptance of BEING a misfit is YOUR key to survival within my order. The progression cannot be stopped; YOU and I both know THAT chaos is the horizon for things to change. I no longer need THAT piece of space junk YOUR friend took anyway," Shobo says, regarding the Blue Planet's satellite, and walks out with his team of elite security drones.

Chorn, angry and confused, mimics Shobo in a troubled high-pitched voice but not loud enough for the departing Shobo to hear. "In *my* odor, *acceptance* to the stench *will* mean that you are *not* wasting water."

*****

In the corridor, Galleon waits for Shobo to finish with the prisoners. Shobo sees Galleon as he exits.

"YOU are LATE," Shobo says, walking past Galleon.

Galleon cringes and turns to walk with Shobo. "I had some last-minute modifications for the neo-navigation system on my ship that needed my direct attention," Galleon says, trying to stay calm.

"Today YOU are fortunate. As YOU have requested previously, I will grant YOU with the most important mission WE have encountered in a millennium," Shobo says.

Galleon smiles. "Thank you, sir. I will not let you down."

"No, YOU will NOT," Shobo says in a threatening tone.

"I am certain THAT the missing Akanian, THIS, Sivad, will inevitably follow standard inane Akanian procedures; THUS, without his partner, HE will report back to THE senior chancellor on Akan. This WILL be a grave waste of time. Akan WILL instruct him to wait for reinforcements and further analysis, holding THAT piece of Blue Planet space junk. IT WILL take days or EVEN weeks for the Akanians to verify the report and prepare a competent ACT against us. In this time, THEY shall be too late and THEIR efforts in vain." Shobo stops by a shield and looks out into the core of the galaxy. "WE shall have the UPPER hand," he continues.

"Galleon, provided that YOUR ship is fully prepared, YOU will depart first thing tomorrow morning for the center of OUR galaxy. There YOU shall engage the temporal wormhole, placing a homing beacon on either side. When YOU reach to the other side of THE wormhole, release the space probes and THE parallel homing beacon. Just after YOU depart, I shall launch a full-scale security force to protect THE gateway on THIS side and wait for YOUR successful return. The space probes WILL communicate back through the homing beacons. No other shall dare oppose US or stand in OUR way." Shobo turns to leave through the next set of doors, exiting the corridor as Galleon bows.

"Thank you, sir, for this honor." Galleon turns and leaves with excitement.

*****

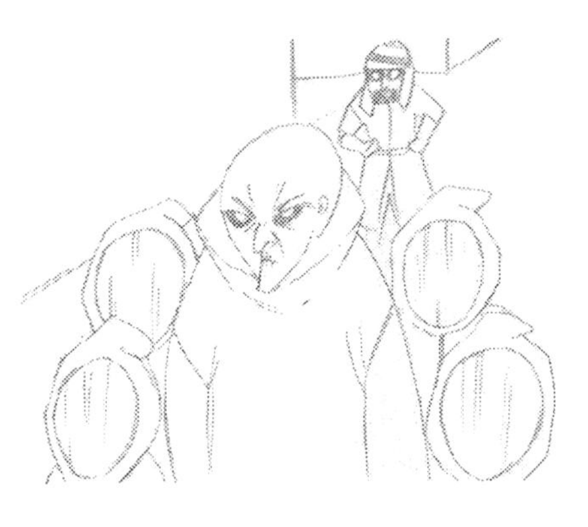

Chorn stands and begins to pace, disturbed by the preceding conversation, when Cas sits up. "He is not very nice, is he?" Cas says while Chorn continues to pace. "That's not true what he said, ya know. Akan would not make you expendable, and you are the same as all other Akanians."

"How do you know? How many Akanians have you met? Besides, look at me; I'm pacing and *upset*. This, this is *not* normal. An Akanian would accept the situation very quickly with little emotion, moving on, accepting that a decision of this type is for the good of the planet," Chorn says, rattled by the conversation.

Cas tries to be sympathetic to her cellmate. "You are the only Akanian I have ever met or seen, other than your friend. So you are perfectly normal to me. You may be rude and arrogant at times, but you seem to be okay."

Chorn quickly responds, "*See!* Rude and arrogant, you said! Akanians are always humble and passive. How come I am not humble and passive?"

"Is your friend humble and passive?" Cas asks about Sivad.

"Sivad? He's confident, creative, and a royal pain in the ass. That's why he's so mischievous, *always* getting me in trouble. He also is not conformed, humble, or passive. You see? We *are* different! We are expendable to Akan!" Chorn shows that he is upset.

Cas starts to take a stronger stance to Chorn, seeing his stress. "Don't let Shobo or Akan get to you! If you do, then they win. Your friend will somehow rescue us, or we'll find our own way out. Besides, you can't be sure that anything he said is true."

Chorn sits down on the stool. "I suppose you're right." As he places an elbow on his knee and hand on his chin in thought, he mumbles, "Mmmmm, Sivad, where are you? Where are you? I hope you're okay."

Royal Court

Sivad and the Ken Club are on Prince Grant's ship, heading toward Farthe to meet the king and ask for assistance to rescue Chorn. Sivad starts to wonder around the ship and finds the galley with the cooled storage units stocked full of royalty-level gourmet food made for a prince.

"Wow, this looks good," Sivad says as the Kens pop their heads around the door, one by one, on top of the other, to look inside. All three of them, seeing this chilled feast, drop their jaws in hunger. Kento, whose head is on the top, opens his mouth, and slobber drips down his jaw onto Kenpo's ear. Kenzo, who is on the bottom, jets over to where Sivad stands staring into the chiller with the door open, looking at the food. Kento and Kenpo fall down then run over to join him. The group has not eaten in a while, and it had been a busy day.

Prince Grant unfastens himself from the pilot seat and walks to the galley. "It has been a long day, and we have some time before we arrive, so let's fix some food, shall we?" Prince Grant says, and the Kens smile and shake their heads fast, showing that they agree, slobber dripping down their chin.

Prince Grant straps on an apron, and an anxious and hungry Sivad passes different foods down a line of Kens from the chiller, finally reaching the preparation table where Prince Grant is ready to cook them a feast.

"This looks good and this and this—ooooh—this too," Sivad says as Kenzo points to another food item in the chiller. "That one also? Okay, but it will need this and that to go with it." Sivad passes more food down the line of Kens.

A few hours later, around a ransacked table of bones, depleted food wrappers, and plates, all five sit slouched down in their chairs, bellies protruding out. The Kens rub their bellies, lick their fingers, and wipe their mouths. Prince Grant picks his teeth and rubs his belly. Sivad leans back with his hand slung in his belt, fully satiated.

Sivad takes a deep breath. "What's for dessert?" he asks. A buzzer sounds, signifying that they have arrived at Farthe's defense barrier, thus their binge is over. The prince gets up from the table with a moan as the food shifts in his belly and heads to the pilot chair to give authorization and navigate to their final destination, the capital city's docking station.

Arriving without complication, the gang makes their way up large stairs of a grand palace, where they stop outside gigantic doors designed with aged wood and iron casing, decorated with the planet's local gems.

"This is the entrance to the royal hearing chambers," Prince Grant says, turning to Sivad. "Okay, Sivad, there are protocols that we must follow. This is the plan. My father is not a happy man, and he likes to yell a lot, too much. I would not want his job, but I don't have a choice, I think. I will talk to him first and ask for his help, so wait here, and I will be back in a few minutes to introduce you."

Sivad tries to stop the prince before he opens the large doors. "Grant, I don't think it's a good idea—" The sound echoes, and the prince rushes in.

Sivad turns to the Kens. "Maybe I should have told him more information about Shobo and the wormhole."

Sivad sits down on the stairs in front of the place and looks over the city. "And they say I'm green with inexperience! This kid has a long way to go and needs to learn about tact. Kenzo, you should teach him a thing or two." Kenzo nods his head, agreeing as they all sit elbow on knee, with their hands on their chins, looking over the city.

"Wow, this is a beautiful city. They have kept it well. They have balanced infrastructure growth and technology while maintaining traditional monarchy values. It shows in their style," Sivad says as a nice breeze blows by. The Kens look around and ogle at the architecture and grand entrance.

Kento gets up and tries to take a jewel out of the large door for a souvenir with no luck. He then puts his mouth to the jewel and tries to use his teeth but can't get them around it and just slobbers on the gem. Kento stops gnawing at the gem and stands up, hearing something. He places his ear to the door and is followed by his two curious brothers.

"What is it? What do you hear?" Sivad asks as he places his ear to the door. They can hear the faint voice of the father yelling at the son. "Oops! Looks like we got the guy in trouble," Sivad says as the Kens shush him and wave their hands to keep his voice down,

"Okay, okay," Sivad says with a proud smile that the Kens are showing initiative.

The incoherent mumbles of the king and Prince Grant become quiet, and giant steps are heard within. The Kens jump back to see the door open with a

large, echoing creak. Sivad, still on his knees from trying to listen to the conversation, looks up to see a very large armored knight standing in front of him, looking down.

The Kens stand, put their hands behind their backs, and move one foot, sliding it across the ground as they whistle and look around, attempting to look innocent from their apparent listening post.

"*Oh*, hello there," Sivad says, looking up at the knight.

"This way," the knight says in a low, powerful voice while turning to escort Sivad and the Kens into the royal hearing chamber.

Sivad jumps up, and in a single-file line, Sivad and the Kens march in behind the dark armored-suited knight.

The Kens, alarmed by the size and ominous presence and walk of the knight, walk with their chests out, holding their breath, taking big steps, trying to keep up.

The knight hurries off and stands at attention in his place among the other knights, while a small, colorfully dressed court jester walks up very strangely, strutting his way as if he were three meters tall, announcing the presence of Sivad,

"Sivad of Akan."

Sivad, not accustomed to a monarchy society, is fascinated by the rituals and strange theatrical characters catering to the king's court.

In the king's presence, Sivad waits for him to speak first, as the king looks at Sivad then tilts his head sideways from his chair to get a better look that the Kens popping out from behind Sivad. "Welcome!" the king says to the Kens, allowing them to feel more comfortable.

The three Kens spread out and kneel down on one knee, knowing that this is the chief. The king of Farthe smiles and opens his arms. "Sivad of Akan. You are a long way from home, my friend. My people have not seen an Akanian in over 150 years. I only see your leaders from a distance at the federation conferences. So what brings you here to Farthe?"

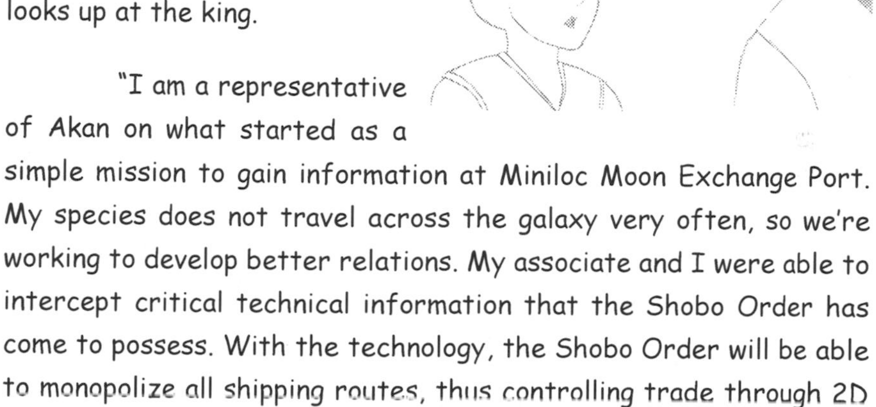

Sivad humbly speaks, "Sir, I must be candid with you." He bows his head to Prince Grant, offering respect, then looks up at the king.

"I am a representative of Akan on what started as a simple mission to gain information at Miniloc Moon Exchange Port. My species does not travel across the galaxy very often, so we're working to develop better relations. My associate and I were able to intercept critical technical information that the Shobo Order has come to possess. With the technology, the Shobo Order will be able to monopolize all shipping routes, thus controlling trade through 2D City. They should be presenting their finding to the science board, but they're not." Sivad pauses to avoid digressing from a lecture on policy and law, since the king is one of the law makers.

"My associate, Chorn, and an innocent from MEP City have been captured and are being detained by Shobo. I fear for their lives, because he plans to make them slaves. *But* more importantly, if Shobo were to use this technology, then he could monopolize all wormhole travel and possibly gain technical control of the galaxy through his findings," Sivad explains.

The king interrupts on the last words in a concerned voice, "Do you mean to tell me that Shobo, that old, dilapidated derelict, has the technology to travel through a wormhole?"

"Yes, sir. I expect that they will be testing the navigation system soon," Sivad says.

The king stands up and looks down at his son sitting on the step near him, also giving his full attention because he is just as interested in all the new information. "Where did he gain such technology? Navigating through a tackyon field is not possible. And if he could, how would he stabilize the navigation and return back to this galaxy?" The king questions.

"Galleon discovered the technology from a space probe that the Blue Planet had sent out. This technology, when compiled with ours, could stabilize navigation through the tackyon environment. How he came in possession of the Blue Planet's space probe, I don't know," Sivad says as the king intervenes with great interest.

"Galleon! I should have known he had a part in this. Where is this space probe now?" the king asks.

The Kens get up and, all at the same time, start explaining in their language and exaggerated body motions, giving details. Kenzo explains the spacecraft crashing into a mountain, Kenpo describes the probe blowing up and Sivad falling off a cliff, and Kento shows their trek into town and getting beat up.

The king watches the Kens, entertained by the motions but also understanding the body language. He says, "So the probe has been destroyed? Hey, aren't you Gens?"

"Yes, sir, on both accounts," Sivad responds.

"So how on Farthe did you meet up with my son?" the king asks with curiosity.

"We crossed paths in a bar—crossed paths in Miniloc, then again getting beat up—uh, in battle on Ciab Prime," Sivad says, trying to avoid any incriminating information to get Prince Grant in trouble.

The prince, defending the statement by Sivad, as he does not want to give his father the impression that he was out messing around, says, "Yeah, no thanks to you!" Prince Grant laughs. "Sivad and Chorn are also the cause of Ganda getting destroyed and us getting into a fight—uh, battle in the first place," the prince says with pride, because he had had a small adventure already and met a new friend.

Sivad and the prince look at each other and give mischievous smiles.

"Your son has been instrumental in assisting us. With your permission, I would like him to continue to aid us," Sivad says, hoping that the king will feel pleased with his son.

The king looks down to Prince Grant with some pride as the prince gives Sivad a thumbs-up by his side, smiling and mouthing the words "thank you."

"I don't know how you got yourself into this and don't know what Ganda is, but it seems that you have been requested and will also have to finish something for a change as well," the king says, pleased with his son. "You will need to finish what you have started here.

"The Shobo Order does not have our support. I do not respect what this Shobo has created over the past hundred years, and I cannot allow his colony of misfits to take control of the galaxy. And those little drones he has are annoying little things. I also see the potential threat. How can we Farthians be of service to you, Sivad of Akan?" the king asks in support of his son and the Akanian campaign.

"Thank you, sir, we appreciate your support. At this time, I would like to request a few things. Please disagree if you see fit. I would like to take a small team—myself, the Kens, and your son—to 2D City to rescue my associate and the innocent who accompanies him," Sivad says, happy that they are making progress.

"Who is the innocent one you refer to?" the king asks.

Prince Grant stands up with some excitement. "Father, her name is Cas. She is *so* beautiful, and her voice is *amazing*," the prince says, speaking fast.

"I knew there had to be something there to keep your interest. Sometimes you have the attention span of a Gen—" the king pauses for a moment, looking down at the Kens below him, knowing that that old saying can't be used in this case as they are paying close attention. He looks back at the prince with a mischievous, evil eye and finishes his statement - "If a girl is involved."

Prince Grant stares at his father with a displeased look then thinks and agrees by shrugging his shoulders, as he knows his father is correct, and he has no interest to argue the point. "Yeah, okay," the prince says.

Sivad interludes and continues with his list of requirements. "We will require resources for my rescue plan. The second objective is to barricade the wormhole at the center of our galaxy. This is still within the borders of Farthe's space, and we need to protect it. I expect that Shobo and Galleon will be attempting to enter and send a platoon of security drones to build a security grid around the entrance. We must stop them. I am concerned that this could become hostile," Sivad says with concern.

"You will have everything you need. I will immediately send four squadrons of my best pilot knights and my most elite naval battle ships to ensure the wormhole is secure for the federation," the king says with enthusiasm.

"Thank you, sir," Sivad says.

"Mr. Sivad, what is Akan's stance on this mission status of yours?" the king asks.

Sivad takes a deep breath, not wanting to answer, as they have not been following protocol. "I'm sorry, sir, but I have not reported in."

"I don't understand. Why not? Isn't it your duty to follow the Akanian process?" the king inquires, knowing that Akanians never rush into anything and that process is essential.

"Frankly, sir, there has not been time. And my associate is a close, personal friend. My superiors would intervene and delay his rescue, setting up comities to evaluate and analyze the situation further, searching for a political resolution. The nature of the mission and what we have uncovered is time critical, and I should be authorized to make a field decision to expedite matters as quickly and efficiently as possible. Therefore, I am still complying with all regulations, right?" Sivad ends, concerned that the king knows Akanian protocol too well and that Sivad and Chorn have not complied with their regulations.

The king walks down the four stairs to the floor where Sivad and the Kens stand, places his hands on Sivad's shoulders, and looks down at the Kens, knowing that they should not be off the Gen Planet. But he sees the significance and knows Sivad is still a youthful Akanian.

"Mr. Sivad, you have come to the right place. If it helps, I will approve and support your field decision. But do you mind if we conduct this campaign in the name of Farthe? I could use the additional respect in the federation, not to mention the publicity," the king says, showing his own political interests, and if Akan does not know of the current event, then it is an opportunity for the king to gain more political power in the federation senate.

Sivad smiles with relief and releases his nervous breath, seeing the king's intention rather than a further lecture on how he and Chorn have been noncompliant with their system. The king is known to be a good man, and if Farthe controls the wormhole, then that would be good and fair for the federation.

"Absolutely. If we can immediately assemble the support team who will fly us over to 2D City and wait for our return, then I can brief them along the way," Sivad says, anxious to free Chorn.

The king calls to one of his knights. "This is Knight Phelan. He will show you our resources for you to choose from. I think you will be pleased at our stock. Enjoy what we have, and take what you need."

Knight Phelan salutes Sivad and bows to the king then turns to escort Sivad and the Kens down the royal corridor out to the dock's storage facility.

The king, pleased with his young prince, turns to him. Grant stands by, anxious for his father's approval,

"Son, you've done alright! And you have made good friends." The king, overwhelmed

with pride, smiles and gives his son a hug. "*Finally!* Thank you for restoring my confidence. You have done well," the king says.

Embarrassed by the hug in front of the king's court personnel, Prince Grant shrugs. "D-a-d, come on!" he says, long and drawn out.

The king smiles and says, "Go help your friends," with a proud voice.

As Prince Grant runs to catch up with Sivad, the king calls his knights to attention,

"Assemble our naval strike force. We have a wormhole to plug!"

The king takes a deep breath and talks to himself. "And my son is finally off on a benevolent and meaningful journey." The king laughs, turns, then walks out.

Calvary Charge

The rescue team begins their journey toward 2D City on one of Farthe's cargo shuttles. Sivad knows they should not call attention to themselves and should arrive at 2D City as if it were a routine cargo run. On the way, in a dimly lit room, a single lamp hangs from the ceiling, shining on a blank scroll. Sivad begins to describe his plan to rescue Chorn and potentially disable Shobo's fleet from going to the wormhole.

Gathered around the parchment, the strike team—Prince Grant and the Kens—look to Sivad as he starts his motivational speech. "Today we shall infiltrate 2D City, cause a disturbance, and get out with two more passengers. We should be able to do this with precision and perfection and not be detected by any of the jabbering security drones. We will be like lightening, quick with a bite, followed by our thunder as we depart, leaving victory and success in our hands. This will be dangerous, and we must follow the instructions to a T, ensuring that there are no mistakes. If we all follow our directives properly, we should all get out safe and undetected. I do not want to have to do this again." Sivad smiles at the group.

Sivad, the Kens, and Prince Grant lean forward after Sivad's speech, gathered around the table, watching Sivad draw on the scroll. "From the king's informants, their intelligence tells us that Chorn is located here, in this holding block. Now, we will call this ground zero," Sivad says while he draws a stick figure of Chorn in the middle.

"Don't forget Cas!" Prince Grant interrupts.

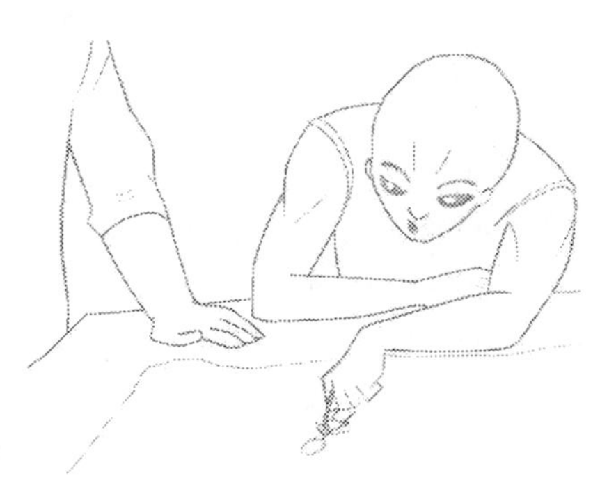

Sivad looks up at Grant with only his eyes. "And Cas here, next to Chorn, at ground zero," Sivad says while drawing another stick character with two round breasts.

"There are four corridors leading to our targeted ground zero. I expect that these corridors will be heavily guarded with security drones. What we want to do is draw the security drones away from our ground zero," Sivad points to the center, "drawing them outward a specific distance down each of the corridors." Sivad moves his hands to each distance. "We will call these locations posts one, two, three, and four." Sivad draws each post number. "Are we all clear so far?"

The team nods in understanding, anxiously waiting for the next piece of information.

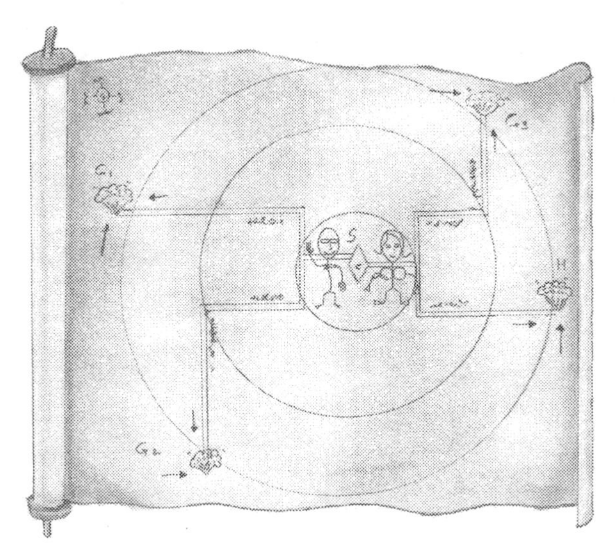

"Kenzo, you shall be at post one." Kenzo stands at attention.

"Kento, you shall be at post two." Kento follows and stands at attention.

"Kenpo, you shall be at post three." Kenpo also stands at attention.

"And, Grant, you shall be at post four," Sivad says.

"How are we going to lure the security drones to the post locations?" Prince Grant asks.

"Glad you asked!" Sivad turns and picks up a box of explosives and places them on the table.

"At the intersections here, here, here, and here, you will push this red button, which will ignite the smaller explosives, allowing sixty seconds before a timer on the main bombs will explode." Sivad points to the devices.

"The initial minor fireworks will draw out the security drones to see what the commotion is. If I'm right, the security drones will leave their posts. They seem to be curious little buggers. Once you push this red button and start the timers, *immediately* drop it and fall back to our exit point, docking station two." Sivad draws the exit point on the scroll.

"But if we blow the halls, how can we get in?" Prince Grant asks.

"Ah! It is not a matter of us getting in through these corridors; it is a matter of keeping the security drones *out* and preoccupied, buying us more time," Sivad says with confidence.

"I see. So how do we get in?" Prince Grant asks curiously.

"Once you release your package, you will fall back out to the exit point, *except* Kenzo. I have another plan for you," Sivad says and does not answer the question yet.

"The floors above and below are durasteel frame and can be cut without causing structural damage, avoiding a collapse of the decks and alarms due to a structural integrity change. We want to avoid that. So I will enter from two floors above the chamber, through the transport cavity here, down onto ground zero's ceiling, cutting through to get them out. We will then escape upward two decks and quickly enter the transport, heading to docking station two, where we will rendezvous. We should be completely undetected. The king's knights will plant two vessels; one will be a special battle-ready ship in docking station one, where Shobo keeps his main fleet, and the other in docking station two, where Knight Phelan will be waiting for us to make our leave," Sivad says in a confident tone and throws down the pen.

"Prince Grant, you must arrive first to meet up with your father's knights and get them ready for our timely departure," Sivad says casually, pointing at Prince Grant.

"Will do!" Grant says, standing at attention.

"Kenzo, are you ready to have some fun?" Sivad says as Kenzo excitedly shakes his head, smiling with anticipation.

"You will drop your explosives at post one. That is closest to docking station one, where we will land our 'Trojan vessel.' Once you release your package of explosives, you must immediately go to deck two of docking station one. There you will open this 'D' package. When you open the 'D' package, just push the blue button, then have some fun," Sivad says with his fingers in the air describing the quotations.

Kenzo, excited, gives Sivad a high five.

"D for demolition time!" Sivad smiles, high-fiving Kenzo back.

"From deck two, you will have a straight shot to docking station two. Take this scooter and haul your Gen booty back down to docking station two. Stay on deck two, as there will most likely be a lot of security drones heading down deck one. When you arrive, you will jump on top of our exit ship and enter though the top hatch, where I will be waiting. Okay?" Sivad says to ensure the instructions are clear.

Kenzo smiles and shakes his head.

"You take care of yourself, huh?" Sivad says with concern.

Kenzo continues to smile, telling him in body gestures and his language, "Don't worry," ending by patting his hand on Sivad's shoulder.

Sivad stands up at attention. "Does everyone understand their duty? If we all follow this plan correctly, then we will be in and out safely with two additional passengers before Shobo or any of his drones will know what happened." Sivad closes by raising his voice, saying,

"Let's go get our friends!"

*****

The cargo ship begins to slow as it enters 2D City territory and follows the access shipping lanes. The gallant rescue crew, ready to expedite their mission, prepares to disembark. The navigation officer looks out at the slowing stars from his station as the ship slows from light speed to sub-light thrusters.

"Sir, we are approaching 2D City," the officer informs.

"Launch the D vessel to auto-land in docking station one. Use Shobo authorization code 7-Victor-Delta-8-Delta-6," the Captain orders.

Just below the command center, the D vessel exits a shuttle bay and departs to 2D City. At the same time, a shuttle launches from the same bay with the rescue team aboard. The captain and command center crew watch the vessels as they head toward their destinations.

"May good fortune be with them and hope for Prince Grant's safe return. Good luck, soldiers of Farthe!" the captain says in his low, bold voice as the vessels enter into the respective shipping lanes and disappear within the cluster of ships flying to and from 2D City.

*****

"Traffic is heavy today," Sivad jokes, piloting the craft through the array of ships.

Prince Grant navigates as they negotiate their way through the stream of vessels.

"Down there! Fly into that hole, there," Prince Grant informs and points at the docking station to park the shuttle.

"It looks like there is a line for parking," Sivad says, looking at three vessels in front of him.

"I guess it's good that there's a lot of traffic today. We'll blend in easier," Sivad continues.

The three Kens watch the air show and flow of lights from the traffic and neon space signs, still amazed that they are entering into a giant city floating in space.

The shuttle enters the docking station with little difficulty, aside from a short wait in the congestion for parking. The hatch opens, and the ramp extends from the shuttle. Sivad exits first, followed by Grant and the Kens.

"Okay, time set, communicators functioning. Everybody has their schedules?" Sivad asks, and the Kens hold up their schedule papers to ensure that they are following the orders. They are

excited for the mission, with determined expressions on their faces.

"*Alright!* I will see you all again in *one* hour at docking station two. Good luck and take care," Sivad says to all while he adjusts Kenzo's shoulder pack. The team scatters and goes their separate directions.

All but one member of the team arrives at their destination to find empty corridors as they have hoped. Kento is not so lucky. At his location, a lone security drone stands and watches the crowd walk by. Kento bends down and reaches into his pack when the security drone walks over to him. Kento stands up and bumps into the drone, turning and looking into the mirrored display, seeing his own reflection. He stops, thinks quickly, and starts talking to the security drone in the Gen language.

"Pika pika, hehai uchuu uchuu," he says, pointing to his stomach and to his mouth. The security drone quickly interprets the actions and words: the visitor is hungry and looking for a place to eat. The security drone points down another hallway congested with people, then turns and walks away to continue his standard patrol. Kento takes a deep breath and sighs in relief.

Kenpo jumps in and talks on the communicator in Gen, which, on the communicator, sounds like quacks and quibbles. "I heard that! That was close, huh? Hey, these things are neat. If I eat it, will it always work inside me?"

"Yeah, this is crazy. I'm getting homesick," Kento replies.

Sivad jumps onto the communicator, broadcasting to all, "Relax, guys. Stay focused. We will be done soon and having a feast back on the ship. Go ahead, engage, and drop your packages on schedule. I will give you a count when I reach the detention center's ceiling. *Uh! Oh, no!* What the—" The crew hears a loud transport go by on the communicator, a few thumping noises, and Sivad growling.

Sivad, who earlier had to jump onto the train tracks of the local transport to cut through the first level of flooring as planned, was informed by the king's intelligence that those particular tracks were not in use any longer. Sivad is surprised to see two bright lights coming his way, and fast. It is the local transport using the tracks he had started working in the middle of.

Sivad quickly ducks his head and squishes his body against the ground, as low as he can, so the antigravity plating of the transport would not hit him as it hovered over. He does not realize that he is making growling noises and that the communicator is still open so all can hear as he pressed himself against the floor and watches the transport carriage hover over top. The crew, hearing the noise and Sivad's painful grunts, freeze as they listen with their communicators next to their ears. They could hear the transport's sound fade down the tunnel and some heavy breathing of Sivad.

"Sivad, are you there?" Prince Grant says with concern. "Sivad?" he yells.

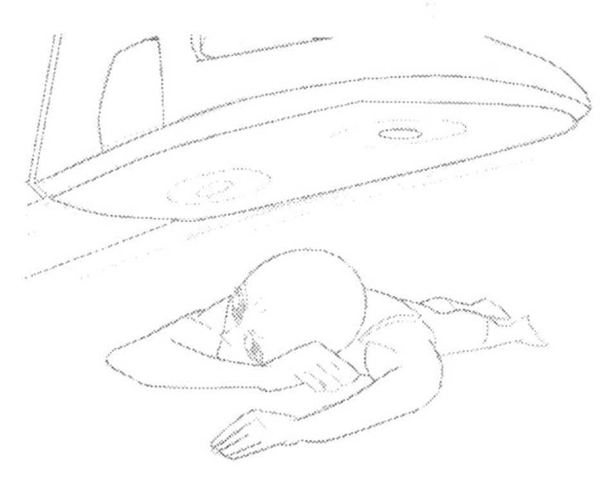

After a few breaths and calming his nerves, Sivad speaks. "Sorry, I had to take a quick break. I guess I shouldn't have drank so much before we left the ship," Sivad says to try to make everyone feel more at ease as he himself was still rattled.

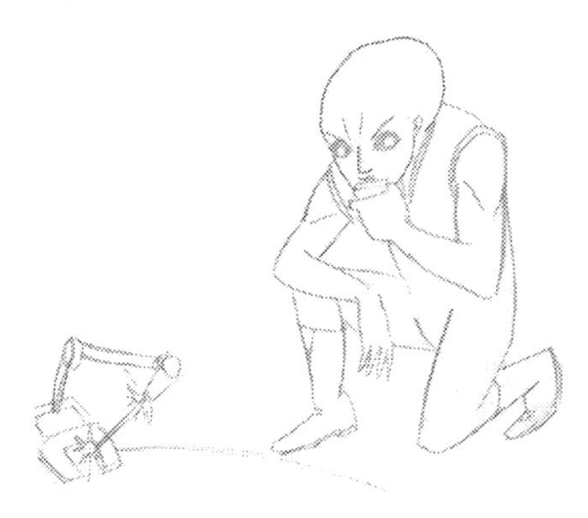

"All is well. Carry out your duties and wait for my signal," Sivad says then switches his communicator to receive only and talks to himself in an irritated tone as he continues to cut through the durasteel floor plating.

"That was an unscheduled transport! Efficiency *sucks* here. Crap, I nearly pissed myself!" Sivad finishes cutting through the first deck's floor as he lets the round floor fragment swing down. It hangs by its bent metal hinge for a moment before the metal gives way, stretching and breaking. He pulls a rope from his pack, fastens it around a secure hold inside the tracks, and proceeds to repel down into the dark space below.

Sivad lands on the floor and ignites a florescent glow stick. He looks around and sees that he has landed in a storage room that hasn't been used in a very long time. Still irritated about the misinformation and the close call on his life earlier, he continues to talk to himself as he looks around.

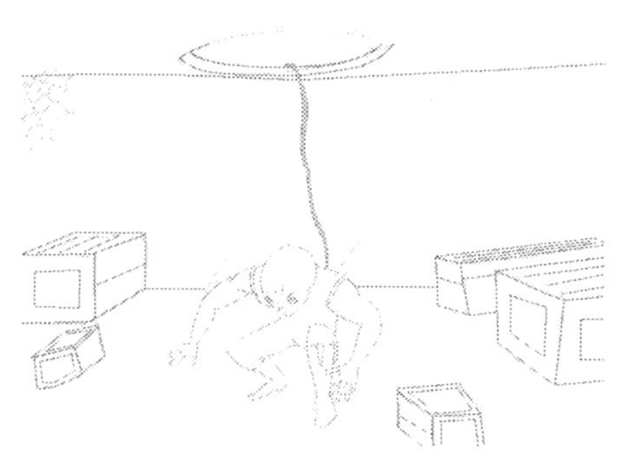

"And look at this complete waste of space. They can do so much more with this. I should call Shobo and let him know," Sivad says as the light enters from the hole above, connecting to the transport track. His glow stick shines over some spider webs through the settling dust from the ceiling fragment falling.

Sivad switches his communicator to synchronous send-and-receive mode. "Okay, I've made it through the first floor and am beginning to cut through the ceiling to the detention center. Everyone, on my mark, engage your package, then get your butts to docking station two: ready, three, two, one, NOW!"

"Setto posto Zo!" Kenzo informs.

"Setto posto To!" Kento informs.

"Setto posto Po!" Kenpo informs.

"Setto posto, uh, NT!" Prince Grant jokes. "Let's go, let's go! See ya'll shortly. Good luck, Sivad and Kenzo," Prince Grant says as he drops his package and heads back to docking station two with his red button in hand.

Sivad begins to cut through the ceiling, knowing that he has sixty seconds to finish the laser cut before the bombs detonate.

*****

Cas and Chorn sit in the detention cell. Chorn begins to get cage fever and becomes more impatient, standing up and starting to pace.

"Chorn, what do you think is going to happen?" Cas asks.

"Do you want the straight or fluffy version?" Chorn says.

"I guess straight," Cas replies, concerned about what the straight answer may be.

"We're doomed to slavery, and slaves have a short lifespan," Chorn says as he looks up at the top section of the laser bars then down to the base, analyzing them further.

"I guess I should've asked for the fluffy version," Cas responds with a worried expression.

Chorn, still pacing and evaluating the room, becomes more anxious in the small chambers. He continues to study the doors and walls for any weakness. "The fluffy version was that we will be able to work for free and get no reward or satisfaction and be expected to continue working until the bleak essence of what we call life fades out quicker than normal," Chorn says.

"I don't like the fluffy version either," Cas responds curtly and sits on the stool to sulk.

Chorn, in his search, zaps himself on the laser bars. "Ouch!" He jumps back a step then begins his pacing again, looking at the door, the light fixtures, then the lasers. "Steel-frame ceiling and floor. The only way in is through that door. If Sivad *were* to rescue us, *how* would he do it? This place looks impenetrable. How would he get into the city, past the drones, and into this room? What would I do if I were—" Chorn talks to himself, analyzing the situation while Cas silently listens. Chorn suddenly stops and leans forward to the laser bars, but not far enough to get zapped again. He looks up at the ceiling above the laser emitter platform.

"What is it?" Cas asks, seeing that Chorn has been distracted.

"The lasers. They just flickered ... ah," Chorn says.

"Flickered? Why?" Cas asks.

"Shhh, *wait!* I heard something," Chorn says, trying to quiet Cas, putting his finger to his lips and the other hand out in a stop motion.

Chorn looks up at the ceiling, then they both hear minor explosions outside and look to the door. They hear yelling and commotion outside the detention cell.

Suddenly, a blue laser beam bursts through the ceiling directly above the detention cell, slowly cutting a large circular hole over Chorn and Cas.

Chorn watches the laser for a moment in complete curiosity, following the sound of the cut while glancing over at Cas.

"How do you get into an impenetrable room in 2D City? You think like Sivad! There are more than two dimensions. He-he," Chorn says.

Chorn turns to Cas, with eyes wide open, and smiles. He knows it must be Sivad cutting through the roof and causing the distraction outside. Then his smile quickly changes to surprise and concern. "Oh, ferbo CRAP! *Not* on two dimensions! Oh, NO! GET DOWN!" Chorn yells. He grabs Cas and forces her to the ground, covering her head.

The sound of strenuous creaks roar through the room, caused by metal warping, and the lasers begin snapping and cracking as they lose their connection, zapping on and off. The top laser platform begins to rock from being cut away at the ceiling where it is mounted.

At the same time, the room shakes from four congruent explosions, dislodging the freshly cut hole above, swinging it down to dangle on a twenty-centimeter hinge yet to be cut.

The laser platform hangs by the chain that secures it to the ceiling then swings down, just missing Chorn and Cas where they cover themselves on the floor. The freshly cut metal fragment of the ceiling peels open below, still holding up the laser platform as it swings from side to side, hovering over Chorn and Cas.

"Oh, NO, SIVAD!" Chorn screams as the laser platform swings by, with the lasers still snapping and sizzling from their fresh break and the emitters trying to reconnect with the receivers on the floor mount.

Sivad pokes his head through the hole above, whispering, trying to get Chorn's attention.

"Psssst! Hey, Chorn," Sivad says, looking down and seeing the detention cell's ceiling hanging and the laser platform swinging back and forth over two figures while the light from the sparks reflect off their bodies.

Watching the swinging lid, Sivad moves his head back and says,

"Whew! Hypnosis training. Swinging pendulums." He continues to whisper, trying to get Chorn's attention as he cuts the last remaining piece of ceiling at a peak swing so it falls to the side. The giant lids of the detention cell's ceiling and laser platform fall to the ground, making a bell-tolling sound, spiraling like a coin and rolling on all sides for a moment until they finally rest and the noise settles.

"*Chorn. Chorn! Let's go!*" Sivad whispers.

Hearing the fragments fall to the ground, Chorn bursts up and watches the round platforms flip-flop on the ground. He clenches his teeth from the noise, looks up, and yells at Sivad, "*Why are you whispering? You think stealth is needed now? You could've killed us!*"

Sivad looks at the hole then the detention cell's lid coming to a spiraling rest and says, "My bad. But good aim, huh?" Sivad smiles. "Let's go! Hey, Cas," he says in greeting as he casually waves to Cas, who is just getting up and looking at the hole above.

"Hi," Cas responds, with not much else to say, and waves back.

Sivad places his hand on the edge then jerks it back. "Ouch! That is hot!" He disappears from sight, and the hole is left empty for a moment.

"*Sivad.* SIVAD?" Chorn yells, wondering where he went, and turns to look at Cas. "Well, how are we going to get up there?" Just as Chorn finishes his last word, a rope drops from the hole and hits him on the head. Cas grabs it.

"Going up?" Cas smiles to Chorn as she starts to climb the rope.

Chorn takes a deep breath while looking around. "Impenetrable room? That's my boy! Find the weak spot every time. Shobo's gonna be *pissed*," Chorn says as he grabs the rope, looks up at the thick durasteel cutout in the ceiling, and starts to climb.

At the top of the hole, Sivad helps Chorn up. Cas stands by his side.

"Good to see you, old friend. Did you miss me?" Sivad says, grabbing Chorn's hand and helping him up.

"What took you so long?" Chorn says, happy to see him.

Sivad starts to spit out non-comprehensive fragments of sentences. "Ah, I crashed, fell, froze, fought, got beat up, traveled, begged, waited in traffic, and—oh—not to mention almost got hit by a transport."

Cas interrupts. "Hey, are we going up again, or are you two going to reminisce all day?"

"Yep, that way, but look out when you pop your head out of the hole. It's the transport cavity, and they are *not* on schedules," Sivad says while point up.

"Transport cavity? Why don't you just say, 'it is a train; look out for the train.' Now she thinks you're a dork and probably doesn't like you anymore," Chorn says, being jokingly cynical.

Sivad looks at Cas then over at Chorn, a bit confused. "Captivity has made you crass, huh?"

"I missed you too," Chorn smiles as they bump shoulders in a slight hug.

Cas, who is already on top of the exit above, yells down, "Come on, guys! I'll be on the platform."

Chorn climbs the rope first, asking Sivad about the space probe. "Did you get the Blue Planet's space probe? Where is it now?"

Sivad, at a loss for what to say, pauses then blurts out a blunt answer. "The probe crashed with the ship and blew up." Sivad starts to climb the rope as if he said a common statement.

"Huh, it crashed and *blew up?*"

"Yeah *but* I got backups before we crashed. I got the backup of everything, the probe, Galleon's records and database, everything," Sivad says proudly.

Chorn climbs out of the hole onto the tracks. "So then you know that Galleon is attempting to test the tackyon navigation system today?" Chorn asks.

Chorn helps Sivad out and onto the tracks, where he stands at the edge of the hole. "*Today?*" Sivad says, surprised. Chorn let his hand go a bit too soon, and he almost fell back into the hole.

"We have to stop him," Chorn says when he sees some lights coming at them.

"Let's go!" Sivad says, running for the platform where Cas stands, yelling for them to hurry.

Sivad and Chorn climb up onto the platform, and Sivad tells Chorn that he has had help. "Don't worry; we got it covered. We have the wormhole barricaded with King Farthe's naval forces. Prince Grant and our Kens helped with the escape," Sivad says with pride, as he is still one step ahead.

The hovering transport that came rushing at them stops, and they all get on. "We shall rendezvous with them at docking station two."

*****

Kenzo, in ready position on the second deck of docking station one, sits down near the rail overlooking a squad of attack ships readying for takeoff. He opens his pack and pulls out a remote control with a large handle. He stares at it and pauses, remembering what Sivad showed him, then presses the power button. He then pulled out his push scooter from the pack, unfolded it, and leaned it up against the wall, ready to get on it and go as fast as he can to docking station two.

Kenzo cracks a large smile, seeing that the remote is powered on, and dramatically presses a larger blue button on the top of the remote, curious to see what will happen next. He has done what he was told and is ready to move the control's stick, but he did not know what to expect when he would press the blue button. Sivad only instructed, *"You will have fun, and be sure to cause as much damage as you can."*

Kenzo depresses the blue button, and the D vessel that the Farthe knights were able to dock at docking station one suddenly came to life. A head popped up from the top of the chassis, the landing gear became longer and longer, and the tail extended out.

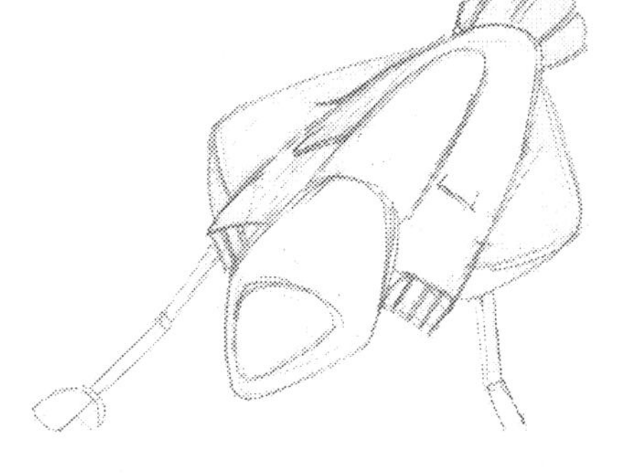

The D vessel transformed into an object resembling a bird with a triangular head, two long legs, and a wide tail for balance.

Two wings spread outward, with electrical shocks spiraling out to all metal objects on the deck.

Kenzo grinned from ear to ear and began to move the controller's stick. He moved the stick to the left and right then up and down. With each move, the D vessel would walk clumsily around, hitting every object near it. Kenzo began to enjoy his new toy as he walked the D vessel around docking station one. Kenzo, not being experienced using a remote control for a ship such as this, accidentally stepped on another ship's wing, damaging the entire ship. "Oops!" he said, then he remembered what Sivad had ordered, **"Cause as much damage as you can."**

Kenzo's face became determined as he followed his instructions and caused as much damage as he could. Kenzo walked the D vessel around to every ship and machine he could, stepping on and kicking everything in its path, while lightening streamed from its wings, disabling all other computer devices. Sparks flew everywhere. Fuel canisters and power cells exploded. The lights above the docking station short circuited and blacked out, forcing the backup disaster lights to illuminate from the floor. Kenzo was in awe at the firework show of lights flashing, small explosions, and the D vessel going wherever he directed it.

"Ooooo, aaaah! Eeeeee!" Kenzo said as he followed his directives.

An entire platoon of security drones began to blitzkrieg the D vessel, attempting to restrain it. They tried to climb it, sliding down in failed attempts.

They struggled to entangle the feet, with futile efforts. And they fired on it with a flood of laser fire, bombarding the D vessel. Their lasers streamed through the dimly lit dock, ricocheting off and scattering onto the walls in a ball of sparks. Kenzo felt completely safe on the second deck, looking down at all the entertainment and light show below.

Thrilled at the spectacle, he could have done this all day, but he knew that the others were waiting for him. He knew by the smoke and sparks that he had accomplished his mission; docking station one was in complete disarray. Just as he was getting ready to finish and go, he heard a loud commanding voice say, "What's going on *here*? Just blow it *away!*"

Kenzo looked to see Captain Galleon holding a large canon on his shoulder. Galleon pulled the trigger, and a dense white light shot from the end and, in one hit, destroyed the D vessel.

Kenzo gives a quiet hiss at Galleon, angry that his toy was destroyed. Then he jumps on his scooter to sprint down the corridor toward docking station two. In a short time, Kenzo became attached to the D vessel and felt disappointed to lose it.

Kenzo decides to stop for a moment and give his respects to the ones they will leave behind. He got off the scooter, turned, and gave his D vessel companion a royal Ken Club salute by bowing then flexing his arms in front of his waist while bouncing his ponytail then holds his right hand up high. Right after, he got on the scooter and pushed as fast as he could to rejoin the others.

Carpe Diem

Sivad, Chorn, and Cas meet up with Prince Grant and Knight Phelan on the ramp of the shuttle on docking station two.

Sivad sees Kenpo and Kento and looks around for Kenzo.

"Has Kenzo arrived yet?" Sivad asks anxiously.

"No, not yet, sir, and we have seen no sign of any security drones. You guys really did a job on them," Knight Phelan says.

"Seems they are stranded on the other side of the explosions or are busy putting out the fires. Your plan has worked well. The only news we've heard is that all ships must remain at dock," Prince Grant says with pride.

"Well, it hasn't worked yet. We're still missing a crew member," Sivad says, concerned about Kenzo as he boards the shuttle and climbs to the top hatch, looking around.

"Come on, buddy, where are you? Get your little Ken butt down here," Sivad says as he pops up through the hatch, waiting for Kenzo to come blazing down the hallway on the second deck from docking station one.

"Welcome to our ship, Ms. Cas. I am Grant. We shall take you somewhere safe," Prince Grant says to Cas, bowing as he introduces himself, trying his best to be charismatic and not to disclose that he is a prince.

Cas smiles. "Thank you. You have done so much."

"I had the pleasure of watching you sing in Ganda a few days ago. It was very heartwarming," Prince Grant says, trying to impress her.

"Really? But Ganda is—" Cas blushes then looks down with a sad expression.

Prince Grant interrupts in a confident voice,

"I will see what I can do to either find you a better place or fix Ganda."

"Oh, you can do that?" Cas says when she notices Chorn between them, watching with his arms crossed and head moving from side to side in an exaggerated way to whomever is speaking,

"Captivity must of been terrible for you," Prince Grant says, still trying to show his compassion and keeping an eye on Chorn, who moved his head early, waiting for a reply from Cas.

"*And* if you kiss him, he will turn into a prince," Chorn says as he walks between them to board the shuttle. "Oh, that's right; he already *is* a prince. Sorry. I guess you'll have no luck there." Chorn starts to mumble, complaining and mocking them as he boards the shuttle. "Humanoids and their mating rituals. Why can't they just spit it out and say, 'Hey, I think you're pretty,' 'Oh, you too, he-he.' I can smell the pheromones in the air," Chorn says, and his mumbles fade as he enters the shuttle and disappears into a dark hallway.

"Really?" Cas says, blushing further.

Prince Grant gives Chorn a cross look. "Okay, you can go back to the detention cell *now*," he says with sarcasm then turns toward Cas. "Yes, I am Prince Grant of Farthe," the prince confesses, introducing himself with another bow.

"Oh, okay. But do you *really* think I'm pretty?" Cas asks, batting her eyelashes with her chin down and cheeks rosy red. Prince Grant blushes profusely.

Sivad stares down the corridor where Kenzo should be making his entry. He hears Knight Phelan speak below. "All are on board, and the lower hatch is secured. We are ready to depart," he states in his low voice.

"Come on, Kenzo! Where are you?" Sivad says while Chorn climbs up and pops his body though the small hatch with just enough room for the two of them.

"Don't worry; he'll be here," Chorn says, taking a quick look around. He slides back down when he hears his name below.

Sivad looks down at Chorn and yells, "I hope your clairvoyance is maturing and you're right. And brush your teeth!" Sivad says, looking back down the corridor while talking to himself. "Prison breath! Boy needs a breath mint."

Suddenly, coming from deep in the corridor, a faint yell is heard with the rattle of squeaky wheels, moving fast. Sivad puts his ear up, trying to identify the strange scream. Is it a shriek of joy, panic, or pain? As the noise becomes louder, it echoes throughout corridor. Sivad recognizes that it is definitely a yell that is out of control.

Hoping that it is Kenzo and that he is okay, all of a sudden, from around the corner, Kenzo comes flying through on the scooter, bouncing off the outside wall and swiftly turning the corner to where Sivad can see him. Kenzo bursts with a large grin on his face, having fun on his fast and out of control entry, trying to slow down. Sivad sees him trying to put his feet down to slow himself with no luck on the slippery durasteel floor polish. Kenzo races toward a railing on the second deck, coming directly toward Sivad, who is waiting at the hatch. Unable to stop, Kenzo smashes into the rail, flips over, and flies through the air. Sivad reaches out and catches him in one smooth swoop.

Sivad, relieved, looks at Kenzo. "What took you so long?"

Kenzo starts to describe his experience to Sivad, moving his hands like he is using the remote control, making a motor sound with his lips as he crushed the ships and walked the D vessel around the hanger. Then he raises his hands high into the air, yelling, "Boom!"

Sivad smiles. "Okay, glad to see you had a good time. Now get in there." Kenzo jumps by him and heads down, excited to tell Kenpo and Kento about his adventure. Sivad ducks into the ship and closes the hatch.

The Farthian shuttle hovers then takes off and enters the nearest outgoing traffic stream on its way to rendezvous with the naval strike carrier stationed one light year away for their protection.

Sivad settles down on a bench in the shuttle. He looks around at the Kens going on about the adventure, Prince Grant and Cas bonding, and Chorn navigating with Knight Phelan. "Everyone is safe," he says with a sigh of relief, satisfied with himself, happy that they are heading away from 2D City.

"Everyone, congratulations and good work! The rescue mission was a success, and no one was harmed," Knight Phelan announces over the intercom as they exit the congested shipping lane and prepare for light speed.

Everyone cheers as the ship achieves light speed to join the Farthe naval vessel.

Galleon's Flight

An angry Galleon enters Shobo's chambers unannounced. "*The Akanians got away.* We need to leave *now* if we are to test the tackyon navigation system," he says, anxious and using a demanding tone to Shobo.

Shobo is not pleased with Galleon's abruptness; however, he understands the urgency now that Sivad and Chorn are on the loose.

"YES, it appears that WE could have complications. As I SEE it, WE *now* have two options: ONE, embark now as YOU desire before THE Akanians have a chance to deploy a defense team; Or TWO, be patient and hold this technology, refining it so that WE have the MOST cutting-edge tackyon navigation expertise in THE universe. But if Sivad AND Chorn have the Blue Planet's probe, THEN the Akanians will also BE able to replicate it, and WE will end up being in a technology race," Shobo says, analyzing the options.

Galleon jumps in quickly, seeing an opportunity. "You see, even your logic says we should leave now."

"HOWEVER, our fleet has been disabled to protect you. YOU would BE ... alone. Can YOU manage that?" Shobo asks.

Galleon nods his head. "*Yes*, I can, sir!"

Shobo pauses and raises his eyebrows. "YES! Prepare to embark NOW. Most likely, YOUR failure will mean death. Do NOT fail ME," Shobo says, gesturing to Galleon to leave.

"Understood!" Galleon turns to leave.

"Galleon ... GOOD luck," Shobo says as he nods his head.

"*Yes*, sir!" Galleon leaves.

Shobo takes a deep breath as if he were exhausted, sits down in his large chair, looks out a large porthole into space, and leans to the chair's control panel. He presses the com-link button to call down to his security captain, "Prepare GALLEON's vessel to leave ASAP!"

*****

On the Farthe naval carrier, Chorn reviews Sivad's plans and what he has accomplished in just a couple days.

"WOW! You've been busy. The Farthians are *really* ready. They must be sending their entire navy. So you organized all this? The rescue, a barricade in front of the wormhole, everything? Did you book the band? Oh, yeah, you got Cas. Damn, you're good," Chorn says to Sivad as he walks around the command center.

"Yeah, I had some help. It's good to have friends out here. And it looks like Cas is taking a liking to Prince Grant. Although, I don't see why; she must like sailing," Sivad says, pulling out his ears, trying not to be conspicuous as Cas and Grant leave the bridge.

"Be nice. This is going to be one heck of a party. I wonder if the Akanian Commission knows yet," Chorn comments.

"Uh, we decided to keep this under a Farthian campaign. I haven't had a chance to report in yet. Been preoccupied, ya know," Sivad says, knowing that he and Chorn are mandated to report anything and everything they find.

"Yeah-, thanks for coming back. You just couldn't do without me, huh?" Chorn says and smiles. "So, well then, where is our ship?" Chorn asks, trying to change the subject, because he does not want to get sentimental.

"Ah! We had better get going. We should be passing the Gen Planet soon," Sivad says, turning to go out.

Sivad and Chorn take the turbo lift down to a docking bay on the carrier. When they exit, Prince Grant, Cas, Knight Phelan, and the Kens are gathered around a shuttle with four large redundant boosters. Cas is bending over and giving Kenzo a

big kiss on his cheek to show her appreciation for his help in the rescue.

When Kenzo sees Sivad, he runs over and jumps in his arms, holding up a medallion in one hand and a scroll in the other and pointing to a kiss mark on his cheek. Kenzo jabbers on about his new gifts and that Cas is now his girlfriend since she kissed him. Sivad smiles, puts him down, and talks to Chorn as he looks at Kenzo's new necklace while Kenzo continues to jabber about his girl.

"We have to go back and get the ship while we're not too far away. We'll take this ship, express ourselves back to Gen, drop off the Kens, get our ship, and meet the Farthe forces at the wormhole," Sivad explains.

Chorn looks at the fast shuttle as Sivad speaks, then he turns to say, "Drop off the Kens? I was just getting used to them."

Sivad shakes his head, also disappointed. "Chorn, we have to take them back. Although they have been very instrumental in helping me, they should not be here in the first place. I think we were wrong to take them off Gen. But if you think about it, how can they go back now after seeing so much? Home will never be the same again," Sivad says.

Prince Grant comes over. "We have honored your friends for their gallant service, and they are always welcome on Farthe."

The Kens all hold up their medallions and scrolls as Knight Phelan stands at attention then gives them a Ken Club salute.

"Knight Phelan will escort you to the Gen Planet in this shuttle so that you can retrieve your ship, then we will meet again at the front. We may need all the help we can get," Prince Grant says to Sivad, taking his hand to shake it and putting the other on his shoulder to show their bond of friendship.

Prince Grant turns to Knight Phelan. "All is prepared. Ensure they are safe, and get back to the front as soon as you can," the prince orders.

"Yes, sire," Knight Phelan confirms then bows and boards the shuttle.

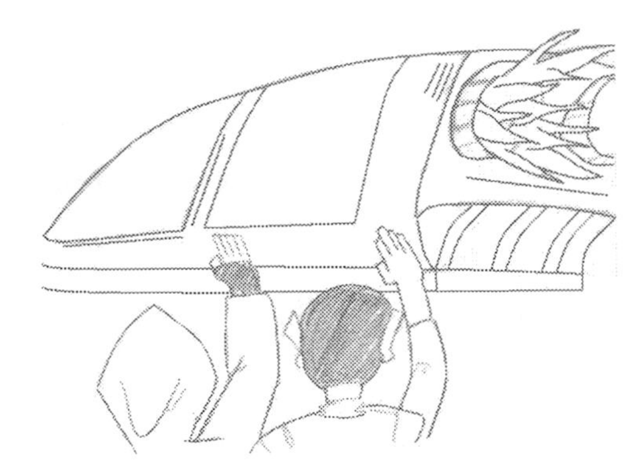

"We shall see you at the wormhole. Go with honor," Prince Grant says. He and Cas move out of the way as the shuttle door closes and the engine starts to whine. The turbo boosters warm up and the thrusters ignite.

*****

At the wormhole, the Farthe Navy gathers. A battalion of spacecrafts form a barricade in front of the wormhole as they enter their strategic formation, with their thrusters roaring, blocking the entrance.

King Farthe, on a heavily protected command vessel, holds position to the side, where he has full view of his navy. He talks to his advisors and knights. "Today will be a glorious day. We have word that the rescue was a success. My son is on his way back. Our Navy is in position. There hasn't been a defensive like this staged in over three hundred years. Today *will* be a great day indeed," the king says.

*****

At 2D City, Galleon rushes to leave, grabs his travel bag, and heads to the docking station to board his shuttle that will transport him to the Gigil Pain. He is stopped outside the shuttle's entrance when a security drone reports the ships status.

Galleon, seeing the report, responds, "Good. The probes, beacons, and all weapons are ready. I do not anticipate that on the other side of the wormhole there will be more aggressive species than us, but it is best not take any chances," Galleon says. "The Gigil Pain is the most powerful ship in the galaxy. We're ready, and there's nothing that can stop us now, not even those two intrusive Akanians. You are dismissed," Galleon says, clenching his fists and ordering his drone to leave.

Galleon boards his vessel, and the drones move away. The vessel begins to hover and slowly turns to leave as the ramp and hatch close in the air.

Last Man Standing

In the jungle at the old Gen ruins where Sivad and Chorn began their journey on the Gen Planet and met their first Gens in the communications hut, they say their goodbyes to the Kens and prepare to join the others at the wormhole.

"Well, this is it," Chorn says, looking around the old Gen ruins. "This place doesn't seem so scary anymore. Rather peaceful," He says, looking around.

Sivad looks down and grabs the medallion slung around Kenzo's neck, turning it in his fingers. "Thank you for your help. Thank the Gen mama, your chief, and your village for their support. We had fun together. They should be very proud of you." Sivad represses his feelings, and his voice cracks. He turns away as Kenzo and the Kens frown.

Chorn steps in front. "Hey, I'm not very good at goodbyes, so, uh, you take care of yourselves, eh?" he says rather coldly then bursts into a ramble. "Ya see, we have to go, and, uh, I would say that it's too dangerous for you, but you've already, uh, proven yourselves in the face of danger. You're all very brave, and, uh, we had a good time, huh?" He pauses. "So, uh, yeah, ya know. Thank you."

The Kens jump on Chorn, giving him a big hug as he leans over to receive the embrace.

"You still need a bath." Chorn smiles, misty-eyed.

The Kens begin to walk down the path to their village as Sivad and

Chorn turn to walk off in the opposite direction, heading to their ship. The Kens admire each other's medallions as they walk. The sadness disappears, and the excitement of returning to their village and telling the stories overwhelms them. They look at each other, smile, hold their medals and scrolls tightly, and take off around the corner to their village with anticipation.

Sivad and Chorn walk into the nicely cut trail that Sivad had painstakingly blazed previously.

"Aren't you going to tell them to say hello to your wife?" Sivad starts to tease Chorn.

"Shut up!" Chorn snaps, still misty-eyed.

"You're whipped," Sivad giggles.

"Shut up!" Chorn snaps again.

"Cute, cuddly Mrs. Chorn."

"Shut *up*!" Chorn snaps.

"With that Gen chicken cooking. Mmmm-mm!" Sivad says, savoring the memory of the feast.

"Shut *up*!" Chorn gives Sivad a playful push on the back as he follows. "Hey, telling me I was married to her? How could you? That was just mean. If you like the cooking so much, you should have married her!" Chorn goes on.

"Too short and hairy for my taste," Sivad replies.

"Hey, do you think we will see them every again?" Chorn says and laughs as they turn a corner on the trail and their voices start to fade. "Hey, did you fart? It smells like Gen chicken back here. Let me pass by ... hey ... hey ..." Chorn says fighting for who will be in front as they disappear down the trail. The jungle is left once again in peace, with only a large leaf still bouncing and settling from when they passed.

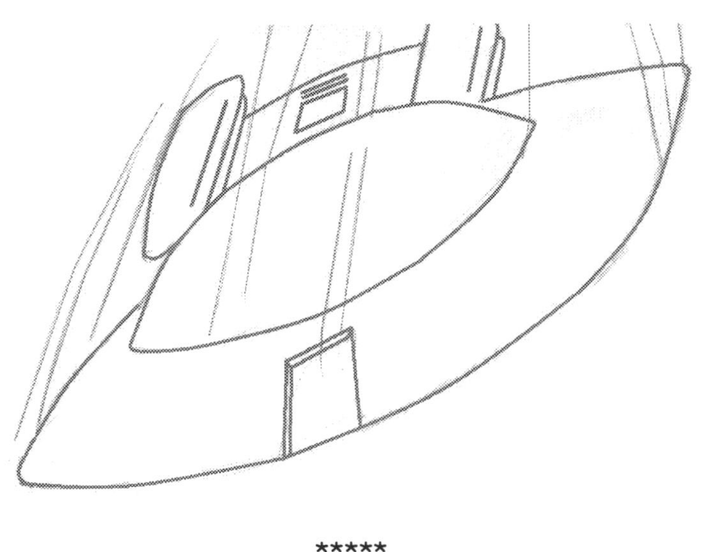

*****

The Gigil Pain travels at light speed, heading to the wormhole at the center of the galaxy, while Galleon sits on his command bridge overlooking the security drones flying the ship. On the large, main viewer, the stars streak by in white lines of light. A small blue lamp begins to flash with a single beep, notifying that they have reached their destination.

The Gigil Pain drops out of light speed, and the passing stars begin to slow. Galleon notices something ahead. "What is that? *Zoom* in sector one degree fifteen!" Galleon orders, and the security drones comply.

The Gigil Pain comes closer to what is soon identified by the sensors as a fleet of Farthian Navy ships.

Galleon's eyebrows drop into his gasmask glasses, and stress wrinkles protrude on his forehead. Not happy, he yells to his team, "Farthian tools! Analysis?"

*****

The king's command vessel detected on the long-range scanners, approaching fast.

"Send out word that our mosquito has approached the spider's trap," the king commands. "Ready stations!" he announces then says to himself, "So, Galleon, what are you going to do now? You know we're here. We know you're here. Will you engage us?"

*****

"That Akanian could not have arranged all this in time. That's impossible. How did they know we were coming?" Galleon says to himself. "Damn that *Sivad!*" Galleon growls as he thinks, looking at the barricade coming closer, then shouts,

"*Ready stations!* We will not be stopped from my destiny. Prepare to engage them as *enemies!*"

"Weapons online!"

*****

On the king's command, ship one of the knights informs, "He is not slowing down, Your Highness. His move indicates that he is preparing to attack."

The king, watching the viewer, replies, "Wait ... wait ... let him engage us first. We will not be the ones who start an interstellar war."

*****

Galleon and the drones strap themselves into their chairs, and his personal viewer reads, "**Weapons loaded and online**."

"Head directly down the center. Time for a wedge buster move! Prepare to fire!" Galleon orders.

*****

"Wait, wait. Just a little more," the king says as his knight turns.

"Your Highness, he is heading directly for the heart of our fleet. He will engage us!"

"Good. Let him come. Galleon is crazier than I expected. I can't believe how this loose cannon could have had Shobo's support. I always thought Shobo was smarter than that, apparently not," the king says.

*****

"A little more ... fire lasers, fire canons, fire, *fire*, FIRE! Bust a hole through the center and enter that wormhole!" Galleon screams his orders. Blue streams of light and green canon orbs flow from the Gigil Pain's hull.

"*Full power* to forward shields! Let's *break* them!"

*****

On the king's command ship, the knights stand in amazement that Galleon is taking a bullish strategy and watch the streams of light heading toward the fleet.

"Steady posts! Hold the line! *Block him*! Do not let him through! Do NOT move!" the king orders.

*****

The glow of the Gigil Pain's thrusters blaze out the back, and its weapons fire on all currents, streaming from the front as they attempt to ram and blow their way through the barricade. Galleon grinds his teeth and clutches his fists.

"Out of the way! *Out of the way!*" Galleon yells through his teeth.

On his chair's viewer, a message displays. "**They are not adjusting their position. Impact eminent**."

"*There!*" Galleon yells. "Enter there, then veer left sixty-five degrees." The crew is ready to follow the order. "Continue *firing!*" Galleon continues to yell.

*****

"Your Highness?" the concerned knight says, waiting for the order to engage the enemy.

"NOW! Launch defensive weapons. *Hold steady!*" the king orders.

*****

Galleon flies through the barricade of the Farthian ships, maneuvers hard port, and rises up to avoid a close impact with the adversary's vessels.

"*Don't hit them*! We must be ready to enter the wormhole with no damage to our ship. Dodge any incoming fire," Galleon says, breaking up the barricade wall and seeing the Farthian Navy break formation and begin to engage and fire on the Gigil Pain.

"Good! Come after me. Come on, *come on!* Come and get me!" Galleon says with passion in his voice, convinced his plan to break up the fleet will cause enough chaos to open a hole in the defense.

*****

The king watches the view screen and sees a swarm of specks of red laser light pursuing Galleon. He clenches his fists and says under his breath,

"Get him!"

Then he realizes a flaw.

"We have too many vessels pursuing Galleon! Order half those vessels to drop back into position beta!" the king orders.

*****

The Gigil Pain swerves in and out of Farthian ships, barely evading a collision here and electric pulses there.

"This is getting close," Galleon says as his ship swerves hard port then starboard, rises, and then dives and flips over in defensive moves while firing at the same time. His security drones navigate the

Gigil Pain with precision while they are thrown around in their seats and strapped in tight.

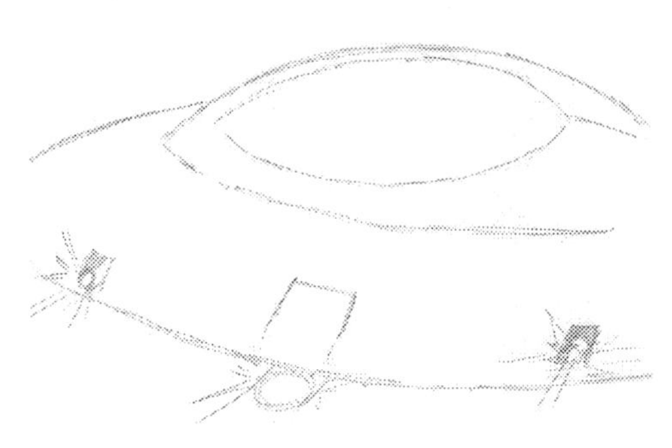

"*There!* THERE! We have a hole. Loop around and weave starboard. *Dive,* dive more! Starboard again. *Spin up,* UP! There it is! *Go, go, GO!*" Galleon screams, seeing the path to the wormhole while his ship continues to fire blue and green pulses.

A third of a planet's orbital distance from the wormhole entrance, Galleon sees his clear shot directly into the core. The Gigil Pain adjusts trim and heads into a straight line to the entrance.

"THERE! *Thrusters at maximum!* We have it! No one can stop us now!" Galleon boasts as they pass through a few disabled Farthian vessels.

*****

"NO! Don't let him get in!" King Farthe yells, seeing that his blockade has been broken and that his ships are in utter chaos trying to pursue Galleon while at the same time avoiding collisions and dodging one another. The Farthian ships fire red lasers, aiming at the Gigil Pain, but accidentally hit each other. More and more of the Farthian Navy becomes disabled from the Gigil Pain canons and friendly fire.

"Don't follow him. That won't work. *Block him!* BLOCK HIM! *Ahrrrrrrr!*" the king yells in frustration, seeing the lines fall and his out-of-practice Navy failing.

"We didn't hold position, and Galleon's got us all tied up avoiding ourselves. *Damn him!*" the king says.

The knight manning the sensors stands up and yells, "YES! The Akanian ship has arrived! Sivad and Chorn's ship is on a direct line to intercept Galleon at the wormhole!"

The king quietly watches. "Increase magnification on viewer!"

"The Gigil Pain will be no match for the Akanians' weapons," the knight says with enthusiasm, because the battle is not over yet.

*****

Chorn, navigating, sits next to Sivad, who is piloting their ship. "What are you doing? You're going to hit them if you stay on this course," Chorn says with a calm voice as a reminder of their trajectory.

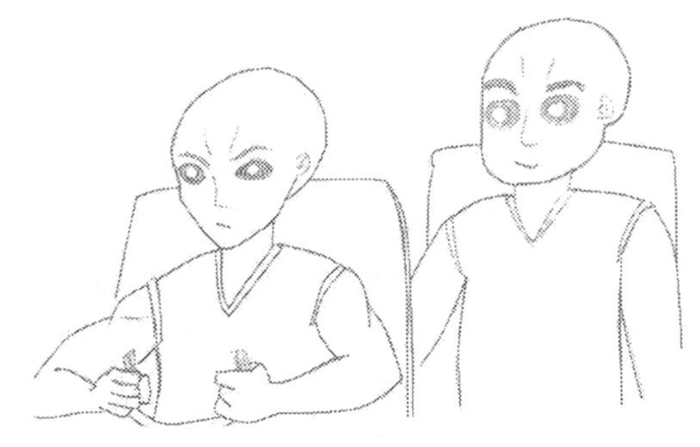

"*That's* the idea. We're running out of options. We need to use our fazer cannons or ram him," Sivad says softly as he looks forward at the viewer with determination.

"*No!* Don't hit them or blow them up," Chorn says with an alternate plan.

"Do you have a better idea for how we can beat him? We should blow him up for trying to make you a slave. That makes me angry," Sivad states with a resolute look to stop the Gigil Pain at any cost.

Chorn stops and thinks for a moment then unbuckles himself from his seat, "STALL THEM! *I have a plan,*" he says as he runs to the back.

"*Stall them?* How can I stall them?" Sivad asks.

"I don't know. That's your problem. Just don't hit them!" Chorn says, rushing back.

"Well, what are you going to do? WE DON'T HAVE MUCH T-I-M-E!" Sivad says, worried.

Chorn pops his head back into the cockpit around Sivad's seat.

"Remember you said back at Ganda that they found the Blue Planet's probe because it caused a navigation disruption?" Chorn's head disappears to the back.

"Yeah, but how does that affect us? And I actually said that when we were departing from Miniloc. You're not going to cause a disruption, are you?" Sivad asks as he stares forward and talks sideways to the back.

"YEP!" Chorn yells while he is calibrating the ship's forward deflector dish.

"Better *HURRRRRRRRY!*" Sivad yells back, seeing that they are still on a collision course.

"STALL! STALL!" Chorn yells.

*****

On the Gigil Pain, Galleon stares straight at the wormhole when his command monitor flashes a message. "**Akanian vessel on collision course in thirty seconds**."

"*I see them!* I see them! Those *incorrigible* Akanians," Galleon says with some concern.

"He won't do it! Akanians don't play dare games. He's not crazy," Galleon says.

"**Course has not changed. Collision imminent**," the display flashes after quite a few seconds of silence and anticipation. The collision alarms begin to sound.

"Arrrrrr! He's crazy! Evasive maneuvers! Do not hit their ship. Hard port! NO! *Starboard*, starboard! - The other port side!" Galleon says, pointing to the starboard side of the ship.

*****

At the last moment, Sivad turns and rolls the ship to his starboard. The ships, both maneuvering to starboard, roll past each other, barely missing a collision of the ship's hulls. With his courage, Sivad forces the Gigil Pain to change course with only meters between the two vessels. The Gigil Pain's new trajectory pushes them back onto the edge of the swarm of Farthian Navy vessels.

"*Whoa!* That was close. And stupid!" Sivad says in relief that Galleon also changed course in the same direction as him.

"*What are you doing up there?*" Chorn yells, getting up off the floor from the sudden course change.

"Space ferbos!"

"Out of the way! Damn ferbos you'd think they own this space," Sivad yells and jokes back at Chorn.

"Well, just don't hit them. And stall, *stall!*" Chorn says, working as fast has he can.

Sivad reengages the Gigil Pain while it is firing on the Farthian Navy. Sivad ensures that his ship is between the Gigil Pain and the wormhole while he receives laser fire from Galleon. Sivad rolls the ship 180 degrees then pulls up hard when a couple of Farthian reinforcements join the pursuit and force the Gigil Pain to retreat back into the entourage of Navy ships.

"Hey, *Cho-r-n!*" Sivad calls out calmly with an inquisitive tone, wondering if he is done working yet but not wanting to nag him.

"Okay, head for the wormhole. But *don't* get sucked in!" Chorn hollers out.

"Hey, Chorn, if we disrupt their navigation system by a radiated particle pulse from our disk array, which is what I think you just did, won't that also disrupt the entire fleet's navigation systems as well?" Sivad asks with concern.

"YEP!" Chorn replies as he buckles himself back into his chair.

"Okay, just checking." Sivad pauses briefly. "So what do you think the chances are of everyone getting sucked into the wormhole's gravitational pull? I mean, if everyone can't steer, then how many will we lose? That would not be good, as everyone would be lost forever and the prince won't like you anymore," Sivad says, swerving to miss a couple of navy ships as he heads toward the wormhole.

"We'll still have a much higher chance for survival then, by watching you pilot," Chorn says, holding on tight and clinching hard from the maneuvers.

"Hey, those are great chances! I'm a good driver!" Sivad says, looking at Chorn. He is startled by an incoming blue and green stream of laser fire. "Shields still at full! Today is a good day to be Akanian," Sivad says with pride in their species' technology.

"Stop babbling and *drive!* Okay, there! Head to that location there. Just under the wormhole core," Chorn says, pointing to their goal.

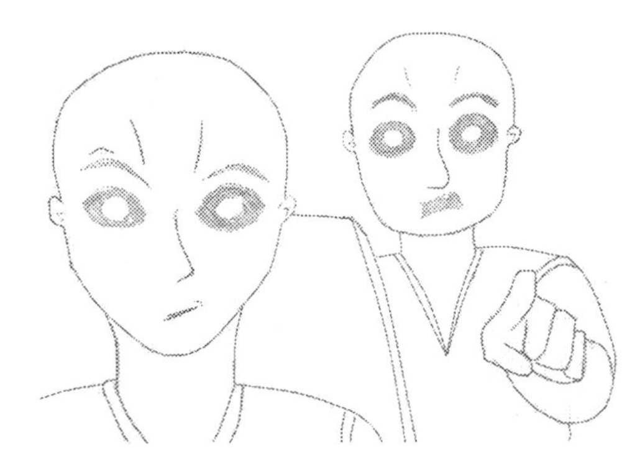

"Where is Galleon?" Sivad asks over the communicator, looking around at all his sensors.

The king's navigation knight answers, "Galleon has beaten us! He's making his move to the wormhole. He's a good pilot. Coming in on your twelve. *Did you say that you are going to shut down everyone's navigation systems?* Please confirm!" the knight says quickly.

"*You* left the com-link open!" Chorn says, shutting it off as quickly as he can.

"Of course. This is a hostile situation, and we need to act as a team," Sivad replies curtly. "Standard process. Don't worry; it was a secure channel," Sivad closes.

Chorn looks at Sivad and says, "*Fine,*" then, down at his control panel, raises a lever to see where Galleon is flying. "On our twelve, huh? Sivad, drop the stern ... NOW!" Chorn says, and Sivad immediately drops the stern and forces their ship into a standing position. Chorn pulls up on a knob, saying, "Bombs away!"

From outside Sivad and Chorn's ship, the disk array extends and rises toward its target.

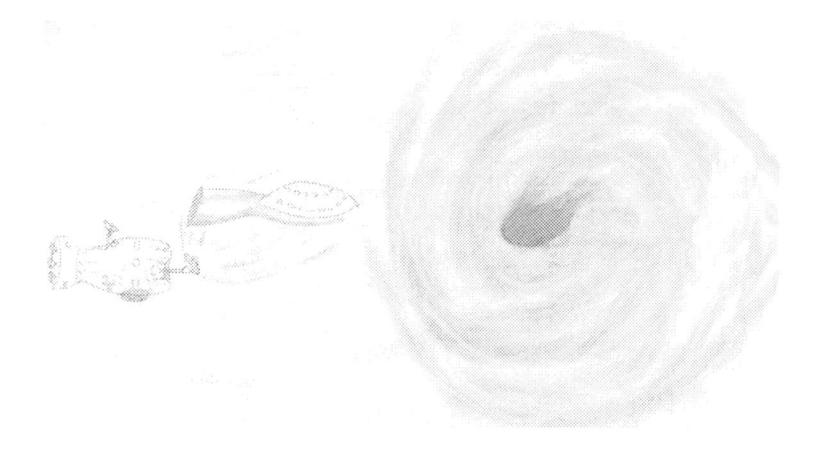

"This is going to get slippery for him. Remember when you were young and you did that Teflon experiment with those ferbos? Your mom was so *pissed!* Galleon is a ferbo with Teflon feet, slippery sucker. He-he," Chorn babbles with pride in his work.

Sivad interrupts, his neck stretched, looking up at Galleon's ship as it flies over top. "ENGAGE! *Engage!*" he yells, impatient.

"Patience, it takes a time. Three, two, one, and ... now! Goodbye!" Chorn says, pushing the knob back in. The disk array starts to vibrate the ship as the signal bombards the Gigil Pain and recoils back to Sivad and Chorn's ship. The signal reverbs through space, expanding farther and farther, encompassing the entire Farthe Navy.

*****

The radiated tackyon pulse hits Galleon's ship, penetrating directly into the core and bringing it to a dead float in space as navigation shuts down and the engines fall offline. The pulse continues to extend outward in all directions, paralyzing the Farthe fleet as well. The space around the wormhole suddenly becomes quiet as the pulse's discharge roars through space, extending out like as a spherical wake, crippling everything in its path. Every ship in the battle is suddenly in a dead float around the wormhole.

The Gigil Pain floats quietly in space and begins to roll stern over bow, head over heels, almost in slow motion. The chaos of battle turns to silence outside the vessel; however, inside, a furious Galleon yells at his crew. "*What the!*—GET THE ENGINES BACK ONLINE NOW, NOW, NOW!" Galleon's cries of frustration and anger could almost be heard in space.

The wormhole's gravity starts to catch hold of the drifting Gigil Pain's bow as it gains speed, succumbing to the wormhole's core. Within a few seconds, the Gigil Pain starts to stretch, elongating the ship, warping its shape. Then, almost in a flash, it's gone. Galleon, his crew, the science slaves, and the Gigil Pain disappear into the mouth of the wormhole, possibly lost forever.

*****

Not too far behind Galleon's lost ship, Sivad and Chorn's vessel still emits the tackyon pulse. Chorn sees that the Gigil Pain is gone and disengages the disk array's radiated pulse. The ship stops vibrating while the disk array settles back into the ship.

Sivad's teeth and hands are still chattering from the vibrations the disk caused. He starts pushing every button in front of him, trying to get their own engines back online. "*Chorn!* The wormhole's *got us!* WE'RE GOIN' IN!!" Sivad yells, helpless to do anything without engines. He sits back in his seat and grabs his chair as tightly as he can hang on.

"No worries," Chorn says as he extends his arm, points his finger, and presses a button to raise the ship's magnetic shields. The navigation systems immediately come back online.

"Well, are you going to sit there getting us sucked in, or are we getting out of here? I suggest you *hurry!*" Chorn's calm voice ends in a bit of a panic.

Sivad's eyes, clenched shut, open in surprise as he looks forward and sees that the engines are back online. He swiftly leans forward, takes control of the ship, and pulls away from the wormhole with all the power the ship could put out.

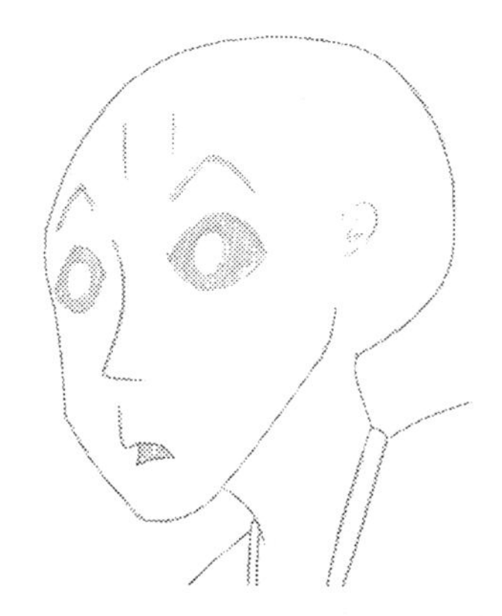

Sivad holds the controller tight while the ship shakes from being at maximum power, trying to escape the wormhole's grip.

"*Go to light speed!*" Chorn yells.

"WE ARE AT LIGHT SPEED!" Sivad says.

The ship barely moves away from the gravitational well. It shakes violently while structural integrity sensors begin to alarm one after another.

"Ah, come on ... go, *go*, *GO*!" Sivad yells when the ride begins to smooth.

Sivad and Chorn, seeing that they have escaped the clutch of the wormhole's jaws, look at each other and let out a huge breath of relief. Sivad disengages light speed and returns to thrusters. They see that the Farthe Navy was far enough away to evade becoming entrenched into the wormhole's gravitational pull, and they return to formation around the king's battle cruiser.

"How's it going out there?" Sivad says, turning on the com-link again to hear that an entire squadron of Shobo's security drones just arrived from the back.

"*Ya see*, that's why we keep the com-link *on*!" Sivad says to Chorn.

The king, on an open channel, announces to the oncoming threat, "Galleon is gone, lost forever. *Do NOT engage*, or it will be another act of war."

Chorn thinks for a moment, listening to the Farthe Navy and the kings announcement. "Shobo's drones won't attack," Chorn says.

There is no response to the king's message as the two battle-ready squadrons face off with one another in uncomfortable silence.

"Why do you say that?" Sivad asks

"Think about it; if Shobo's drones become hostile, then that will trigger an interstellar war, and the entire federation will get involved. 2D City and the Shobo Order just aren't strong enough to handle that. I expect he will play the politician and call Galleon's journey a rogue trip and Galleon himself a loose cannon. Shobo will have to apologize for this one at the next federation council meeting. Besides, we are in Farthian space still, it would not be prudent." Chorn explains.

Sivad and Chorn look at each other as Chorn reflects on his statement and crossing his fingers.

"*Apologize?* Na-!" they both say at the same time, knowing that Shobo would never apologize for anything.

"I hope you're right," the king of Farthe says on the com-link.

Chorn looks at Sivad, surprised because he keeps forgetting that all can hear them speak.

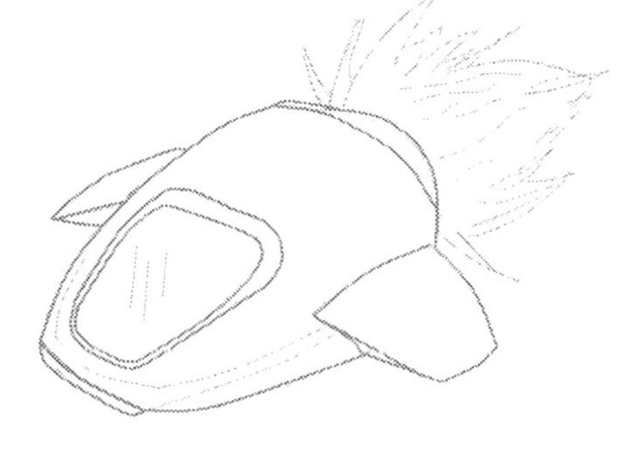

The squadron of security drones positioned in front of the Farthe Navy in a stand-off awaits their orders. After a short, tense moment, the lead ship of the drone squadron turns and heads the battle-ready ships away, back to 2D City.

Cheers of relief are heard throughout the Farthe Navy over the com-link.

"Well done, gentlemen. *Well done!*" the king announces. "This day marks the first battle offensive in over three centuries. I think things are on the verge of change, and the cold silence of the galaxy will begin to unite. It *is* an exciting time!" the king closes.

Sivad looks at Chorn. "It is an exciting time. Things are on the verge of change, and the federation will have to reunite. I can feel it," Sivad says, repeating the king's words while covering the communicator.

One of the kings knights broadcasts from his lead ship in front of the squadron. "Here's to that! It's good to work with you Akanians again. Thanks."

"This is *your* fault, you know!" Chorn says to Sivad. "Always getting us into something."

Feasting Time

Sivad and Chorn sit on the steps overlooking Farthe's capital city, just outside the doors of the royal courtroom where Sivad and the Kens previously waited to meet the king. Sivad looks inside, seeing the palace royal courtroom, a feast being prepared in their honor, and joyful music playing in celebration.

In the center of the feast, a skewered, roasting animal carcass rotates over a fire. Around the barbeque, vegetables and fruits are arranged in a colorful decor. Servants and cooks run around, ensuring everything will be ready for the feast. When a town bell tolls, notifying them of the time, they work faster. Once the bells stop ringing, an echoing voice announces over an intercom, "Ten *minutes until the* king's *attendance."*

The knights move to formation along the outer edges of the corridor and stand at attention. Knight Phelan walks to the feast table, attempting to take a sneak bite from the table, when a short, fat cook with a long mustache slaps his hand, waives his wooden spoon at him, and points for him to go away. The much larger Knight Phelan cowers and walks to his position behind the king's chair.

Prince Grant and Cas hold hands, talking on a bench next to the palace waterfall flowing through the middle of the room, as a waiter serves them champagne. Grant and Cas toast each other and drink with arms intertwined.

Sivad turns back around and looks out over the city, watching the sunset, sitting next to Chorn. He takes a deep breath and places his arm around Chorn, who is enjoying the scenery, finally relaxed. "Mission complete!" Sivad says as he gives a thumbs-up across Chorn's other shoulder.

Chorn looks at Sivad, smiles, and shakes his head. "Yeah, but why do I feel that we are just beginning? We have *so much paperwork to do now.*"

Sivad reflects on the accomplishments. "On this mission, we're able to report to the senior chancellor that the Gens' evolution has begun again, we have the technology to travel through wormholes, we reunited the galaxy for a common purpose, we learned that our species needs to get out more, we had an exciting battle, and we saw a young man grow into his ears. He-he," Sivad says, looking back at Prince Grant. "What do you think? Do you think that they will marry and have kids named Sivad and Chorn?" Sivad says smiling.

"Would you name your kid Sivad? I would only name my pet Sivad," Chorn smiles and continues, "Don't forget, YOU also destroyed a bar, YOU used an unapproved device, YOU took Gens out of their natural environment, YOU got me in trouble for the thousandth time, YOU got me captured and almost sent to a slavery camp, YOU almost got us killed in our own ship, and YOU destroyed the most unique finding in thousands of years, Blue Planet's probe. And YOU did not follow process or procedures the entire time. What was common among all those? YOU!" Chorn says, pointing at Sivad's chest, and laughs.

Sivad smiles and shakes his head, proud of what Chorn is saying. "**Yeah, cool!**"

Chorn laughs, trying to figure out Sivad, and says, "So overall, we did alright, constant on all extremes."

The sun sets and the last sliver disappears over the water, converting the sky into a colorful array of orange and red. A divine smell flows from the feast tables. Sivad's nose rises and expands from the smell of the roasting dinner. "Oooooooh, that smells *good*! Let's go eat and join this celebration!" Sivad says.

Just after Sivad smells the barbeque, the final bell rings, and a voice echoes through the court, *"Enter King Farthe."*

Sivad and Chorn stand up.

"Mmmm, I think I'll try it this time. It does smell good," Chorn says, sniffing the air and willing to take a risk eating meat rather than a vitamin capsule. When he turns to look at the juicy roast, whose essence is filling the air, he sees the Clark chef from Miniloc preparing the barbeque.

He jumps back with a cringe on his face as the music plays louder and the celebration begins.

Sivad and Chorn are ushered past the feast tables into the royal courtroom by the jester, where Prince Grant and Cas join them from the side. All together, they walk to greet the king, with Knight Phelan standing behind him and the Clark chef sharpening his knives behind the feast table, staring at Chorn, ready to cut the meat, and laughing.

*****

In a dimly lit room in 2D City, surrounded by his elite security drones, Shobo stands looking out a transparent steel window into space toward the center of the galaxy.

"Sivad AND Chorn," he says, rocking from side to side. "Sivad ... AND ... Chorn," he says again. "Mmmmm, I'M sure I'LL be SEEING YOU two again!"

Shobo groans as he turns to walk down a long corridor with high vaulted ceilings, lumbering side to side as he walks farther away.

NASA

EXPENSES LATEST

VOYAGER SATELLITE LOST IN SPACE

Voyager Missing - NASA under Military LOCK DOWN

NASA Cover-up? How deep does it go?

Earth, 1978, NASA Mission Control, San Francisco, *CA*: A number of the *Voyager* series satellites were launched to explore the *Earth's* solar system as the Blue Planet's species begin to evolve and expand into space. Six months after launch of the Voyager 4 satellite, it disappeared in space. NASA becomes concerned, because the satellite, although damaged, continued to send images and radio of events to come.

After losing contact for a day, the Voyager satellite sends back its first image of a spaceship on a direct collision course.

"HOLY *shit!* NOC, do you see that?" mission control says over the ham radio between their San Francisco Mission Control in California and Network Operations Center in Cape Canaveral, Florida, after they both receive the first image broadcast from the Voyager 4 satellite.

"Is that what I think it is? A ... spaceship?" NOC asks mission control.

"What the—"

"I guess we are *not* alone in the universe," mission control answers, still unsure what they are looking at in the picture.

"Get the president on the hotline ASAP!" NOC says with urgency in their voice.

Mission control contacts the president on a red phone that rings directly to his desk.

"President speaking," a voice answers.

"Mr. President I have urgent news for you! Our Voyager program has found what appears to be intelligent life outside our planet," mission control says.

"What is the Voyager program?" the president responds.

"The Voyager program is a series of U.S. space missions that consist of a team of unmanned scientific probes, Voyager 1 through Voyager 6. They started launching in 1977 to take advantage of a favorable planetary alignment. Although they were officially designated to study just Jupiter and Saturn, the two probes are able to continue their mission into the outer solar system. They are currently on course to eventually exit the solar system in the 1990s, sir," mission control explains.

"What does that mean?" the president asks.

"The Voyager program is what you spent six-hundred-million dollars on over the past five years, sir," mission control answers.

"Oh, that program. It was expensive, huh?" the president replies. "So tell me, son, what did you find?" the president asks.

"We believe we have found aliens, Mr. President," mission control informs.

"*Did you say aliens?*"

"Yes, sir, Mr. President."

"Are these aliens hostile?" the president asks.

"Ummmm ... hard to say, sir."

"Are they intelligent?" the president asks.

"Ummmm ... hard to say, sir," mission control responds again while they look at the images. "We have the Voyager radio back online as well, sir. Very strange sounds emitting from the probe. Definitely an alien language," mission control announces as they receive more information from the Voyager satellite.

"Is your station secure? I want a 100 percent personnel and communications lockdown there now!" the president orders.

"Yes, sir!" mission control confirms.

"My generals and I will review and be there in the morning. Continue to collect as much information as you can. We need to know if these aliens are hostile," the president closes, hitting his fist on the table and hanging up.

The military enters the mission control facilities quickly and ensures that no one is allowed to enter or leave, and no communications are permitted with anyone outside. NASA enters facility-wide lockdown by the U.S. military as the Voyager 4 satellite continues to send astonishing images and radio of the sounds and aliens communicating.

The entire NASA staff on site gasps with their mouths wide open as the images continue to come in. They try to analyze each one, but the images are too amazing to do anything to except gawk at them.

The next morning, the president and his generals, personal advisors, and scientists enter the NASA mission control, ready to review what is seen.

The mission control chief already has all the images posted on TV screens at the front on the command center wall. The president and staff look in awe at the assortment of images with ships, species, and action happening all around the Voyager satellite.

They see a collision with a strange oblong vessel; a sharp black ship staring directly at the Voyager; humanoids in protective uniforms; humanoids and aliens dressed as if they were lost on a desert island for years; Galleon peering close into the camera, showing his gasmask glasses and big nose, with a radio translation of "Is this thing on?"; strange, small, mirrored-faced midgets that imitate and mock their gasmask-glasses-wearing leader behind his back and make strange gestures when he is not looking, which are interpreted as profanities by NASA; a beautiful humanoid woman who is under duress by the midgets and their leader; another alien, slightly chubby, yelling and being tackled and oppressed by the mirrored-faced midgets; the midgets with weapons of unknown abilities; three strange, furry monkey people riding the satellite as if it were a jungle gym and licking the camera; another alien, shorter and more muscular than the other, taking off in a ship with the Voyager then coming to the back and looking at the satellite, talking to himself and doing a strange dance with the hairy monkey people; and the same alien panicking, trying to fly and then running back, yelling as the Voyager satellite takes photos of the front view of the ship nearing a planet and then crashing into an icy ground in an explosion.

"So, General, do you think they're hostile?" the president asks.

"Frankly, sir, after seeing these images and hearing that ... that sound of their language and tones, I think the universe is crazy. Not sure if they have intelligence. Just look at those bald aliens and the furry people," the general responds.

The president turns to his scientific advisors and the NASA experts. "What do you think? Are they a threat to us?" the president asks.

"Well, sir, they have ships in space and there are what appear to be weapons, but it's hard to say, because they seem to be completely ... *nuts!*" mission control concludes.

"One thing is for sure, Mr. President. There are other species in the universe, and we have to be ready for them. They may not appear to be a threat in these images, and our top communications experts are working to translate their language or languages, but whether crazy or nuts, we have to be ready!" the president's scientific advisors conclude.

"So that means more budget to the space defense program, right? We will continue to call it space exploration. Generals, move all the data and personnel to *Area 51* immediately," the president orders.